N.J. SAULD

The Broken and Damned

Book One of the "My found family" series

This book was professionally typeset on Reedsy.
Find out more at reedsy.com

"Life breaks everyone Nikita. The very good, the very strong, the very kind, and the very tough."
John Wilson

"So we armour ourselves in the wrong we've done. We lead with the things we hate most about ourselves. Do our best to drive people off before they can leave. Because if they leave, it cements the belief we already have, that we are not worth staying for."

Kelsey Shelman

Contents

Preface

Note from the author: This series is a fictional story following a group of hurt and damaged people as they explore themes of love, loyalty, redemption, survival, and the psychological impact of past abuse and trauma. The story contains themes and depictions that may be distressing to some readers, including but not limited to: vulgar language, graphic violence, physical and emotional abuse, sexual exploitation, torture, trauma, war, murder, and mental health episodes.

Reader discretion is advised.

Acknowledgments

Special thanks is owed to:

My wife Elisabeth for her unceasing encouragement
Shanae for hearing all my rants during this process and designing the covers
Mel the ultimate beta reader

Without them, this series could not have been written

Prologue

I've been staring at this blank Word document on the computer for what feels like an eternity. At the start I made a cup of tea, watching steam swirl upwards until it sat forgotten and cold beside me. I reheated it in the microwave; terrible idea, disgusting. I tipped it down the sink and made a second cup. Only to get lost in thought once more, and it too grew cold, untouched. I feel utterly lost, unsure of where to begin or what to write.

The therapist I see—a woman with kind brown eyes and calming voice—suggested it might be a good idea to write about the things that happened. 'To process what happened,' she had said. I can't see how putting it on paper will help. As Kelsey once said, "there's no fixing what's wrong with us."

But I do think writing down what happened might be a good idea for different reasons. I doubt anyone else will read it. But if they do, I hope they see I wrote to honour them. To remember them, my found family.

Ken, with that powerful confident swagger, like a well-muscled pit bull walking the streets unafraid. Thomas, quiet and sweet and savage. Amana, with his deep calming voice and massive presence. Jean-Paul, elusive and hard to define, a puzzle of a man. Kelsey… every woman should have a friend like her. Sarcastic, witty, beautiful and could fight like you would not believe. Buster, who was always there when anyone needed him. And John; kind, ferocious, gentle, strong, man-with-a-plan John fucking Wilson whose presence made you feel like everything was going to be okay simply because he was there.

Oh God, I'm crying already, that's not a good sign. I think that rather than write from my own point of view I should write in the third person. That way if someone does read it, it'll be like a little fly-on-the-wall written documentary about us. That will also make it easier to retell the conversations and events I was not actually there for, as well as how I now know what people were thinking and feeling at the time. Anyway, this is my family, this is their story and by extension my own. I hope I tell it right. I wonder where to start. I guess in South Sudan, about twelve years after the second North-South war. That's where everything changed, where it all started.

1

Chapter One: Jabori Wildlife Reserve

John- South Sudan, East Africa.

"Go help Kelsey, I want her, a field surgery kit, and the immobilon on that troopie pronto; tell her I'll brief her on the drive. And Amana? Make sure you and Sefu bring your rifles, mine too just in case! I'm going to let Amy know we're off- we're gone in ninety seconds. Let's move!"

John strode across the dusty compound toward the classroom as his team raced about around him. He'd been living in Africa for the last five of his thirty-four years working as an anti-poaching veterinarian and reserve manager dedicating himself to protecting Africa's endangered wildlife. It was a hard and unforgiving calling, but it was where he had met Amy, his wife. She was all that was the best in him. They had met when John was in Botswana protecting elephants. She had come to see the world, make a difference, and had found her passion teaching underprivileged children. When John accepted the role as manager of Jabori wildlife sanctuary, he did so with the condition that he be permitted to build a classroom on the grounds so the local children could receive an education. These children were wary of men, especially armed men in fatigues, and so John always made a special effort to smile and have a happy go lucky demeanour around the them.

He made sure a broad grin had broken out upon his face when he entered the classroom.

"Hey kids how are we today?"

"Good, Mr. Wilson," came the chorus from the children.

John strode over to his wife at the front of the class still with the grin across his face.

"Bull elephant, over by three-mile lagoon," John whispered as he hugged her. "Pretty bad from what Amana says, multiple gunshot wounds. We probably won't be back till after dark, don't wait up."

"You know I will. And be safe, they might still be in the area and you're not invincible, no matter what you think."

"Course I am." John whispered. He kissed Amy, the children giggling as he did so, and broke away from her.

"You be good for Mrs.Wilson, okay?" he asked with that ever-present grin.

"Yes, Mr. Wilson," came the children's reply.

John stepped out of the classroom and let the smile fall from his face. He strode toward the gate as the vehicle rumbled through the compound and stopped at the entrance for him.

"Mrs. Wilson is in charge while I'm gone," he instructed Thimba, the guard on duty. John swung up into the back seat beside Kelsey as Amana passed his rifle back to him.

"We got an elephant injured out past three-mile lagoon," he shouted to Kelsey as the truck left the compound. "Amana says multiple gunshot wounds to the chest and stomach; poachers might still be in the area. When we get there, you'll be the primary for sedation. Amana, Sefu, and I will secure the area, then you and I will do the surgery; the lads can keep watch. If there is gunfire, hit the dirt don't do anything brave, yeah? Leave the stupidity to us."

Kelsey grunted in acknowledgement, her brow furrowed in concentration as she prepared the drugs for the tranquilliser gun.

***

"Tough old bastard" John commented as he lowered the binoculars and passed them to Kelsey. "See his back right leg, just below the ankle? Look like a snare injury to you?"

"Oh boy, yeah, they must have really wanted him. Poor guy. As if he wasn't in enough pain already."

"Fucking ivory poachers," he muttered.

The were three main types of poachers. Bush meat, ivory, and pet trade. Bush meat poachers John could empathise with. A lot of them were just trying to feed themselves and their people. It was still his job to stop them, but he understood where they were coming from. Pet trade poachers looked to steal young animals, often by orphaning them and selling the young as pets, and ivory poachers looked only for elephant tusk and rhino horn.

It had taken the small team till mid-afternoon before Sefu, sitting up in the lookout, had managed to spot the resident elephant heard. Sure enough, a half hour later they sighted the old bull still following. As Sefu and Amana checked for any sign the poachers were still in the area, John and Kelsey had taken the opportunity to observe the bull from a distance while planning their approach.

"Lads are back," John stated nodding to the returning Amana and Sefu. "How we looking, guys?"

"No sign of them," Sefu answered. "I think maybe they wait for him to die in the night, come for his tusks tomorrow."

"Okay, Here's what I'm thinking. On one hand I think he's so slow and weak right now that if we dart him, he might just lay down where he is, and even if he does take off, he's going nowhere fast. We're a good distance away from the lagoon. I think if we're going to do this, then this is the spot. On the other hand, he's very injured. I counted at least ten bullet wounds that I can see from here, most likely he's got a few more we won't see till we get up close. On top of that Kelsey and I noticed he's also got a snare wrapped around his right back leg that's also going to have to be seen to. It's what, 4:30 now? If we dart him and start a four-hour surgery, that means we're going to be out here at night under spotlights. That'll pick us out for any poachers or predators that hunt this area for miles around. I don't want to put you guys at risk if all we're going to do here is prolong that poor fucker's misery. If that's the case, I'd rather put him out of it now and take his tusks back to the compound for burning. What's everyone's thoughts?"

Kelsey held her tongue to give Amana and Sefu an opportunity to speak their mind. She knew that if she said her piece now, they would chorus their agreement with her in order not to look weak in front of a woman. She had every intention of continuing with the surgery no matter the risks. But if they were to run into trouble it would be Amana and Sefu that would face the consequences first as they tried to protect her.

"I no think poachers come back tonight. I think they wait for him to die, come in morning." Sefu put forward. "And if they do come back tonight, there will be less poachers in the morning." He patted the rifle in his arms. "I am fine with this. Amana still guides this area sometimes, maybe him know who hunts here?"

"Predators won't be a problem." Amana spoke now. "Some leopard and the usual assortment of scavengers. No lion prides come this far, you might get an outcast male but I doubt a single lion would be so bold as to come into the light. Sarba's hyena clan does visit but they are only small, maybe four big enough to hunt. I'm more concerned about the poachers returning but I agree with Sefu, I think they'll wait out the night and return in the morning, unless of course they see us saving the elephant, but that's the hazard of the job isn't it?"

Kelsey took her opportunity to speak now. "Risks or not, this is what we're here for. If I was happy with a boring risk-free life, I would be back in Sydney at my little vet clinic telling people not to feed their fat golden retrievers so bloody much. But this is the life we all chose so let's just get on with it. I want to dart him and take a closer look. If we can operate, we will, doesn't matter how long it takes. However, if we get up close and see that all we can really do is prolong his suffering with no hope of a positive outcome for him, then we'll do what John said — put him out of his misery and take his tusks for burning."

"Well let's pray it doesn't come to that, shall we?" John concluded. "Everyone back in the truck we'll drive a little closer and do the final approach on foot. Sefu, you take the right-side Amana you're on the left. Let's go."

The truck slowly crept towards the old bull until the team was within fifty meters. As soon as Kelsey applied the brake the four of them silently disembarked, assuming their positions as they approached their target. John and Kelsey in the middle, focusing solely on the elephant. John with his rifle slung over his shoulder, Kelsey with the dart rifle. Between them they carried the field surgery kit, a large foot locker filled with medical supplies. Fifty meters to their right and slightly ahead of them, Sefu vigilantly kept watch, his head on a swivel scanning for threats and his rifle cradled in his arms. Amana was doing likewise fifty meters to the left of the two vets.

"You should take the job." John grunted as he and Kelsey set the locker down. "Monarto is a good zoo, got some excellent breeding programs from what I hear. A head vet spot there at your age is a real feather in your cap."

"Offer's for a senior vet, not a head vet. But by rights yeah, I should take it."

"I'll keep his attention, give you a clear shot." John offered.

John slowly approached the old bull head on, talking to him in a calm reassuring tone. "Hey handsome man, you're alright. Kelsey here's going give you a nice little jab and you'll start to feel all better." He was careful not to get too close, or look like a threat. Weak and wounded as he was, the bull was still easily able to kill him. He was in pain and there was every chance Kelsey's dart would startle the elephant, causing him to lash out.

However, he didn't even seem to notice the dart smacking into his meaty hindquarter and sticking, he just continued to stare at John.

"Is it even in?" John asked after a few minutes had passed with the old bull showing no sign of feeling the drug's effect.

"Ha ha ha, what Amy asks you every night. He's a big boy. Give him some time."

"Every night I wish! I'm married you know. Got another dart ready just in case."

"Of course."

John's fears turned out to be unfounded as a minute or two later the bull had started to sway as he fought the drowsiness the drug bought on. As his legs started to give way John nimbly darted forward and seized the bull's trunk, holding it and pulling it forward. John's timing had to be perfect. Had he waited too long to grab the trunk, there was a chance the bull could have landed on top of it and suffocated himself with almost no hope of them being able to save him. Conversely, had John gone too quickly, even in his current state the bull was easily capable of seriously injuring him.

As soon as the old bull went down, Kelsey was on him monitoring his vital signs.

"So why don't you take it?" John started again as he dragged the footlocker next to the elephant, "The job at Monarto, I mean."

"It would be nice." Kelsey responded. "Regular hours, clean sheets, hot water-"

"Civilisation, actual money in return for your work, not being shot at while operating-" John added.

"Food that looks and tastes like real food, an actual sterile theatre to operate in."

"Reliable electricity, oh and air conditioning!"

"And I'd be able to see my family more often. I can't say it wouldn't be a good job."

"But…" John prompted.

"Well, it's not Africa, is it? I mean yeah, we complain about things here, and yeah, we get angry, our work here has its demands and its risks. We go through a roller coaster of emotions on a weekly basis. We've saved lives, we've lost friends. We get shot at, and we get actually shot. I've still got that bullet in my hip from Rwanda."

"Rwanda, God that was fucked."

"Point is, I'm supposed to trade the family we have built here, the work we do after all we've been through, for what? To go back and complain about rosters in some staff room or the cost of living while sipping lattes? How am I supposed to get along with people that have no idea what I, what we, go through out here? I just don't think I could do that."

"Yeah, like you said, 'it won't be Africa.' For all its faults, we do get to live a unique life. Where else are you going to see a sunset like that?" The two friends stopped momentarily to gaze at the sky as shades of tangerine and salmon slowly faded into deep purples and blues, with the last remaining sliver of sun casting a golden glow against the horizon.

Less than two hours later the small team was loaded up in the jeep headed back to the compound, jovial at a job that hadn't been as bad as it looked. It had appeared the poachers were not very experienced and had haphazardly shot at the three-ton giant with a smaller calibre weapon resulting in the bullets only just penetrating the old bull's thick, leathery hide. The snare had been the worst of it. An older injury, the snare was not at all designed to withstand an elephant's strength but the wound had become infected. Without the complications from the snare, the bull probably wouldn't have required any veterinary intervention. It had taken John and Kelsey less than an hour from when the bull first went down to Kelsey injecting the anaesthetic reversal drug. Kelsey ha methodically extracted the bullets and cleaned the wounds while John worked on the snare injury and monitored the elephant's vitals. The team had then given the bull a huge one-off dose of antibiotics before reversing the sedatives. They then backed away, remaining vigilant as they observed their patient from the jeep, ensuring it came out from under anaesthesia and was up and moving around well enough to fend for himself before leaving.

The four friends were laughing and singing; Kelsey produced a hip flask filled with Irish whiskey and four small shot glasses. "Picked it up on my last stay in the city. Come on," Kelsey prodded John as she offered him a nip. "We had a win here today; injuries weren't as bad as they looked. We saved an elephant, no one was injured. It's not too often we can say that. We should celebrate the times we can."

Amana had offered to drive since he didn't drink. Sefu had broken out into song, singing something in Swahili and Amana had joined in. Kelsey didn't know the song, but it didn't stop her belting out the three words she recognised. Only John remained quiet, studying some of the slugs Kelsey had pulled from the elephant. "Doesn't make much sense, does it?" he said to Kelsey when she had stopped singing. "I wouldn't use these to stop a rottweiler, let alone an elephant."

"People do stupid things when they're desperate," Kelsey shrugged. "It's definitely not the work of our usual poachers. I wonder what drove them to it."

2

Chapter Two: The Lord's Resistance Army

John-

It was just before eight o'clock when the jeep ambled back into the compound. Mossi was now the head guard on duty when they arrived.

"Boss, Mrs. Boss says for me to tell you to see her as soon as you get back."

Like that's not what I do every time I get back, John thought to himself. "Thanks Mossi."

"Alright guys, Amana can I get you to refuel and park the truck? Sefu, you help Kelsey move that footlocker back into the supply shed and you two can refill it with anything we used today. Then I want you all to get something to eat. Mossi, where is Mrs. Boss?"

"In your house, Boss."

"Thanks mate. I'll go see what she wants."

As the small team went about their work, John paced toward the little onsite cottage that served as home for him and Amy. He ran a calloused hand through his thick black hair, as he stepped inside and looked around.

"Amy? Ahh, shit!" He tripped and fell heavily. *The fuck was that?*

John started to pick out the shape of what he had tripped over; it was a young male.

John reached for the small bear claw style knife he carried clipped to his belt in the small of his back. "Who the fu-"

"John! Language in front of the children," Amy scolded as she came around the corner turning on the light to see her husband knife half drawn staring down the two frightened children.

John quickly stood back up absolutely disgusted with himself for nearly drawing a weapon on children.

"What are your names?

"I..I'm Issa," stuttered the older of the two boys, "this is my little brother Tau."

"Issa and Tau," John started, getting down on one knee to be closer to the boys' height and putting the smile back on. "I am sorry for what I said, and for giving you guys a fright. I didn't mean to. You scared me too, alright? Now stay right here, I'm going to talk to Mrs. Wilson and then we'll be back."

John got up and followed Amy into the kitchen, shutting the door behind them.

"I'm sorry," John got in first.

"It's alright, you couldn't have known. And I love how protective you are of everyone here. The boy's village burned this morning. We got word while you were gone."

"LRA?"

"LRA. I didn't know where to send them. Obviously, I couldn't send them home. I'm not sure if any of their relatives survived."

"They can stay here for tonight. We'll figure out a longer-term solution in the morning. Have they had something to eat.?"

"No, they don't want me to leave them and they're too scared to leave the house. Mossi spotted me moving them from the classroom to here and helped. But we decided to wait til you got back as to what to do next. Everyone knows about an LRA attack, only you, Mossi and I know about the boys."

"Alright, I'll sort food for them. The LRA, huh? This far south?"

"Worst kept secret in camp right now, everyone knows about it, no one's talking about it."

"I'll go to the hall and nip this in the bud. Get some food and bedding sorted while I'm there."

"How'd the elephant go?"

"Much better than we thought. Had gunshot wounds but the morons had used a light round. He had a snare wrapped around an ankle as well that had been infected. But we were expecting much worse. Everything went fine; he's up and running again and we didn't have any trouble with poachers or predators."

John stopped and smiled at her. "You worry for nothing." He kissed her on the forehead and headed back to the two boys.

"Stay here with Mrs Wilson. I'm going to go get some food for you guys and some bedding. I'll be back soon. Amy, how about some hot chocolate for the boys?"

"Oh, what a good idea. Issa, Tau come into the kitchen we'll make some hot chocolate."

John maintained his smile until he was out of the house and jogging down the cottage's front stairs. But his smile quickly faded when thoughts of the LRA's actions came back. The Lord's Resistance Army, often referred to as the LRA, was the biggest rebel group in that part of Africa. What made them more terrifying than most was their frequent use of child soldiers. They would go to a village, round everyone up, burn the village down, and force the children to kill their own parents. With no home to return to, and the shame of killing their own family hanging over their heads, most of the children would never even attempt to escape and would become indoctrinated.

John strode into the hall with a heavy heart for the conversation that was to come, his broad shoulders sagging a little as though a great weight had settled upon them. Most of the rangers were eating and chatting, a few were playing cards. Thimba had joined Amana, Sefu, and Kelsey in discussing the elephant they had saved. John made his way over to them and addressed the small group of friends.

"Sorry to interrupt guys, but I need Amana's voice."

John turned to the massively built Amana, "I need everyone's attention, the whole room." Standing at five foot ten and nearly a hundred kilos of solid muscle John was by no means a small man. But Amana was positively gigantic, standing nearly head and shoulders above John. And with such a large frame came a booming voice to match.

"Sure thing boss. EVERYONE, MR. WILSON GOING TO TALK TO US NOW. HE NEEDS EVERYONE TO LISTEN."

John stepped up onto one of the long bench seats that ran along the tables so everyone could see him. He felt every eye in the room on him.

"As some of you may have heard, a village not far from here was burned. The word is it was the work of the LRA." John heard the muttering, a few scattered gasps. It was one thing for them all to have heard of an LRA attack, it was another thing entirely for their boss to stand up and openly acknowledge it. He pressed on. "Two of the boys from Mrs. Wilson's school belonged to that village. Small mercy the attack happened while they were here. But now they have no home to return to, and we don't know if any of their family survived. So, until we find a more long-term solution they shall be staying with us. I would impress upon you all that these are frightened children and ask that you go out of your way to make them feel safe and welcome here. After this I'll need some help organising some bedding and food for them. If the kitchen staff would be so kind as to make a little extra?"

John took in a deep breath as he examined the grave faces before him.

"Now about the LRA. It's unlike them to come this far south, given the army barracks at the city are only a day away. I don't see them coming down here to cause us trouble, but I can't rule it out either. We are a tougher nut to crack than some poor village, but we do have things they want. Weapon stocks, fuel, vehicles, food, water, and the like. Not to mention that they fund themselves from criminal activities that we impede, like poaching. Make no mistake, they do stand to gain if they can defeat us. Until we get word they have moved back up north, we are going to prepare for the possibility they might come here. Everyone is to clean and check their rifles before they go to bed tonight; I will be inspecting them in the morning. Until further notice all travel outside the compound will be subject to my approval and starting tomorrow morning, we shall be preparing the compound to withstand assault. If those motherfuckers want to come and try us here, they'll find us more than ready. These are just precautions, but we must be prepared for the fact they might not be. Lastly, I understand facing the LRA is not what you signed on for. I know some of you have family in the villages around here. If for any reason you feel like you cannot stay, that you need to leave to see to your family, or if facing the LRA is not something you can do, please come to my house tonight and talk to me. I think that about does it, any questions?"

"Next villages are behind us boss."

John searched for who had spoken, he found Kenyatta staring right at him. Kenyatta could not be less like Amana if he tried. Where Amana was tall and heavily built, Kenyatta was short, tough, and wiry. Where Amana was essentially a kind and gentle giant, Kenyatta spoke with a hard edge and had a sneer that could curdle milk, his eyes and demeanour exuded an utter contempt and hatred of all those who oppress others that could only come from someone who had been deeply and horrifically wronged. Kenyatta was not a talker, but in

John's few conversations with him he had told of how he had been a child soldier in the service of a group like the LRA until he was able to escape. Despite his hard edge, Kenyatta was always respectful to others and had a particular soft spot for Mrs. Wilson. Perhaps most importantly given the circumstances, Kenyatta was never found to be wanting during a confrontation.

"What are you getting at Kenyatta?" John replied confused.

Kenyatta stood up now so everyone could see him. "All other villages in this area the LRA might attack lie between us and the city. If you have family in the villages, know that the LRA must come through here before they can attack them. You have a much better chance of stopping them here than leaving to see to your family. For me, I hope they come. Give me one chance, and I'll cut out Lord's heart and feed it to him." The utter hatred Kenyatta had for the LRA and for Lord in particular was unmissable in his voice.

"I think we're all on the same page here," John stated when Kenyatta sat back down. "Everyone finish your meals and clean your rifles. We start building defences in the morning. I'll let Mossi know what's going on."

"I hear you, boss." Mossi called out from the gate. "I am with you."

"That's sorted then, oh and here's food," John said as one of the kitchen staff placed a tray down on the table beside Kelsey. As John took a seat, another of the kitchen ladies placed a second, covered tray on the table beside him. "For the children," she said. John smiled his thanks. He turned to the small group of friends around him.

"Now about bedding for the boys, we have room for them in the cottage, but no spare beds."

"There are some extra cots in the store room." It was Amana who spoke. "Nothing special, same as the ones we sleep on, but clean and spare."

"They'll do. Help me grab them when I finish here?"

"You two grab the beds, I'll take the food over," put in Kelsey. "We should all get going, got some big days ahead of us. Night then." The four men mumbled their goodnights to each other and left the hall. Sefu and Thimba for their dorm, Amana and John for the storage shed.

"Boss what'll happen to the children if none of their relatives survived? Where will they go?" Amana asked as he and John opened the store room.

"Don't really know," admitted John, picking up one of the cots. "Mrs. Wilson and I can't keep them indefinitely, much as Mrs. Wilson might like too. The Sam Childers orphanage is an option. Though I don't like it, and Childers has his hands full as it is. But they would be safe there. Thing is, I've never known you to be someone who starts these kind of conversations without an idea of your own. So, let's hear it."

Amana hesitated as John closed and locked the storeroom. He started as the two friends picked up the beds and carried them toward the Wilson's cottage. "They are welcome in my home," said the big man. "My wife and I have a place in the city; they'd be safe, go to school, have food, running water and a roof over their head."

"Will your wife cope with the extra numbers? How many children do you have now?"

"My wife…we cannot have children of our own, boss. She would be filled with joy to welcome those two in our home."

John looked across at his friend. Amana would make an excellent father. He was calm, good natured, and wise. His wife Auni was a lovely lady and a devoted wife. The two boys could certainly be worse off than living with Amana and Auni.

"They'll stay here for at least the next few days. Beyond that we'll just have to wait and see. If we can find their family, that's obviously our first choice. But if it comes to it, I know you two would care for them like they were your own."

After the two beds had been made up in the spare room of the cottage and the boys put to sleep. John and Amy retired to their room and as was their custom every night, sat down at the little table in the corner of the room. He took her hands in his, they bowed their heads together, and prayed. Then after kissing his wife goodnight, John pulled a large canvas roll and a long hard plastic case from the cupboard on the other side of the room, collecting his rifle on the way out. John made his way out to the long table on the outside porch. Kelsey, who slept in the other room at the cottage had also had the same idea and was already there with her canvas roll along part of the table, laying across the canvas were an assortment of firearms she was cleaning and inspecting.

"Mind if I join you?" queried John as he set his own canvas roll down already knowing the answer.

"By all means. Make me feel like less of a serial killer sitting here mucking around with guns on my own."

John set down his rifle and the long hard plastic case against the wall, quickly ducking back inside and came back with two small glasses and a bottle of scotch, pouring a glass for both Kelsey and himself.

"Singleton?" Kelsey asked, "Isn't that your best scotch? Sure you want to waste it on tonight?"

"It's not my best scotch, it's my favourite, which is different. And if there was ever a time for scotch, it's now."

"Can't argue with that," Kelsey replied. The two friends clinked their glasses together in salute and took a sip.

John took another before he started again.

"Look I just wanted to say, normally in a situation like this I would ask you and Amy to leave, take those kids with you. And I haven't asked you that, not because I particularly want you guys here if we are attacked…" he got no further before Kelsey cut him off.

"Idiot, we are safest here. I know that, you know that. If we left and tried to reach the city with the LRA around, it'd only be dumb luck if we made it. I know that if you thought we'd be safer elsewhere, you'd be telling us to go. And you know that I'd refuse. Besides," Kelsey continued, waving her hand over the assortment of firearms on her canvas roll. "How many times do I have to prove to you I can hold my own?"

John chuckled. "Which brings me to my next point. I've never asked, and you don't have to tell. But I'm not stupid. You carry a sig sauer, you're surgical with that M4. You basically have an armoury on that damn roll, and that shot in Rwanda? That was over a kilometre, from one mountain to another, water in the middle with no spotter to help you. I couldn't make that shot, no one without world class training makes that shot. You've got the best eyes here, you're the best shot, and I know you remain calm under pressure. So, when you've finished with your stuff, I want you to prepare this." John lifted the long hard plastic case onto the table and opened it to reveal a Dragunov SVD rifle. "Tomorrow morning, I want you to take Thimba and build a nest wherever you feel is best, somewhere up high that gives you good line of sight over the compound and the outside. If we do get attacked, I want you on over watch, keep us posted of what's going on, and take whatever shots you feel best to disrupt the attack. I'm not going to tell you what to do, I trust you."

"Where have you been hiding this?" Kelsey looked over the rifle. Dragunov's instilled fear in those who faced them, and having a woman wield it, well that would be all the greater insult. John knew Kelsey understood the faith he was placing in her. They had that bond that only comes from shared danger. Where neither talked about their past, yet each understood.

As John started pulling apart his day-to-day rifle, a lever action .308, Kelsey, without looking at John, started to speak.

"I wasn't born in Australia, as you know. My mother is Australian, but my father is Israeli, and I grew up in Israel. My father insisted I be able to fend for myself and every Israeli man and woman is required to do two years in the army when they turn eighteen. At twenty I moved to Australia and enrolled in vet school. I worked very hard to lose my accent which is why…" Kelsey's voice trailed off before she burst out laughing.

"How do you still have that ancient piece of crap!?" Kelsey exclaimed gesturing to a pistol gripped sawn-off double barrel shot gun that looked as if had been made well before either of them had been born.

"What? It's never let me down before. It has its job."

"What role could it possibly fill that wouldn't be done better by your .308, or your Styer or that equally ancient .357 you wear?"

"I like having it tucked in the car door or by the bedside table for that first exchange, just easier to let a doorway have both barrels knowing it'll hit something and give me a second or two to get sorted."

"Well do me a favour? Don't fire that thing anywhere near me. It's just as liable to blow up in your hand as it is to fire."

"Don't worry, I plan to have you up nice and high before any shooting starts."

It was well into the night by the time the two friends finished cleaning their weapons. Further still by the time they finished the scotch and turned in for the night, both well aware that another opportunity to sit, relax and talk would not readily present itself over the next few days.

3

Chapter Three: Preparations

John-

The camp next morning was a hive of activity. Wilson had everyone up by 6:00 am. He'd inspected every rifle and had divided all the staff into work parties, filling hessian bags with sand and building them up in key points around the compound as well as fortifying the gates and walls. He had then ordered that everyone was to head in and have breakfast before starting work.

By 7:00 am, John was eating his breakfast and discussing the plans for the day with Kelsey, Amana, and Amy, who had Issa and Tau beside her. John's thinking was that the boys knew what was coming, so hiding it from them and pretending everything was okay wasn't fair to them. It was better to have them helping in preparing the defenses.

"You and Thimba find a good place to build your hide?" John asked, turning to Kelsey.

Kelsey, halfway through a large mouthful of her toast, motioned for Thimba to answer.

"The water tower gives the best view of the area. But it's obvious and very exposed. The next best space is the roof of two block."

Kelsey stepped in for him now, "We'd like to build a nice big hide at the top of the water tower." Seeing a confused frown come over John's face she quickly continued. "We're going to build our actual hide on the two-block roof but have a nice big hide on the water tower so if they do see shots coming from our direction they'll hopefully think it's coming from the tower and target it instead of us. The only issue is that you can't see the whole way around the compound from any one spot. It's a matter of finding where the best spot on that roof is. That'll be this morning's job."

"Fair enough," John replied. The three of them staring at the rough map in front of them. For ease of communication Kelsey had labelled the front of the camp "A" side, the right "B" side, the back "C" side, and the left "D" side. The buildings were identified with either names or numbers. "Although I don't think you have to worry too much about the C side. They'd be foolish to try cross the river and attack us from the back. Between us, the crocs and hippos none would make it across. It's just the A, B and D sides you'll have to worry about."

"I'd have to agree with you." Kelsey said thoughtfully.

With thoughts of defensive measures and expecting an actual attack on the compound the mood had grown quiet and somber among the friends. Everyone clearly heard the call come from the front gate.

"STAND TO!"

The mess hall erupted in a frenzy of activity.

"Everyone to your battle positions!" bellowed Wilson. Giving Amy a quick kiss, he continued. "Issa, Tau, you stick close to Mrs. Wilson and Kenyatta okay, do what they say." John had assigned Kenyatta the role of protecting Amy and the two boys in the event the compound was attacked and knew he would take his duty seriously. Kelsey was now also shouting above the din. "Thimba!? We must get to the roof! Go!"

At this, John shot a quick glance at Kelsey and their eyes met for no longer than a second or two. No words were spoken and yet an entire conversation was had. John and Kelsey had been through these kinds of situations before and had those wordless conversations before. He tore his eyes away. "Amana! You're with me. You drive." And with that the two friends ran out of the mess and piled into the truck outside. As they pulled up to the front gate Amana turned the vehicle sideways so that it not only blocked the front entrance of the camp but so that he would be able to use the engine block as cover. As Amana and John exited the vehicle John's earpiece crackled into life.

"John? Kelsey. How copy?"

"Solid copy. See anything?"

"You got three Toyota Hiluxes. In convoy, on the road, coming straight for the front gate. Gotta say, doesn't look like a rebel attack."

"Okay, Kels. Wait one."

John stepped up into the watchtower where Sefu was on duty. He had sounded the alarm.

"What do we have, mate?" John could see the dust cloud kicked up by the vehicles and could make out a white pick-up as the lead vehicle.

"Not sure Boss. We not expecting any arrivals today, so when I seen them coming, I sound alarm. You always said better to yell too soon than too late. Hope I have not caused too much trouble?"

"No, you did well. Like you said we aren't expecting any visitors. So, who they fuck are they? Good job, Sefu."

"Your Styer is on the rack Boss, and your armour is on the desk."

Strapping his body armour on John turned on the PA system. "Everyone, hold your fire. This doesn't look like a rebel attack, but we don't know who they are or what they want, so remain on alert." Picking up his Styer out of the rack, John stepped out of the watchtower and onto the main road into the compound. He took a second to look behind him and check everyone was in a good position behind cover. He noticed Amana behind the engine block of the truck and walked over to him with half a grin on his face. "Amana, when this all kicks off, check your targets before you fire, hey? If you shoot me in the ass, I'm going to be un-fucking-happy, alright?"

A chorus of nervous chuckles came back to him as the small joke cut through the tension each man was feeling.

Now the cars were within fifty meters of the compound. John strode back to the centre of the road, released a deep breath, and held up his hand to signal to the small convoy to stop…

4

Chapter Four: Nikita

Nikita- St. Petersburg, Russia- Fifteen months after the events in South Sudan.

Nikita stood outside the office. Waiting, with her head bowed, to be summoned inside. The bass of the Red Dragon nightclub vibrated the floor beneath her feet in low rumbles. Nikita did not know why she had been sent for, nor would she ask. Questions had long been taken from her. She could no longer remember her birthday, if Nikita was her real name, or what her favourite movie was, if she ever had one.

It had been that way for years now. She hadn't understood at first, been too young to grasp what was happening. Her father had taken her to a house where money changed hands, telling her he would be back soon and that these kind people would look after her until then.

Father never did come back.

The first night wasn't so bad. They fed her, let her watch television. But by the second day, the smiles had vanished, replaced by cold commands and locked doors. A woman, stoutly set with blue eyes and brown hair now greying with age, educated her for the next few years. Nikita learned to read, write, cook, clean, and obey without quarrel.

Then came the men. With hungry eyes and rough hands, they educated her in a different way.

Five years passed as Nikita was trained. Five years of being passed from one handler to another, learning new languages through necessity rather than choice, learning to play the piano so she might better entertain guests. Five years of having her personhood slowly stripped away until she became only what they wanted—shattered and worthless, empty and perfect. A shell of a woman that did not ask questions, did not argue, did not hope, just obeyed.

Training had been brutal. But life afterward was no easier. Having invested so much into her education, her teachers sold her. Since then, Nikita could not tell how many times she had been sold. Nor how many years had passed. She reasoned that she was not yet thirty and had to be at least twenty-four. But accuracy beyond this eluded her. Some masters had been callous, some business-like, others liked to pretend to be virtuous and kind. None of them compared to her current owner, Mr. Sokolov.

In addition to his day job, Mr. Sokolov was a part owner of the Red Dragon nightclub. On a good night, Nikita would work there in the private lounge. On a bad night, things would be much, much worse. Sokolov was a movie director of sorts. What he and his associates were capable of drove terror into her heart. A mere look from the man made her chest tight and her head scream even as she stayed silent. Above all others, she feared this man.

And so there she stood, head bowed, in the hallway, waiting to be summoned. Not knowing why and knowing better than to wonder; or worse, to ask.

"Nikita. Come in," Sokolov's voice commanded from inside.

She obeyed, keeping her eyes down as she entered. She did not speak. Doing her best to control her breathing, Nikita could see Sokolov from the chest down and, out of her periphery, another man. Though she could not see his face, he seemed tall. His long bony fingers came into view; he moved slowly yet could easily gain a good distance in a few, easy steps.

"This is the one I spoke of," Sokolov spoke again. Interestingly, again in English, not his native Russian.

"She is pretty, might be good." The other man spoke in English with a distinct French lilt. *So that's why, neither must speak the other's language. They have to communicate in English.* Not unusual, many in Europe spoke varying levels of English as a second language for this exact reason.

Nikita did not dare speak as the Frenchman circled. She felt an icy prickle stretch across her skin under his gaze. "She will need to be cleaned up to be suitable for the job."

"Leave it to me," Sokolov replied. "She'll be ready."

The Frenchman cleared his throat before replying, "I leave this in your hands." Nikita couldn't see, but she felt the two men walk toward each other, heard them shake hands, before the Frenchman walked past her and out the door.

The door clicked shut behind the Frenchman, leaving Nikita alone with Sokolov in the suffocating silence of his office. The bass from the nightclub seemed to throb in time with her heartbeat, though she kept her face carefully blank. Her eyes fixed on a spot on the floor, counting the pulsing that thudded in her ears.

"Look at me," Sokolov commanded.

Nikita raised her eyes slowly, meeting his gaze with practiced emptiness even as her chest seemed to constrict in on her. Her mouth remained closed but if someone bothered to look, her nostrils flared rapidly as her breathing spiralled out of control.

"You have a new assignment," he said, drawing from his cigar before exhaling a cloud of smoke that drifted between them. "An Australian. Mr John Wilson. You will be working as his personal assistant."

Personal assistant. The words meant nothing. It was always the same story dressed in different clothes.

This was not unusual—being assigned to men of business or politics. What was unusual was the level of detail Sokolov provided. Typically, names were unnecessary. She was simply told where to go, what to wear, what to do. Nikita remained still, waiting for instructions.

"This man is an anti-poaching and wildlife specialist in Africa. Our French friend requires him to accept a position at Leningradskiy Zoo and is paying me handsomely to make that happen." Sokolov's calm words were menacing in their explanation. "We are offering him a supervisory position with salary, accommodation provided, and a personal assistant to take care of his every need."

Every need. The words hung in the air, their meaning unmistakable. Nikita kept her face expressionless even as her stomach pooled with dread.

"Your job is simple. Make him comfortable. Make him... want to stay. Whatever that requires. You drive him to and from work, shop for him, cook and clean, whatever is necessary to keep him here and happy."

He reached out, his thick fingers brushing her cheek. Nikita didn't flinch, though everything inside her screamed to recoil.

"Johnathon is not like the others. He's a cruel and savage man. He's spent the last six years killing his way through Africa. Before that he was military. What he's capable of makes even me nervous." He ceased his caress momentarily before seizing Nikita by the throat, lifting her off her feet before slamming her against the wall of his office.

"I don't care what he wants. I don't care what he does to you. You exist only to keep him here and happy. If you fuck this up for me, or if he decides to quit or leave before the Frenchman pays me... you will long for the kindness I've shown you thus far. I will make sure your next video is... exquisite. Understand?"

Nikita nodded as best she could with Sokolov's fingers pressing into her throat. The pressure wasn't enough to cut off her air, just to remind her who controlled it.

"Good." He released her, straightening his cuffs as Nikita's feet hit the floor with a dull thud. "You begin as soon as he accepts the role. You'll be moved to an apartment near his. Make yourself presentable."

She rubbed her throat gently when his back was turned. Dropping her hand immediately when he faced her again, pulling a manila folder from his desk before handing it to her. "Memorise everything. His habits, his preferences, his history. By the time he gets here, I want you to know him better than he knows himself."

Nikita took the folder; her throat still throbbed where his fingers had been.

Back in her small room, Nikita read the papers under the harsh fluorescent light. The first page held a photograph—a man with hard eyes and sun-weathered skin, his expression unreadable. Jonathon "John" Wilson. Not smiling. Not scowling. Just... watching, as if he could see through the camera lens to whoever might be studying his image years later.

She traced her finger over the sparse details. Five foot ten inches tall, solid build, hazel eyes, black hair. Born in Cloncurry, Queensland. Military service. Advanced qualifications as a medic and in enhanced interrogation techniques. After discharge, six years in various African countries combating poaching operations. A wife- no longer around. No children.

The file contained newspaper clippings too, they detailed wildlife conservation efforts, quotes from local officials praising his work protecting endangered species. Secretly Nikita had always thought Africa a magic and wonderful place. Back when she had hope, she thought she'd like to visit there one day. This Jonathon... there was no doubt he was dangerous, but something didn't align with Sokolov's description. Although Nikita knew better than to question, the mere fact she was being bought to him was proof enough of his cruelty.

Nikita memorised the details as though her life depended on them, it did.

5

Chapter Five: St. Petersburg

John- Saint Petersburg, Russia. Three months later.

"We're pleased you finally accepted our offer, Mr. Wilson. We are looking forward to having you bring your expertise to our team. Do you have any questions? I trust they showed you your apartment and gave you the keys already? It is satisfactory?"

It had been eighteen months since the incident in Sudan. Eighteen months since he'd lost her, eighteen months since damning himself. He'd spent that time contracting, well contracting and drinking. He fought rebels in Equatorial Guinea, tracked poachers in South Africa, trained rangers in Angola, hunted problem animals in Mozambique- where didn't matter. There hadn't really been a plan, just wake up, drink, and deal with the day. There hadn't been any shortage of work for men like him. Men with his skills that didn't have a plan, who didn't care if they lived or died.

After bouncing around Africa on various teams in a drunken haze, John came to the realisation that despite how hated himself, whenever put in a position where he might be killed, something deep within him resolved to fight, resolved to live.

He had decided to leave Africa, and unsure of where to go accepted an offer to join the St. Petersburg Zoo managing their Africa exhibits. They'd been offering it to him for about three months. Russia was as about as far from Africa as one could get, and the job even came with an apartment to live in. Nothing fancy, one bedroom, one bathroom, with a shower over the bathtub, combined living/dining space and a small kitchenette- but better than how he had been living lately.

He'd moved in yesterday, if you could call it moving in. Everything he owned fit into two bags. It was his first day on the job as it were, and John was meeting with the curator of the zoo — a large thickset man called Aleski, before meeting the rest of his team.

"Apartment's more than fine, moved in yesterday," came John's reply to Aleski's question. "My only concern is that my Russian is quite terrible, bordering on non-existent. Question wise, how many staff do I have? What level of oversight do you want me to have on them?"

A slight confused look overtook Aleski's blockish face. "You have six in staff; you are their superior. Manage them as you like, if you must make changes that is fine. Retrain them, fire them, do what you think is best, they are yours. As for your concern about your Russian, all the staff speaks English, but in differing levels. But we did not hire you to learn Russian, your assistant will act as an interpreter should you need her to."

"Oh yes, my assistant?"

"Nikita," Aleski replied before bellowing into the hall, "Nikita! My office. Meet Mr. Wilson."

John stood from his chair as Nikita entered the room and held out his hand to shake hers. "It's a pleasure," he offered.

"The pleasure is mine," Nikita countered.

John studied her as they shook hands, he wasn't sure what to make of her. She was neat and professionally dressed in a long-sleeved version of the same uniform he wore. On top of that she was one of the most gorgeous women he had ever laid eyes on. Short, with golden hair and piercing green eyes, a small spread of light freckles dotted her face. Fine arms with pale skin ended in petite hands. Five foot three, or maybe five foot two, she barely came to his shoulder high.

Yet there was something off about her. She met his gaze and smiled, but only with her lips; her eyes betrayed a look of disgust, or was it fear? Her mouth remained closed, but her nostrils flared with effort. Maybe she had heard something about his work in Africa? *Regardless, she's right to be disgusted.*

The first day flew by and in what had only seemed like an hour or two, John found himself sitting in his office long after the zoo had closed writing an email to Kelsey. She had been ecstatic to hear of John accepting a real job somewhere he wasn't going to be constantly shot at. Although Kelsey's own news was not without concerns, John was frustrated to learn that she had received a good behaviour bond by the police after an incident at a bar which saw her reject the drunken advances of a man by throwing him through a table. Although it was well and truly dark by the time John had finished up, the time difference between Africa and Russia meant he was wide awake. Nikita was also still at her desk, although it didn't seem like she was doing much.

"Nikita what time to you go home normally?'

"I am your assistant; I go when you go."

"Don't stay on my account go home. It's late, don't you have a family or husband waiting for you?"

"Sorry Mr. Wilson, I'm not to leave until you do. I understand you do not have a car and as your assistant I am required to pick you up for work and take you home when you are finished. If there is anything else that you require to make your stay here in St. Petersburg more comfortable, I am to assist in making that happen for you."

For fuck's sake. John sighed and looked across at Nikita. "I will go home, if that means you'll go home too, deal? Let me just send this email and we'll be out the door in five minutes. Do you want to get yourself ready?"

"Should I make a stop for food, Mr. Wilson?" Nikita inquired as the two climbed into the car.

"Again, it's John, and nah I'm good. Got sorted with most of my needs yesterday. General groceries here are quite cheap. I imagine the average wage here is not a lot?"

"Most people are just getting by, those with money flaunt it, but the gap between the haves and the have nots is massive. There is not much of a middle class in Russia. Do you have anyone here with you in St. Petersburg, or are you living alone?"

"You already know I live alone. I'm not a moron Nikita, I mean I'm not particularly smart, but I'm not stupid. I'm aware you probably know all about me, my background, my work in Africa." He let his voice trail off. "That I lost my wife…"

An uncomfortable silence hung in the air. *That'll teach you for asking stupid questions.* A few minutes later they pulled into the curb in front of the apartment complex.

"I'll escort you up," stated Nikita as she went to exit the car.

"What on earth for?" Came John's tart reply. "Do you not have someplace to be? Isn't there anyone waiting for you at home?" He checked his watch. "It's nearly nine o'clock for crying out loud."

"Well, I don't have anyone waiting for me at home and I was thinking, maybe I could come up and you could tell me stories about Africa and if there was anything you needed help with tonight, you know cooking or company… after all I am your assistant. I'm to help you with whatever you may need during your stay."

Awfully bold, yet John couldn't help the feeling that Nikita didn't really want to be around him, that she didn't actually want to come up. *Is it fear? Does she simply not like me? Why's she being so forward then?*

Or maybe I'm just tired and not thinking straight. At any rate he didn't care, he didn't want her to come up anyway.

"You say you're my assistant and you're to help me out with whatever I need?" John asked.

"Yes, sir," came her quiet reply.

"Well, I need a lift to work in the morning. Be here at seven. Go home Nikita."

***

True to their arrangement, John walked out at 6:58 the next morning to find Nikita's car waiting for him. As he climbed in, she handed John a coffee.

"Milk no sugar, correct?"

"Fuck me, how detailed is the zoo's file that you even know how I take my coffee?"

Nikita smiled in response.

"Thank you," John added. "I want to apologise for yesterday. I was just tired."

"Oh, of course sir, you needn't explain."

"Stop calling me sir. Do you have any family in St. Petersburg?"

"No, I live alone."

"Did you really want to hear about Africa?" John inquired.

"I would love to. I have never been, but I always wanted to go there. What was it like?"

"It's hot as hell and people keep trying to shoot you. But you can't get the views anywhere else. It's honestly amazing." For the first time John saw a bit of a light in Nikita's eyes, her posture still rigid, but she genuinely wanted to talk about Africa. "I'll tell you all about it sometime," John continued as they pulled into the zoo. "You want to join me on rounds? I need an interpreter."

"Absolutely, Mr. Wilson."

The African exhibit frankly wasn't much to write home about. There was a small troop of chimpanzees. A pair of giraffes, some zebras, ten ring-tailed lemurs, three cheetahs which happened to be brothers, and a small African wildcat called a caracal. To make matters worse the enclosures were little more than prison cells. Concrete and bars, the 'cleaning' of the enclosures involved hosing them out, which in Russia left them perpetually cold and wet. For animals evolved to live on the plains and jungles of Africa, this was altogether entirely unsuitable.

John was more than frustrated by the time he and Nikita stopped in at the chimpanzee enclosure.

One of the keepers, Nikolai, had just finished feeding them when John and Nikita arrived. John hadn't had much to do with Nikolai as yet but did know he spoke the least English of his staff. He also seemed to John to be a little haughty and arrogant. However, John was letting this slide so far as he wasn't sure if it was real, or simply a bit of a culture and language barrier. A scuffle between two or three of the female chimpanzees had sent screams through the back halls as John and Nikita approached.

"What was the scrap over? Any injured?" John asked knowing that chimpanzees, like all primates, were capable of inflicting serious injury on each other in a matter of seconds.

Nikolai looked at Nikita to translate and the two had a brief conversation in Russian. To John it seemed tense and curt, with Nikolai almost dismissive in his replies. But he wasn't sure if that was true or simply how Russian sounded to him.

Nikita turned back to John. "The fight was over food" she said with a bit of an unsure look on her face. Nikolai added something in Russian.

"What was that?" John asked.

"Ah… apparently it is not uncommon, it is not anything to be concerned about." although John thought Nikita didn't seem like she was accepting of the answer herself.

"Horseshit. Chimpanzee fights are always something to be concerned about. Also, what lazy dickhead just dumps food in one big pile? Of course they're going to fight over it. Translate that to Ivan the moron," John threw at Nikita. "And why are the females fighting over it? Isn't there a dominant male in this troop?"

Nikita hesitated and then began translating to Nikolai. Nikolai spat something back to her in Russian before waving his arm to the back corner of the enclosure and uttered something with a sneer.

"What was that?" John turned to Nikita.

"The male chimpanzee is at the back of the cage. He stays there with his head pressed to the ground."

John noticed that Nikita seemed a little hurt, like whatever Nikolai had spat at her before had found its mark.

"How long has he been doing that?"

"For a long time, Mr Wilson. He's been doing that since before I started here."

"Alright. Have all the keepers meet us in the break room after their rounds, this can't go on. And stop calling me Mr. Wilson, for fuck's sake!"

An hour later in the break room shortly before the keepers started to wander in, John took Nikita aside. "My Russian is rudimentary. Would you mind translating something I heard today?"

"Sure, John."

John replied with a clumsy attempt at the words Nikolai had spat at Nikita earlier. Nikita flinched as if she had been struck and looked back at John. She took a long breath, but before she could reply Nikolai walked in the room, closely followed by two other keepers. "We'll finish this conversation another time," John offered her, then turned to the men. "Have a seat, lads."

Over the next hour or so John laid down the law with how the animals were to be cared for. Enclosures were to be raked and swept instead of hosed whenever possible, enrichment programs designed, feed distributed throughout enclosures, not just dumped in one pile for the animals to fight over. Keepers were to alert John of any animals in their care that they suspect may be injured or sick, and training programs needed to be written.

"What are we training for sir?" the question was asked by Mikhail, one of the younger keepers. Smaller than Nikolai, he was in excellent shape and moved with the ease of a youth who had yet to suffer wear and tear or injuries. He also spoke the best English of the five keepers and John found he didn't need Nikita to translate for him to talk to Mikhail. The young man was a hard worker and humble, looking after his animals as well as he knew how, but still young and quiet.

"The question was what are we training for?" John repeated prompting Nikita to translate for the rest of the keepers. "We're not training you; we're going to train the animals." He continued.

"The enclosures they're in are not the slightest bit suitable. The zoo has acquired the vacant land behind it, and we are going to design and build a new African precinct to open late this year. We're going to train our animals to make transporting them to their new home easier and safer as well, making it less stressful to provide them veterinary care. I'll write the programs and provide training on how they should be implemented. If you have any questions or concerns about your animals, the training, or the new enclosure designs, feel free to chat to me about it. Otherwise, go and have your lunch."

John spent the rest of the afternoon writing basic training plans in English, which Nikita would then translate in Russian.

"You have an excellent grasp of enrichment and training theory mate. Quite impressive."

She blushed, smiling. "Thank you, I took a few online courses, nothing special."

"I'm having trouble with something, I don't really understand the hierarchy of the keepers," John continued.

Nikita thought for a second before replying. "In Russia, in a situation where everyone is at the same level, you defer to the oldest. If any of the keepers were concerned about something, they'd run it past the oldest of them, and he'd tell them what to do."

"Regardless of if the oldest keeper had any idea what to do?"

"Yeah, that's just the way it works here. It's… not always the best system."

"So, if a keeper was concerned about their animals, instead of coming to me they would go to the oldest keeper first, and if that keeper dismissed their concerns, they would drop it?"

"Yes," Nikita replied. "Even if they knew it was a problem, it's hard to break the culture."

"Who's the oldest keeper? The one everyone must go through?"

"Nikolai, Mr. Wilson"

"Fuck me. Why did I already think that before you said it?" John asked getting prickly. It did not escape him that Nikita reverted to the more formal "Mr. Wilson" in response to his aggravation. He took a deep breath to calm himself and looked into the bullpen outside his window where the keepers typed their notes. Mikhail was the only one still there, John had already noticed that Mikhail's notes were the most in depth and observant of the keepers and an idea struck him. He got up and banged on the window, waving for Mikhail to come into his office.

"Shut the door behind you please, mate." John took a seat, but Nikita had stood. Mikhail stood ridged and facing straight ahead, not unlike a soldier at attention.

"Relax will you. Mikhail? I'm going to ask you a question, and I want you to answer with what you think, regardless of what other people have told you, okay?"

Mikhail looked a little confused but nodded his agreement.

"The male chimpanzee that's pressing his head into the ground, what's wrong with him?"

"I don't know, I'm not a vet. But I would think he has head pain and is trying to get relief. His right eye looks wrong, maybe glaucoma? That would cause head pain."

"Liver issues could have the same effect, especially if the stress of managing the girls gets the better of him." It was Nikita who added the last bit.

John gave her a quizzical look but quickly composed himself. "That's more information in one question than I had the whole time I've been here. To be clear, next time you have a concern with any animal here, you come directly to me, that goes for you too." He turned toward Nikita for that last bit; something was off about her. He really needed to get to the bottom of it. And fast. It was irritating him, in fact Russia in general was irritating him. At least in Africa they shot you and you shot them.

The intricacies and undertones of Russian social conventions were not for him.

6

Chapter Six: Dinner

Nikita–

By late afternoon John had sent out a memo to all his staff: Mikhail was the senior keeper, effective immediately. Although Nikita was sure John would have to lend weight to that promotion until the rest of the staff got the message.

That evening she again drove him home. He was an interesting study this John. Seemed, fairer than she had expected. His conversation with her and Mikhail this afternoon spoke to that. But Nikita knew better, she knew what he was. Knew men like him, that started off fair and pretended to be virtuous only to become cruel later.

She did her best to stay calm. He had refused her invitation last night, perhaps he would again tonight, then again perhaps not. There really wasn't any point in wondering when John would require her, she simply knew that sometime, he would. The when was inconsequential.

"Here's good," John's voice cut through her spiralling thoughts.

Nikita pulled the car to the curb outside his apartment building, her hands gripping the steering wheel tighter than necessary. The engine ticked in the silence as she waited for him to speak, to make his demand.

"You know, you don't have to do this," John stated. His voice was calm and conciliatory. The words hung between them like a blade waiting to fall. She had heard similar promises before—empty reassurances that preceded demands, gentle preludes to violence.

"Do what?" she asked, as though she didn't know the answer.

John turned to look at her then, and something in his expression caught her off guard. Not hunger or anticipation, but something that looked almost like regret and shame.

"Any of it. The driving. The coffee. The offering to shop, cook…" He gestured vaguely, unable or unwilling to explain further.

"It's my job," she said carefully, testing the waters.

"No." His response was immediate, almost harsh. "Your job is administrative work. Translating, assisting me in a professional capacity." He ran a hand through his hair. "Not handling me as though you're a servant."

The silence stretched between them again. Nikita felt something shift inside her chest—not hope, she wouldn't allow herself that luxury—but perhaps the smallest crack in her certainty.

"I should go," John said finally, his hand already on the door handle.

"Would you like me to come up?" Nikita repeated her question from yesterday.

John leaned on the door frame as he replied, "Go home Nikita. See you in the morning."

***

John-

John walked up the steps of his apartment block. It had not been lost on him how Nikita reacted in his presence. Being fair, John knew he was surly and abrupt. He drank too much, spoke too harshly, and he was a killer. Worse than that, he was the lowest of the low. *Maybe the poor girl was simply a sensitive soul? No, there was more to it than that.*

He pushed his key into the lock; flicked on the light as he walked through the door, illuminating the functional furniture and bare walls. Nothing personal adorned the space—no photographs, no mementos, nothing that would anchor him to this place or any other.

He tossed his keys onto the counter and moved to the cupboards, pulling a glass off the shelf and pouring a rough nip from a bottle of Blanton's before slumping onto the worn couch. The day's events replayed in his mind, particularly the look in Nikita's eyes when she'd offered to come up. It was like she didn't want him to say yes, even though she offered. Same as the day before. The whole thing made him uncomfortable and fidgety.

"Christ," he muttered, taking a long sip as he looked out the window, eyes drifting down at the street. Nikita's car was still there, parked at the curb. *Was she waiting to see if he'd change his mind?*

"Fucking oddball," he let the curtain fall back into place.

When he looked out again about ten minutes later, he found her still there. *Fuck it. Guess we're doing this tonight.* He walked out the door and back down toward the car.

***

Nikita-

Nikita saw him coming in the rear-view mirror, his silhouette cutting through the amber glow of the streetlights. Her pulse quickened. *This was it then. He'd changed his mind after all.*

She watched him approach the passenger side door, her breathing shallow as her chest tightened. Every instinct screamed at her to start the engine and drive away, but she knew better.

John tapped on the window. When she rolled it down, he leaned against the car, studying her face in the dim light.

"You've been sitting here for over ten fucking minutes," he said. He spoke calmly, but was no less frightening for it.

"I was just…" She fumbled for an explanation that wouldn't sound pathetic. "Checking my messages."

"Lie." The word came out flat, matter-of-factly. "You didn't go for your phone once."

Heat flushed across Nikita's cheeks.

"I don't understand you," John said, his voice lower now, less accusatory. "You offer to come up, but you look terrified at the prospect. You insist on driving me, bringing me coffee, but you flinch if I move too quickly." He paused, studying her face. "Why? If I'm so distasteful, why not just stick to translating and administration?"

In that moment Nikita understood. *He doesn't know. He legitimately thinks I am just his assistant.*

The realisation hit her like ice water. *Of course he didn't know. Why would he?* The arrangement had been made through intermediaries. Sokolov had placed her here as he had placed her elsewhere before— to serve, to please, to be whatever was required. But this man, this strange, gruff Australian, hadn't been told what she really was.

"I..." Nikita's voice faltered. How could she explain without revealing everything? Without endangering herself? "It's complicated."

"Uncomplicate it."

She looked down at her hands, still gripping the steering wheel as if it might anchor her to safety. "Where I come from, it's important to... anticipate needs. To be useful." The half-truth tasting bitter on her tongue.

"And who told you I needed a personal servant?"

John's voice had softened slightly, his Australian accent seeming more pronounced in the quiet night.

Nikita swallowed hard. "No one specifically. It's just... expected."

"Expected by whom?" He shifted his weight, still leaning against the car door, but his posture had changed—less confrontational, more concerned.

"By..." She hesitated, the risk of saying too much looming over her. "By my previous employers." *Not exactly a lie.*

John's expression darkened. "And what exactly did these previous employers expect from you?"

The question hung in the air between them. Nikita felt trapped between the truth she couldn't speak and the lies she couldn't maintain. Her fingers trembled slightly against the steering wheel.

"Okay, that's enough." He said simply. "We don't need to do this here and now. Do you have any plans for dinner tonight?"

The unexpected shift in conversation left Nikita reeling. *Dinner?* She stared at him, searching his face for the trap she was certain lay hidden beneath the casual question.

"I…" she began, then stopped. *When was the last time someone had asked about her plans? When was the last time she'd had any plans that were truly her own?* "No."

"Good. Come up then. I'll cook something."

The words drove into her like a punch to the stomach. This was it—the demand she'd been waiting for, dressed in the guise of hospitality. Her stomach clenched as familiar dread settled over her like a shroud.

"You don't have to—"

"Neither do you." John straightened, stepping back from the car. "But it's been a long day and I'm bloody hungry. So come up, eat some food, and maybe we can figure out how we can both do our jobs without getting under each other's skin."

Nikita hesitated for a second, knowing she had to accept. Yet something about John's demeanour—his frustrated honesty, hands in pockets, looking more impatient than predatory.

"It's just dinner," he added when she didn't respond. "Nothing fancy either. I'm thinking gnocchi."

"I can cook that for you."

"I can bloody well cook it myself. Are you coming or not?"

"That sounds lovely, thank you."

They walked up to John's apartment in silence. Nikita noticing how

John deliberately slowed his pace to let her set the rhythm of their ascent, deliberately kept distance between them. Small considerations that felt foreign and unsettling. *Stop that you idiot.* She chided herself. *He's literally trained in torture, how stupid do you have to be to think this ends well? When Sokolov tells you a man is dangerous, then he's dangerous. End of story.*

John's apartment did not surprise her. No personal touches, no photographs, nothing to suggest permanence or attachment. It reminded her of places she'd known—places meant to be passed through, not lived in.

"It's not much," John said, catching her assessment. "But it serves its purpose."

He moved to the kitchen, pulling ingredients from the refrigerator. Nikita remained by the door, uncertain whether she should sit or stand or offer help again. The domestic normalcy of the scene felt surreal—watching this man who supposedly dealt in violence and control simply... cooking.

"Sit if you want. You're making me nervous hovering there like you're ready to bolt." He tossed gnocchi into the pan, the sizzling sound sharp in the quiet apartment.

She perched on the edge of his couch, hands folded in her lap, watching him work. His movements were economical, precise. Very unlike his usual jerky, abrupt manner of speaking and moving. There was something almost meditative about the way he handled food, as if this simple act provided him some measure of peace.

The aroma of garlic and herbs filled the small apartment as John worked, the soft sizzling of the pan the only sound between them. Nikita watched his back, the tension in his shoulders as he focused on the task. This didn't fit with what she knew of him—what she'd been told. Dangerous men didn't cook gnocchi for their assistants. They didn't maintain respectful distances or show concern about making others uncomfortable.

"Water?" John asked, glancing over his shoulder.

"Yes, please," she replied automatically.

He filled a glass and set it on the coffee table near her, returning to the stove without lingering. Not hovering, not using the moment to touch her or invade her space. Just… giving her water.

Nikita watched him as he worked, she caught herself wondering what had carved such deep furrows around his eyes. Not age—he was only mid-thirties—but something heavier. Something that matched the careful emptiness of his apartment.

"You're staring," John said without turning around.

Heat rushed to her cheeks. "Sorry, I—"

"No need to apologise." He carried two plates to the small table. "Just wondering what you're thinking."

The question caught her off guard. *When was the last time someone had asked what she was thinking? Really asked, not as a prelude to punishment for thinking the wrong thing.*

"You're not what I expected," she said carefully, accepting the plate he offered.

John settled across from her, his movements deliberate, slow. "Yeah? What did you expect?"

The question hung between them as Nikita pushed gnocchi around her plate, buying time. How could she answer without revealing too much? Without admitting that she'd expected cruelty disguised as kindness, demands wrapped in courtesy. "Someone less… less considerate."

John let out a short, bitter laugh. "That's not a word most people would use."

"Most people?"

"People who know me." He took a bite, chewing slowly. "My wife used to say I had the social skills of a brick wall."

Nikita took another bite, the flavours rich on her tongue. *This is really good. Everything is going well, too well.*

"You're doing it again," John said.

"What?"

"Act like you're waiting for the other shoe to drop. Like you expect me to do something…. unkind."

Nikita's fork clattered against her plate as she set it down, her hands trembling slightly. She looked up to find John watching her with those sharp eyes, seeing too much.

"I don't know what you mean," she said, but even to her own ears the denial sounded hollow.

"That's a lie." John leaned back in his chair, his expression firm but not unkind. "You sit like you're ready to run. You offer things you don't want to give. You flinch when I move too fast. You don't think you do, but you do. You flinch and recompose yourself."

Nikita's chest tightened. This was dangerous territory.

John went on, "I can't figure out if I disgust you, or if you're scared of me, or both. You act almost like you owe me a debt. Like you're terrified I'll collect at any moment. I can't stand it." The admission hung between them, raw and unexpected. He rose and ducked into the kitchen before returning with a bottle of vodka and two small glasses.

7

Chapter Seven: Questions and answers

Nikita-

John placed the bottle and both glasses on the table. "What I propose is this. I have questions for you, and it seems you have some for me. So, we'll go one for one. Ask a question, take a shot. Then it's the other person's turn. Whatever this is between us, I want it sorted tonight."

Nikita stared at the bottle. *This was it. Play respectful, nice dinner, now a drinking game. Get her drunk, take what he wants. And you thought he was different, how stupid. Just obey, it will be over soon.* A thought crossed her mind, one way to find out.

"And if I don't want to play this game?" *Risky, anger him and you'll make it much worse.*

"I'm not holding you prisoner. If you don't want to play, by all means finish your dinner and leave. But this—" he gestured between them "— would continue. The flinching, the walking on eggshells. I can't work like this, Nikita. Can't have you terrified of me every bloody day; and it can't be any picnic for you either."

The honesty in his voice caught her off guard. Not a threat, but something closer to exhaustion.

"One question, one shot?" she asked quietly.

John rose from the table, walking over to the door and opening it before returning to his seat. "One question one shot. And if either of us wants to stop, we stop. You may go first."

John poured two small glasses before sliding one across to Nikita. *It's a trap, but you don't have to make it worse. Something small, simple.* "Where did you grow up?" She took her shot, the burning in her throat heightened by anxiety.

John sighed, "Cloncurry, western Queensland. But you already knew that. Ask again, don't waste your questions."

"How do you know what I know?" The words tumbled out of her before she could stop them. *Oh fuck.*

"Okay, well you've never asked how I have my coffee you simply bring me coffee made exactly how I take it. When I commented that my file must be detailed, you didn't react at all. Means yes there's a file on me and you've read it. If it's detailed enough to know how I take my coffee than it would also have generic details such as hometown, military service, work in Africa. I think we can skip the preamble questions and ask what you really want. Next round of course, you already used your question this round."

John raised his glass, "My turn. You have a decent grasp of zoological practices, and you knew one of the reasons the male chimp could be sick. Why are you not a keeper?" The drained the glass with practised ease.

"It's not the position I was bought in for, it's hard to explain. It's not what the department needed. They needed someone to be an assistant to you." A sad little smile crept over her face and she turned her eyes away.

"Okay, your turn." John prompted, pouring Nikita's glass as she weighed her options. "Why did you refuse me last night?" The question came out before she could second-guess herself. "When I offered to come up."

John's eyes never left hers as she drank. "Because you didn't want to come up and I didn't want you to come up. Again, you knew the answer already. Stop wasting your questions." There was a hard edge to his voice now and Nikita knew she was annoying him. John's bluntness was honest in a way that left no room for the careful games she was used to playing. Nikita glanced at the open door the back to John.

"Okay. Why did you open the door?" she asked.

John's eyes were on her again, but studying her face, not roaming her body as most men did. "You don't feel safe and I need you to need to know you can leave. I get the feeling you don't think you can, and it's important to me that you understand that's not the case."

John raised his glass. "Did you have any choice about being my assistant?" He pressed and took his shot.

Nikita felt the question slice through her defences like a blade. The vodka's warmth had barely settled in her stomach when the chill of his question froze her in place. She stared at her empty glass. The alcohol clouded her mind as she weighed lies against truths, survival against honesty.

"No," she finally whispered. Something shifted in John's expression. Nikita hurried to add to her answer, "I mean, I'm the assistant to that position. You won that position, so I'm your assistant."

"Hmmm, okay," he said, his voice deceptively calm as he poured again. "Your turn."

"Why do you care?" The question escaped her lips before she could filter it. "About my choice, about my comfort. Why does it matter to you?" The words tumbling out of her after several shots. *What are you doing? You're not thinking straight.* It occurred to Nikita that this may have been John's plan all along. He didn't need to hurt her to get answers, just take the edge off and ask hard enough. At this rate he'd know every dark secret by the end of the night.

"Good questions, though still not what you want to ask." His hard eyes never left hers as he spoke. "I get the impression some of your previous bosses treated you like they owned you, maybe got a little rough or handsy. You want to know whether I'm going to be like that, whether I'm going to hurt you, that's what you want to ask."

Nikita's breath caught in her throat as John's blunt assessment stripped away every pretence she'd been clinging to. *They had owned me, but John couldn't know that.* The vodka glass trembled in her hand.

"I…" she started, then stopped. He was right. That was exactly what she wanted to know—needed to know.

John leaned forward slightly, his voice softer but no less direct. "So… ask."

The silence stretched between them, filled only by the distant sounds of the city filtering through the open door. Nikita could feel her pulse hammering in her throat. This was the moment—the question that would determine everything that followed.

"Are you going to hurt me?" The words came out barely above a whisper, yet seemed to echo in the small apartment.

John held her gaze with an intensity that made her want to look away.

"No." The word came out flat. "I am a god-awful piece of shit. But I will never hurt you. Not intentionally, not in anger, not for any reason. I will never lay a hand on you, never take something from you that you don't want to give." His voice was rough now, edged with something that sounded like disgust. "Whatever is in your head, the answer is no."

John poured another glass. "My turn. I was going to ask why Nikolai doesn't respect you, but I get the feeling he's just a disrespectful kind of person. He called you something today, something that hurt way down deep inside. My Russian is not very good, but I did recognise the word for 'whore.' I'm sure there's more to it than that. Explain."

Nikita had known John would ask this again. She knew eventually John would know every little thing about her, down into the parts she tried to close off from the world. The things that she had buried deep inside and wanted no one to ever see. That was the issue though; too many people already knew that secret, they knew how to reach out and touch it like an exposed nerve to cause pain whenever they wished.

"Nikolai…doesn't respect women much, or people in general. It's just something he says."

John looked back across the desk into her eyes. She looked straight back, willing him with every ounce of herself to believe what he was just told.

"Lie," John slowly let out. "Although I'm sure Nikolai doesn't have much respect for people in general, that's not why he called you that. What did he call you?"

Her head swum, there really wasn't any wiggle room from here. But if she said the wrong thing Sokolov would… with tears in her eyes she sat silently staring at the table, trying desperately to think of a way forward.

"Look at me." It was not a question. "I really am not going to hurt you. I just want to know what's going on. You and I both have questions. That's why we're doing this."

"You hurt me to find out. They hurt me for telling. Either way, I get hurt." Tears fell silently "Seems to me only choice I have is who hurts me and how bad. If I am to suffer, then let it be at your hand. You're a good man. I'm sorry, but I can't tell you everything, you would not be safe." *Not that I know much.*

"I'm not a good man, and who are they that would hurt you?"

Silent tears rolled down Nikita face. *Do not answer, no matter what comes next. Better John than Sokolov. You can take it.*

"Not going to talk? You would protect me as I hurt you to find out what I want? That seems silly." Nikita looked at the table, tears blurring her vision. She desperately thought of a way forward and found none. She noticed John go very still, the kind of stillness that reminded her of predators right before they strike. *Here it comes.* She braced herself. But when he moved, it was to rise to the kitchen, flicking on a kettle.

She looked at the open door; it seemed so far away. She doubted she could make it in her current state, and where would she run to anyway? Sokolov? She'd rather take her chances with John.

"How do you take your tea?" The words pulled Nikita from her thoughts.

"That's not rhetorical." John continued, "If you don't answer I'll make yours the same as mine."

"Milk, one sugar please."

John returned with two steaming mugs, setting them on the table before ducking back to the kitchen for a packet of biscuits. "Timtam's, little treat from back home." He explained as he sat.

"I'm not going to torture you with boiling water, if that's what you were thinking." His voice steady and calming. "I made tea because you're crying and you look like you need it."

She stared at the mug. *That had been what I was thinking.* The kindness he showed felt more dangerous than cruelty—at least with cruelty, she knew the rules.

"I am worth less than nothing Nikita. But honestly, there is no part of me that wishes to harm you, and there is nothing that you could be protecting me from that is worse than what I deserve. So, here's what's going to happen. You're going to tell me what Nikolai called you. You can tell me that at least and I in return will tell you what happened in Sudan with my wife. You tell me your secret; I'll tell you mine. We can leave it at that for tonight if you're willing."

Nikita, took a breath. If she wanted to keep anything she would have to give up something. It killed her what she was about to say, but it was the only way forward. *Say enough to satisfy him, no more.*

"He called me 'Shyluka iz Bratsk' it means 'the whore of Brastk' except there are no articles in Russian so we don't have a word for the."

"Brastk is a place?"

"A city on the banks of the Angara River."

"What was he referring to?"

Nikita turned her face away, "Some videos I starred in, before I was an assistant. Starred, ha!" She spat the last part out.

"I see," John said quietly. "I take these 'videos' are not suitable for children."

"Not suitable for anyone really, they are not tasteful. Pain and humiliation was the key focus and unfortunately, they are on several well-known sites."

"Nikolai doesn't respect you because you were an…" he paused as if searching for the term, "actress, before you worked at the zoo?"

"Kind of." He had been kind and respectful in what he had heard so far and seemed satisfied with her answers. "I was sold when I was young and trained to accept what men wanted to do with me. Turns out when men can do whatever they want without consequence, they turn to pain and humiliation. I was good at dealing with that and made a name for myself, each video I was in was worse than the last."

Nikita looked up to see John's reaction as she spoke. The look on his face was not pity, more like sorrow. His posture was soft and his voice calm as he replied.

"But you got out, and got yourself to the zoo. Leaving behind that life is a big thing. You should be proud of that. And if Nikolai continues to bring up your past he will answer to me. That shit ends today." He took a breath. "Your knowledge of animals is really very good, if keeping is something you want to work toward, I would support you in doing that."

Nikita stared at John across the small table, her tea cooling between her trembling hands. His words stilled the air—support, protection. The kindness felt like another trap, yet something in his weathered face suggested he meant every word. She watched as John bit off a corner on his biscuit before dunking it in the tea. He bought it up to his mouth but paused, his brow furrowed in thought.

"N-no," he said softly, almost to himself. He looked at her again. "No, you're not free, are you?" He said it slowly and did not need an answer. "You said you were bought in for this position, to be my assistant, with no choice."

Nikita held her breath and said nothing, able to almost see John's brain clicking and whirring as it connected the dots. *Oh, fuck he knows, I've said too much.*

"You keep telling me you are my assistant to help me with working, cooking, company, or whatever else I require."

He leaned back in his chair now looking away. "The past few days make a lot more sense now. It raises other questions, sure. But I promised we would be done once you told me what Nikolai said, and I keep my promises. I will however, add this." He turned back to face Nikita again. "My wife is gone. But your 'company' as it were, will never be required outside of work or as friends over a meal. Secondly, I am not a good man. I'm literally just shit stacked high. But I will never and I mean ever, lay a hand on you and I will not allow anyone else to either, nor to disrespect you. You have nothing to fear from me, this I promise. Do you understand?"

Nikita looked deep into his eyes. John either was telling the truth, or he at least believed his own lies.

"I understand Mr Wilson... John," she hastily corrected herself. Despite his promises, he was still a dangerous man. She wanted to remain on his good side if possible. "You have no reason to do me any kindness more than what you've already shown. But could I perhaps ask a favour?"

"Ask."

"Could you maybe go along with a show that I am doing what I was bought in for? Nothing too much, but if I could come up sometimes. Stay a few late nights for dinner, occasionally sleep on the couch. It would look as though I am being put to my intentioned use and not raise eyebrows."

He seemed to hold a breath and Nikita thought he might refuse, "I don't want to put you in any danger so yes, I think that's a good idea. Having said that, you will be put to use. I do need an assistant, and I do like good food. You mentioned cooking before. Are you a good cook?"

"Yes sir" she smiled. "It was the one part of my training I actually enjoyed."

"Fantastic, I'd like you to come up a few times a week and teach me to cook some of your dishes. You'd have to stay and help me eat them of course. But tonight is the first decent home cooked meal I've had in a while, and I'm rather rusty."

"I would like that," she said, and for the first time in years, meant it.

John nodded, then leaned forward slightly. "Time to hold up my end." The change in his demeanour was immediate—shoulders tensing, jaw clenching as if bracing for physical pain. "You want to know about Amy. About Sudan."

"If you're willing to share it."

John reached for the bottle, pouring another glass. "I remember it every night…..

8

Chapter Eight: A friendly Visit

John- Jabori Wildlife reserve, South-Sudan, East Africa. Eighteen months ago.

As the Toyotas came to a stop John could notice the decals on the side of the cars, marking them out as belonging to the local police. He had quite a good working relationship with the local police in general, although there were bad eggs as there are everywhere. The officer who got out of the lead vehicle wasn't one of his normal contacts.

"G'day" John started the neutral colloquial greeting. "Apologies for the hostile reception, but I'm sure you've heard about the LRA attacks."

"The same reason we are in convey, Mr Wilson. My name is Sergent Kwame, I was hoping we could have a word."

"We could, what do you wish to discuss?" John stated evenly and without moving. Other officers had begun to exit the vehicles. "Count twenty total," Kelsy crackled into his ear. "Rifles all and armour, they're coming in pretty heavy for a chat."

John tuned away slightly and spoke into his microphone as discreetly as he could. "We'd be going heavy too if we needed to pass through LRA territory. Watch them, but don't do anything stupid." His reply was met with a simple terse, "Copy" from Kelsey. He was going to pay for the 'stupid' comment later he knew. Kelsey's best and worst traits were the same. Nothing got past her, you simply couldn't get up early enough in the morning to pull the wool over her eyes. Whatever tactic people thought to try she was three steps ahead of them. It made her invaluable in the field regardless of the situation. John could not manufacture a better right-hand man, or woman as it were. However, that also meant she was deeply paranoid and sometimes saw threats where there were none. A fact that had caused a considerable about of problems in Rwanda.

"I was hoping somewhere more private." Kwame said quietly

John smiled but with his mouth only, his eyes were steely and threatening. There was something off here. "This is as private as I can offer you," he said evenly. This was turning into a delicate situation. Technically John was the law in the reservation, the police didn't have the jurisdiction here. But in practice, in a place like this sometimes the government employees tended to feel like they had jurisdiction wherever they felt like it.

"Fine. It's come to our attention that you have been undertaking the burning of tusks on this base. As you know, this is not for you to do. You are supposed to hand these over to the authorities to process and dispose of."

Oooh, fuck, John thought to himself. This was not going to be an easy day. "Okay. Well with all due respect Sergent, firstly, 'what is for me to do' is to disrupt poaching efforts on this reserve, and that includes the burning of confiscated tusks or horns should I deem it to serve that purpose. And two, in the furtherance of that goal, we had been marking the tusks we handed over to the police and we kept finding them on jackals trying to move them, which means there is a leak. That's why we started burning the tusks on site instead."

Kwame stepped closer, bristling at the statement. "Are you accusing me of corruption?"

"Not you personally, but there is a leak." Things were getting tricky now. It is entirely possible that Sergeant Kwame had no idea of the leak and had simply been sent to investigate by some higher up. It was also possible that this little visit of twenty armed men was supposed to pressure John to toe the line a little. He grinned inwardly. *Evidently, I've interrupted someone's cash flow.*

"John take two steps to the left; you're in my shot" Kelsey whispered. John had his mike open, and Kelsey had heard every word. "Slap your right thigh and he'll take a deep breath through his fucking forehead," she finished.

"In future, I'm to order that you are to turn over all seized contraband to the authorities for processing."

"I would remind you that on this reserve, Mr Wilson IS the authority." It was Amana now, having come from around the vehicle. His size drew Kwame's attention.

"Enough, both of you" John was growing tired of this conversation and the escalating tensions. He took two steps to his left as he spoke. "Sergent, you've no authority here and you know it. Frankly, this could have been a phone call. I find you coming here twenty men deep as overtly aggressive. So kindly, I think it's time you left. I'll take your 'orders' under advisement. You've delivered your message, now go."

Kwame and John stood nearly eye to eye, Amana to John's right.

"DOWN NOW!" Kelsy screamed so hard into John's ear his head rung. He hit the ground as a he saw a thud hit Amana's chest. Instantly Kwame's head rocked back, and he fell, lifeless. Kelsey's rifle spoke twice more, and two more bodies joined Kwame. His training kicked in and John raised his Styer, letting several shots go. Moving over to Amana, he fired again and in that spilt second it felt as though the world ignited as both sides now erupted into gunfire.

"MOVE MORON!!" John's head rung again. Sefu stepped around the doorway of the tower and swept the cars, covering John as he grabbed Amana and dragged him around the vehicle. "How in the fuck did that start!?" John asked of no one in particular.

"TRAP!" Kelsey crackled again. Her rifle spoke again as she took another life. "There were more under the tarps in the trays."

"How am I?" Amana asked. John examined him quickly, "You'll live. It'll fucking sting, though."

"Right," Amana replied. Rounds whizzed around them finding their way under and through the troopie. Amana gripped the undercarriage and lifted, straining as the car creaked under the pressure before crashing onto its side. The two men took shelter behind the engine block.

"We have a problem. Police were a Trojan horse. There're three groups coming from the tree line. One in front, one coming for the D side, one for B side! They're inside the wire on the front! MOVE!" Kelsey relayed just as a man in a blue uniform tore around the car, crashing into John. They grappled briefly until Amana's mighty frame threw him away. Before the man had even regained his feet, John fired three times into his chest.

"Fuck this," John growled standing behind the car. He bought his rifle up to his shoulder, Amana right behind him. Leaning out he fired repeatedly. Two men ran into the guard house; gunfire erupted briefly and all fell silent. None exited, and Sefu's rifle did not start again. Amana took over while John reloaded. "Kels, Sitrep!" he yelled.

"A side holding, Sefu, Alex, and Mosi down. Second group has hit the D side and will breach. Total over one hundred hostiles. Get to D wall. We'll cover."

"Amana, stay and hold!" John yelled, as he turned into his mike now. "Attention all, shoot every cunt not in a ranger uniform. We break them here. Moving to D in 3,2,1!" John took off, rounds whirring around him. He wondered how he hadn't been hit, or maybe he had and just didn't feel it yet. That had happened before, in Rwanda. *Fucking*

Rwanda, he swore to himself. *What a shit show.*

He heard Kelsey's rifle sing again and a body fell beside him. Taking respite behind a building, he tried to catch his breath and took stock of the battle in front of him. "I owe you," he panted.

"Adding it to your tab," Kelsey growled back.

The rangers had succeeded in taking back the front and had closed the main gates, though they could be breached if rammed by the cars. On the B side wall, rangers were firing outward –the third group must have reached it. However, it seemed that his men had stolen the initiative in this fight. John turned now to the D wall, his blood running cold at what he saw. Men poured over the wall and made their way into the buildings, including the cottage where Amy, Kenyatta, and the children were hiding.

John sprinted across the compound paying no head to the battle around him. "Kels, Cottage!" He screamed hoping she heard. Another body fell even before it had reached the first step. *Kelsey was death itself today.* John raised his rifle and fired, emptying the magazine and dropping several more men. He discarded it now and drew his revolver.

Blood pounded in John's ears as he covered the last few metres. "FRIENDLY!" he yelled as he reached the porch. The front door hung splintered on its hinges, kicked in by the intruders. Inside, chaos reigned—overturned furniture, shattered glass, the metallic scent of blood mixing with gunpowder.

A muffled noise drew his attention and John charged into the living room. Kenyatta lay on his back, a hand feebly trying to stop the blood seeping from a giant wound in his abdomen. Eight or ten enemy lay around the room. "Ran out the back," Kenyatta breathed. "Go, I'm fine," he lied.

For a split-second John hesitated, torn between his search for Amy and the mortally wounded Kenyatta who had defended her.

"GO!" Kenyatta shouted.

"Thank you, brother." John sprinted for the back door. He burst through it to find Amy holding Tau and Issa behind her as four enemy levelled weapons at them. Yet no one moved. *They're just kids.* Lord was notorious for his use of child soldiers, and he had done so here.

The youngest couldn't have been more than twelve, a rifle trembling in small hands that should have been holding schoolbooks. His eyes were wide with terror and something else—*drugs*, John realised. They'd been pumped full of whatever cocktail the LRA used to turn children into killing machines.

"Let them go," John said quietly, his voice cutting through the chaos. "You don't have to do this. You're just boys."

The eldest child —maybe fifteen—sneered with manufactured bravado. "We kill the white man and his woman. Orders."

Amy's eyes met John's over the children's heads. Terror flickered there, but so did trust. Complete, unwavering trust that he would find a way.

"John," Kelsey crackled in his ear. "They've breached the A side again. We must retake the gate, or we'll be over run."

"Little busy here, John replied quietly.

"End it. We need you." Kelsey growled.

Easy for you to say. "Are you seeing this?"

"You're in my blind spot and we're taking too much fire for me to move. Sorry."

John went to raise his revolver, but his hand wouldn't obey. These weren't hardened killers—they were victims, broken children forced into a nightmare. The youngest child's rifle wavered, tears streaming down his dirt-streaked face.

John was faced with an impossible choice. Lose the woman he loved or do the unthinkable, the unforgivable…and every second he hesitated his men, Kelsey, fought alone to save the camp.

Fucking, fuck.

"What's your name?" John asked the youngest, keeping his revolver pointed to the ground. His off hand up, palm facing the children to show he meant no harm.

"Names don't matter. We are soldiers of—"

"That's not true… You are children." John heard Kelsey in his earpiece "Christ, just kids," she just muttered. He took a step forward. "I know you're scared, but you don't want to hurt anyone. I can see it in your eyes."

"Shut up!" the eldest screamed, swinging his weapon toward John who instantly raised his revolver in response.

Don't make me do this, don't make me choose.

"Okay. Okay." John slowly holstered his revolver. Raising both hands now he stepped forward. "See no need for weapons. My name is John. I run this camp. What's your name?"

The youngest boy's lip quivered. "D-David," he whispered, barely audible over the distant gunfire.

"David's a good name," John said, taking another careful step. "My friend David back home, he liked to fish. You ever been fishing, David?"

The boy's rifle dipped slightly. Behind him, Amy shifted protectively over Tau and Issa.

"Don't listen to him!" the eldest barked, but his voice cracked with adolescent uncertainty. "Kill them now or—"

"Or what?" John's voice hardened. "You think Lord cares about you? He made you kill your own parents, filled you with drugs and sends you to do what he's too cowardly to do himself."

"John," Kelsey's voice crackled urgently. "They're inside the wire on two sides. We're a midge's dick from being overrun."

John's jaw clenched. Time was bleeding away.

"But if you put down those guns," John continued, his voice steady despite the chaos surrounding them, "I can promise you safety. Food.

A life."

David's eyes flickered with hope—a dangerous, fragile thing. The eldest boy noticed it too and jabbed his rifle toward Amy. "Enough talking! We finish the mission!" In that infinitesimal moment, John saw everything with crystal clarity. Time seemed to stand still even as the battle raged all around them. No one willing to make the next move. A round ricocheted from somewhere, whining as it sped between the small group galvanising the children into action. The eldest fired hitting John in the chest. The round smacking into him with brutal force, driving the air from his lungs but not penetrating the amour.

Ah fuck! "No" John barely managed to wheeze out. But too late, the younger boys screamed, their rifles swinging wildly in panic as they fired on Amy and her wards. Amy's body tensing to shield Tau and Issa.

John chose. He damned himself, Lord and everyone else; and he chose. His hand moved in a blur, revolver clearing leather with a practiced ease born of nightmares and necessity. The eldest fell first, his head snapping back as John fired, the bullet finding its mark with terrible precision, no heroic disarming shots. This wasn't a movie. This was hell on earth. The middle two boys fired wildly at Amy and her charges, spraying their shots as panic overtook their drug-addled coordination. John made his decision, his revolver booming twice. Two more small bodies crumpled. The youngest—David with tears still wet on his cheeks—stood frozen, his rifle pointed at the ground, his little body shaking so violently he could barely stand.

"Hide," John whispered hoarsely. "Just run and hide." The boy dropped his weapon and bolted.

John turned to where Amy had been standing and his heart stopped almost mid-beat.

Amy lay on the ground; her body still curled protectively around Tau and Issa... One look at her face told him everything. She was gone.

He'd lost her. He had an impossible choice; he made it and lost her anyway.

9

Chapter Nine: Exceptions to the rule

Nikita-

Nikita watched John down another glass, his hands steady despite the amount he had ingested. "There's more to it, but that's the gist of it. We did end up holding the compound, but it was closed a few days later. Most of the rangers transferred to other reserves. The two boys Tau and Issa they lived, we sent them to live with Amana and his wife, once Amana had recovered from his wounds. Kels took a job in Australia at Monarto Zoo. I went contracting, worked all over."

"You blame yourself," Nikita said quietly.

"Of course, I fuckn do." John's laugh was bitter. "I should have seen it coming, if I'd been faster, if I'd found a way—"

"If you'd been perfect," Nikita interrupted, surprising herself with her boldness. "If you'd been something other than human."

"Don't you get it? I'm not human. Everything and anything good about me went with her. What do you think? Because I'm sad, it changes things? My guilt does not absolve me."

Nikita looked at the man in front of her, tears in his eyes and wearing shame like a second skin. *He was broken, like her,* she realised. She had shared her shame, and instead of ridicule and disgust, his response

67

had been to share his own, lowering himself to her level.

Suddenly, she believed every promise he had made that night. As she stared at him, she felt it happen, the smallest fracture in the wall she'd built around herself. A hairline crack through which something unfamiliar might seep—not trust, not yet, but the distant possibility that there might be exceptions to the rules she'd learned through pain. That John might be an exception to the rules of men. She reached across the small table, taking his hand in hers.

"John?" she started softly. He would not look at her. "You didn't start the fight, you were attacked. You didn't do anything wrong."

"DIDN'T DO ANYTHING WRONG!?" he tore his hand away. "They were CHILDREN! They should have been laughing in the sun and playing football, they should have been loved, they should have been protected. And I killed them. I killed them and I lost her anyway. There is no lower of a man than that." His eyes remained averted.

He would not put a hand on her, Nikita knew that now, not even gently. Despite what she was told, this was not a man that revelled in cruelty. This was a man utterly ashamed of his savagery, who felt unworthy of anything other than disgust. He truly was broken, the abrasiveness of the past few days simply a cover. She rose from her seat, "Is there anything I can do before I go?"

John shook his head, still unwilling to look at her. "No mate, just pick me up same time tomorrow."

Nikita made to leave but stopped. "John?" she asked softly. He grunted in response. "There are much lower men than you. You might have done bad things, but I don't think you're a bad person."

Silence hung thick in the air between them.

"I could stay, sleep on the couch. Maybe you shouldn't be alone toni-"

"Goodnight, Nikita. Pick me up in the morning." He still sat at the table.

***

The next morning John once again walked out of his apartment block at 6:58 to Nikita, already waiting for him, coffee at the ready. He looked like he needed it. *Mustn't have gotten much sleep last night,* she thought. Truth be told she hadn't either.

"Good morning, John" she smiled.

"Morning, mate."

They sat in silence for the ride to the zoo. Nikita parked and went to exit the car.

"Wait," John spoke softly. "Our conversation last night stays between us. I will not betray your words to anyone and when you're with me, you're safe. Whatever arrangement brought you to me, whatever debts you think you owe—they don't exist in my apartment. Understood?"

Nikita studied his face, searching for any sign of deceit, finding only the same tired honesty as last night. "Understood," she replied quietly.

John nodded. "Thank you for what you said last night."

Chapter Ten: Enforcing Boundaries

Nikita-

"YA nemnogo govoryu po-russki" Everyone turned to John and froze. The words hung still in the air. Nikolai square with John, his stare boring into him. A stare that would, and had, cowed lesser men. But not John.

It had been two weeks since the dinner at Johns apartment and news of Mikhail's promotion had received mixed reviews. Some keepers accepted it, some grumbled but ultimately gave way. Nikolai however, was furious, and had been letting everyone know about it. All five keepers, plus John and Nikita were in the staff room. John had allowed Nikolai to have his tantrum. That was until, he called Nikita 'that' again and in excruciating detail stated the things she must have done to get John to demote him. *Not that I had any hand in your demotion.*

"YA nemnogo govoryu po-russki" John stated again, before switching to English. "Not much of it, but enough to know what you said. No one, and I mean no one," he glanced along at the other keepers, "will ever refer to Nikita in derogatory language. Not only is she your colleague, but my assistant. To disrespect her is to disrespect me." The last line he growled staring straight into Nikolai's soul.

"Nikolai doesn't speak English, he doesn't know what you're saying," Nikita's small voice said. She was equally parts embarrassed and scared, yet a small warmth grew within her chest. Prickly as he might be, John kept his word. She couldn't remember a time when a man had stood up for her. But here, and potentially outnumbered five to one, John was.

"He gets my fucking drift," John growled, stepping closer to Nikolai. "Apologise, now." The words low and menacing in any language.

Mikhail stood now and spoke to Nikolai. The young man's face set in determined lines as he translated. He had guessed correctly that Nikita would not be comfortable translating to the man who had just called her a whore. Nikolai scoffed and retorted in Russian, pulling out his phone as he did so.

Mikhail looked slightly confused and glanced at John, "He says he'll show you what your sweet little love is."

Nikita's heart dropped to the floor. *John would see, they all would see.* They'd know, and she would have to endure their glances, the whispers as she walked by. And it's not like she could simply resign and leave. She had to stay. Her head had been racing so much she barely noticed John's right hand subtly waving her behind his desk.

"Tell him I couldn't give a fuck what he's trying to show me. He's fired. And if he doesn't put his phone away, I'll bounce his munted head off the floor…"

John had stepped even closer to Nikolai as he said it. "TRANSLATE!" he bellowed at Mikhail.

Mikhail hesitated unsure what to say as there was no Russian word for 'munted.' But regardless Nikolai didn't need a translator. John's words were violent and challenging in any language. He stopped typing at the phone, instead staring right into John's eyes. Thick in the chest and arms, and nearly a head taller than John, Nikolai had made it known amongst the staff that he considered the Australian an upstart. Everyone knew Nikolai thought it was enough that John had been bought into the zoo as his superior. But to demote him, fire him and challenge him over this woman, this thing, this whore. It was a great insult, and if the Australian wanted to test him, Nikolai now made it known he was more than willing to fight

A silent conversation passed between the three men. John, Nikolai, and Mikhail. All three seemed to come to the same decision at the same time as John and Nikolai broke apart a few steps taking off their watches, caps, and rings. Mikhail stepped back, his eyes darting between the two men as they prepared for the inevitable clash. The tension in the air was palpable, like electricity crackling before a storm.

John rolled up his sleeves, revealing tanned, sinewy forearms. Horrific scarring played out along the left one, disfiguring a tattoo there. His jaw set, eyes determined. He was not the same as the man Nikita had seen pictures of. That man had been near a hundred kilos of functional muscle, with a broad back, imposing arms and massive chest. John now couldn't have been much more than eighty kilos and while hard muscled, he was not the same presence he had seemed in the photos. Yet while he was smaller than Nikolai, but there was an unafraid savage energy about him, like a predator ready to pounce. Nikolai's movements were more deliberate, almost casual, as if he were merely preparing for a mild inconvenience rather than a fight. His massive frame seemed to expand as he squared his shoulders, a sneer playing at the corners of his mouth as he seemed to disregard his opponent.

Nikita had retreated behind the desk, the mask she often wore slipping in a show of worry and fear. She knew better than to intervene, but her eyes never left John's face. He didn't use or hurt her. Then he'd promised to stand up for her, now he was actually fighting Nikolai over her. *For what? Her non-existent honour?* She wanted to scream at them to stop but both John and Nikolai were beyond reason now.

They circled each other like feral dogs; eyes locked in a fierce glare.

John struck first, a quick jab aimed at Nikolai's jaw. The Russian dodged, barely, the punch grazing his cheek. He countered with a powerful right hook that caught John in the ribs, causing him to stumble back. Mikhail cursed under his breath at the sound of flesh meeting flesh as the two men traded blows.

Nikolai's size gave him an advantage, but John's speed and nous kept him in the fight. He slipped under another heavy right cross, landing his own cross on the Russian's chin as he did so. Nikolai's head snapped back, but he barely flinched, instead grabbing John by the shirt and hurling him across the room. John crashed into a filing cabinet, the metal denting with the impact. He shook his head, trying to clear his vision as Nikolai advanced, a predatory grin on his face. But the Australian wasn't done yet. As Nikolai reached for him, John lunged forward. Folding his right hand towards his own chest he drove his elbow with all his weight behind it into the bigger man's diaphragm just below his chest, forcing the air from his lungs.

Nikolai stumbled back, gasping. John, pressing his advantage now raining fists, elbows and knees on the Russian's face and body. The Russian was tough, absorbing the punishment and waiting for his opening. It came when John overextended on a wild haymaker. Nikolai ducked under it and wrapped his massive arms around John's waist, lifting him off his feet. With a roar, he slammed John onto the desk, scattering papers and sending Nikita scrambling backward with a yelp.

The impact knocked the wind out of John, and he lay there gasping as Nikolai loomed over him. The Russian's face was a mask of rage, blood trickling from a split lip. He raised a meaty fist, ready to bring it crashing down on John's face. But as Nikolai's fist descended, John jerked his head to the side. The Russian's knuckles smashed into the wooden desk, and he howled in pain. Seizing the moment, John rolled away from the Russian regaining his feet and circled back into the centre of the room resetting himself.

John had started this fight too angry; he knew better than to fight this recklessly. The events of the last few weeks and not sleeping well had done this to him. Sure, the past eighteen months living rough and not caring for himself had taken their toll. He was not as fit and strong as he had been two years ago, but he was still a skilled and savage fighter. And it was time to end this.

His eyes narrowed, his breath coming in controlled, measured pants. Nikolai shook out his hand, rage and pain etched across his face. Swelling already starting under his left eye, his lip and nose bleeding. The Russian's eyes were wild, unfocused. John changed tactics.

John circled to his right, away from the considerable power of Nikolai's right hand. The Australian was light on his feet, hands raised in a classic high guard. Nikolai lunged forward with a left jab. John parried down the awkward punch, and stepping with his left foot in one fluid motion, he brought his right leg up and across, driving his shin into Nikolai's left thigh with a dense sickening thud. Nikolai grunted, his leg buckling slightly. John pressed his advantage, following up with a quick left hook to the face. Nikolai managed to block it, but the force of the blow put all his weight back on that left leg, which John savagely chopped at again buckling the Russian for a second time.

The tide was starting to turn now as John's experience bought itself to the fore. Nikita reasoned Nikolai must have been used to men who were afraid of him and didn't really want to fight. Faced with a man like John, who stood steadfast and willing to engage, Nikolai had needed to use his size and strength to end this quickly. He hadn't been able to and now every chopping arc of John's shin bought the end closer. Nikolai's face contorted in pain as he struggled to keep his balance. John, as if sensing victory was near, pressed forward relentlessly. He feinted another leg kick, causing Nikolai to drop his guard to protect his thigh. In that split second, John drove his right foot into the floor and with all his weight and momentum behind it, unleashed a vicious right elbow that connected squarely with Nikolai's chin.

The Russian's legs gave way, his massive frame sinking and crashed to the floor with a thunderous impact. John stepped back, ready to deliver another blow, but it wasn't necessary. The Russian had been unconscious before he hit the ground. The room fell eerily silent. John stood over his fallen opponent, chest heaving, knuckles bloodied. Mikhail stared in disbelief, his mouth agape. Nikita emerged slowly from behind the desk, her eyes wide with a mixture of fear and admiration. John turned to the other keepers against the wall. "Anyone else?" he asked.

Silence met him. "Is there anyone else?" Mikhail, startled into action, communicated with the other keepers then shook his head at John.

"I'll be fair but firm," John started. "You do your jobs well and we will have no issue. You have a problem with your rounds, your animals, or me, my door is always open. But anyone degrades one of their co-workers including Nikita, and you will answer to me. Understood?"

Mikhail translated again and everyone nodded.

"Get that piece of shit out of here" He gestured at Nikolai as he walked out of the room.

***

John-

Later that night Nikita was again trying to get John to accept pressing a pack of frozen peas on the swelling around his cheekbones. "You should have let me tend you straight after."

"First of all, I'm perfectly capable of holding ice packs on my own," John retorted as he continued not to hold the peas to his face, nor allow her to. "Secondly, if I let you tend me right it would have given credence to the idea that you're...." he looked for the right but still respectful word "sleeping with me. Which was the reason I had just fought Nikolai because he had implied the same thing. It would have been a bad look."

Nikita gave him a quizzical glance. "He did more than imply. I know you don't understand a lot of Russian. But his accusations were very explicit."

John sent her a cold look. "And I made that clear to everyone that it wouldn't fly."

"You did." She left him holding the frozen peas and walked over to the kitchenette where she had had stared prepping some vegetables for dinner. Tonight was a simple steak and roasted vegetables. Nutritious, but uninspiring.

"I never got the chance to thank you," she said. "You kept leaving whenever I tried to talk today."

"You don't need to; I've wanted to hit him for weeks." *No need for her to feel any more indebted than she already does.*

"Well, I want to thank you anyway." She paused. "No man has ever stood up for me, let alone fought for me." She added the last sentence in a quieter voice.

"Well... you're welcome," John said awkwardly.

Nikita turned back to the vegetables, her knife rhythmically chopping through carrots and potatoes. The silence stretched between them, punctuated only by the soft thud of the blade against the cutting board. John shifted uncomfortably on the couch, wincing as he adjusted. He cleared his throat. "Look, ah, about what Nikolai said..."

She paused mid-chop, her back still to him. "Yes?"

"I want you to know that I don't see you that way. You're not... You're more than just..."

Nikita set down the knife and turned to face him, her expression unreadable. "More than just what, John?"

He struggled to find the right words. "You're not some object to be used or traded. You're a person. A capable person who deserves respect. It's important to me you know that."

A ghost of a smile brushed her lips. "I knew you thought that the second you threatened him."

John cleared his throat again. "Does everyone at the zoo know? Have they seen the videos?"

"Not that I know of," she started neutrally. "Although they certainly would have if you hadn't stopped Nikolai from using his phone. Thank you for that," she offered.

John waved her off again. It had not escaped him that she had answered in a way that didn't say that no one else knew. Only that not everyone knew. *She had a habit of that,* he thought to himself, *not lying, but not really answering with the full truth.* He knew she was still hiding something from him, that he was yet to fully gain her trust. He hoped the fight today had gone some way toward that, but he couldn't deny he was a little frustrated.

"I suppose word of the fight has gone around. Everyone will know by now."

Nikita hesitated, her eyes flicking away for a moment before meeting John's gaze again. "Not everyone, but word spreads fast in a place like this. Gossip is the lifeblood of any workplace."

John groaned, letting go of the frozen peas to rub his temples. "Great. Just great. Actually, who fucking cares? He's a cunt."

"It's not all bad," Nikita said, turning back to her vegetables. "Most people are on your side. They think what you did was… admirable."

"Admirable," John repeated flatly. "Getting into a fistfight at work is admirable now?"

Nikita shrugged, placing the veggies in an air-fryer. "In this case, yes. Nikolai has been problematic for a while. You're not the first person he's angered, just the first to do something about it. You should shower. Dinner will be ready soon."

John stepped into the small bathroom, taking off his shirt as he did so, wincing as he caught sight of his reflection in the mirror. His cheek was swollen and starting to bruise, a stark reminder of the day's events. As he undressed and stepped into the shower, he let the hot water wash over him, easing some of the tension from his muscles.

His mind wandered back to Nikita's words. *Admirable.* The thought made him uncomfortable. He hadn't done it to be admired; he'd done it because Nikita deserved better than to be spoken about like that.

When he emerged from the bathroom ten minutes later, towel wrapped around his waist, the smell of cooking meat filled the air. Nikita was setting the table, her movements efficient and practiced.

She glanced up as he entered, her eyes lingering for a moment on his bruised torso before quickly averting her gaze. "Dinner's almost ready," she said, her voice cheerful. "I left some clean clothes for you on the bed."

John nodded, grateful for her thoughtfulness. He retreated to the bedroom, finding a fresh t-shirt and sweatpants laid out for him. As he dressed, he could hear Nikita moving about in the kitchen, the soft clink of plates and utensils an almost comforting backdrop to his tumultuous thoughts.

When he returned to the main room, Nikita was already seated at the small table, two plates of steak and roasted vegetables steaming before her. John lowered himself into the chair across from her, wincing slightly as his sore muscles protested.

"How are you feeling?" Nikita asked, her eyes flickering to his bruises.

"I'm honestly fine mate," came the reply. "Although today has pointed out how much I let myself go. Could I trouble my assistant to find an appropriate gym around here for me?" He asked with a sparkle. He knew allowing Nikita to do things for him made her feel valued and useful.

"Like a boxing gym or weights?" she asked.

"Weights. I need to regain some of my size and strength. Probably eat more and drink less too. The actual fighting itself isn't a problem."

"I'll say," Nikita said with a smirk.

The simple meal did not take long for the two friends to finish. "Thanks for that," John stated.

"Please, this isn't even real food," Nikita replied taking the plates. Then her face lit up. "Tomorrow night, have dinner at my place. Let me cook you a real Russian dish in my kitchen with all my stuff. It'll be good, I promise. Besides, you have that meeting the following morning without me, so you'll need to drop me home tomorrow anyway to keep the car."

"Actually, that sounds pretty good. Maybe I'll dig out some of my Africa stuff to show you afterwards."

"Looking forward to it," she replied as she went to fill the sink.

"Umm no, leave the dishes," John said. "You either cook or wash up, not both. I'll do the dishes, you head home."

"I could stay the night," she offered.

"Not tonight. I know I said you would a few times a week. But not tonight, okay?" It was phrased as a question, but it was definitely a statement.

"Okay. Goodnight John," she called sweetly as she turned to leave.

"Goodnight mate," came the reply. "Make sure you get some good sleep."

Nikita turned back to him again, placing her hand on his chest and gently kissed his swollen cheek. "Thank you again for today."

Two hours later when John finally fell asleep, he could still feel Nikita's lips on his cheek.

$$11$$

Chapter Eleven: Dinner among friends

John-

As always, Nikita was there to pick him up at 6:58am.

"Good morning, mate. How'd you sleep?" John asked as Nikita handed him his coffee.

"Well, thank you. And you?"

"Best I've slept since I got here. Looking forward to tonight."

She was starting to become more comfortable around him. Relaxed, but still professional. John sent out revised rosters. Mikhail's zebra was coming along the best, no surprise there. After lunch Aleski knocked on the door of John's office.

"Heard you and Nikolai had a little...misunderstanding yesterday," he started.

John's jaw tightened, his eyes hardening as he looked up at Aleski. "Misunderstanding? Is that what he's calling it?"

Aleski continued, seemly undeterred as he leaned against the doorframe, crossing his arms.

"Look, I'm not here to take sides. But we can't have this kind of conflict in the workplace. It's bad for morale. Boy, you should have put some ice on that." The last bit was spoken as he gestured to John's swollen bruise.

"You told me these were my staff to retrain, promote, demote or fire as I please. Your words. Nikolai required retraining. When he refused to accept that, I fired him. He also refused to accept that and a fight broke out. It's unfortunate, but Nikolai crossed a line. He needed to understand that his actions have consequences. And for better or worse, everyone else on the team got the message. They are free to leave if they like, but while they are here, they will fall in line."

Oddly, his explanation seemed to satisfy Aleski. He nodded slowly. "Fair enough. I can't argue with that logic. Just… try to keep the fights to a minimum, eh?" John grunted in response, turning his attention back to the paperwork on his desk. Aleski lingered for a moment longer, "I've noticed Nikita's been spending a lot of time with you lately."

John's pen didn't miss a beat; his eyes fixed on the document before him. "She's my assistant," he replied nonchalantly. "It's her job to spend time with me."

Aleski's lips quirked into a sly smile. "I didn't say it was a bad thing. Enjoy her."

John's jaw clenched at his insinuation, but he forced himself to remain outwardly calm. "Is there anything else, sir?" he asked tersely, still not looking up.

"No, that's all," Aleski replied, his tone light. "Have a good evening, John."

As Aleski's footsteps faded down the hallway, John let out a long, slow breath. He rubbed a hand over his face, feeling the tension in his brow. Aleski had struck a nerve. Nikita was… different John had to admit. Her quiet strength, her resilience in the face of her past – it called to something in him. He shook his head. *Cut that shit out, boyo.*

***

That night Nikita showed John around her small apartment.

"Very nice" John stated. In truth it was small and cramped. The walls were a dull off-white colour, with peeling paint in some areas. The furniture was worn and mismatched, with a well-loved couch in the corner and a small kitchen table against the far wall. The air had a slight dustiness to it, making him feel dry in the mouth.

Must've been provided by whomever had arranged Nikita to keep me satisfied, John thought to himself. "What are we thinking about for dinner?" he asked.

"Beef stroganoff, a favourite of mine" came Nikita's cheerful reply. "I prepped most of it last night. It's a bit of a shame we don't have the matching wine. But we shall make do."

"Out of interest," John asked, "What is the matching wine?" He had noticed a liquor store not a hundred yards from her apartment. Nikita's eyes lit up at the question. "Oh, a nice pinot noir would be perfect. It complements the beef beautifully." She paused, a hint of wistfulness in her voice. "But it's not necessary, really. We'll be fine without it."

John nodded, his jaw tightening almost imperceptibly. He glanced at his watch, then back at Nikita. "Be right back," he said gruffly, already moving toward the door. Nikita's brow furrowed in confusion. "Where are you-"

But John was already gone, his heavy footsteps echoing down the hallway. The cool night air hit him as he stepped outside, a welcome respite from the stuffiness of the apartment, not that he would let on that he found it stuffy. He strode purposefully toward the liquor store, his eyes scanning the streets out of habit, always alert for potential threats. Once inside, John quickly located a decent bottle, not bothering with the finer details of vintage or region. He paid and hurried back. As he approached the apartment, a flicker of doubt crossed his mind. Am I *overstepping? Would Nikita think I'm trying to impress her, or worse, buy her affection?*

He pushed the thoughts aside as he entered the apartment. The weight of the bottle in his hand felt oddly comforting, a tangible gesture of… what? Kindness? Appreciation? He couldn't quite name it.

Nikita was stirring something on the stove, the rich aroma of beef and spices filling the air. She turned, her eyes falling on the bottle in his hand. "You didn't have to-" she began, but John cut her off with a small shake of his head. "It's nothing, honestly. You're making dinner, it's only fair I supplied the wine."

Nikita's smile was soft; he could tell she was touched by the unexpected gesture. "Thank you, John. This… this is very kind of you."

John grunted in response, uncomfortable with the gratitude. He busied himself with opening the wine, the familiar routine of uncorking the bottle a welcome distraction from the warmth in Nikita's eyes. A short time later, the two friends sat down to eat at the small table. Nikita hadn't turned on the dining room light. Instead opting to light several candles. He didn't know whether it was the food, the wine, or the intimate candlelight, but John was feeling decidedly nervous. "Can I ask how come the candles? Do your lights not work here?"

Nikita paused, her fork hovering mid-air. A flicker of uncertainty crossed her face before composing herself. "Oh, the lights work fine, just…not the living area one," she said softly, her eyes meeting John's in the warm glow. "But no matter, I thought the candles might be nice. More relaxing, you know?"

John nodded, his throat suddenly dry. He took a long sip of wine, buying time to gather his thoughts. The candlelight cast dancing shadows across Nikita's face, softening her features and making her eyes shine. He found himself staring, transfixed by the way the light played across her skin. "It is nice," he admitted gruffly, looking away and making a mental note to fix the lights. "Good thinking."

Nikita smiled, relief evident in her posture. "I'm glad you like it.

Sometimes it's good to slow down, enjoy the moment." John grunted in agreement, focusing intently on his plate. The stroganoff was delicious, rich and flavourful. He found himself savouring each bite, aware of Nikita's eyes on him. "This is really good," he said between mouthfuls, surprising himself with the compliment. Nikita beamed, clearly pleased. "I'm so glad you like it."

As they ate, John couldn't help but notice the way Nikita's fingers curled around her wine glass, the gentle slope of her neck as she tilted her head back to take a sip. The candlelight casting a warm glow on her skin, making her appear almost ethereal. He shook his head slightly, *Stop that*. This wasn't why he was here. He wasn't supposed to notice these things, to feel this… whatever it was. As they finished their meal, Nikita leaned back in her chair, wine glass in hand. She gazed at John, her eyes soft in the flickering candlelight. "Thank you for joining me tonight," she said quietly. "It's nice to have company."

John shifted uncomfortably, acutely aware of the intimacy of the moment. "It's nothing," he muttered, avoiding her gaze. "The food was good." A silence fell between them, heavy with unspoken words. John could feel Nikita's eyes on him, searching his face for something he wasn't sure he could give. He stood abruptly, his chair scraping against the floor. The wine, candles and Nikita were making him decidedly uncomfortable. He suddenly became painfully aware of how awkward he was and desperately searched for a distraction. His eyes fell on an electric keyboard in the corner. "You play the Keyboard?" he asked.

Nikita's eyes followed John's gaze to the instrument. "It's… Yes."

"That's not what you wanted to say."

Nikita hesitated, "It's not a keyboard. It's an electric piano, a similar but different instrument."

That took guts, correcting me like that. He cleared his throat, grateful for the distraction. "Would you… play something for me?" he asked, his voice gruff but tinged with genuine curiosity.

Nikita stood, smoothing her long-sleeved dress as she moved toward the instrument. "Sure, I'm not very good though, it's been a while." she warned, settling onto the bench. John leaned against the wall; arms folded across his chest. "I'm sure it's fine," he said, his tone softer than he intended. Nikita's fingers hovered over the keys for a moment before she began to play. The melody was simple but beautiful, a haunting tune that filled the small apartment. John found himself closing his eyes, letting the music wash over him. She played well, truth be told.

He didn't even notice when she had finished. He slowly opened his eyes to find her standing in front of him, his body tensing instinctively at Nikita's proximity. Her hand hung in the space between them, mere inches from his muscular chest. For a moment, time seemed to stand still, the air thick with tension. Nikita's green eyes met his, a mix of vulnerability and nervousness in her gaze. "John," she whispered, her voice barely audible over the pounding of his heart. He wanted to step back, to put distance between them, but found himself rooted to the spot. Her scent enveloped him - a subtle mix of vanilla and something uniquely her. It stirred something deep within him, something long buried.

"Nikita," he managed, his voice hoarse. "We shouldn't-"

But before he could finish, her hand made contact with his chest. Even through his shirt, her gentle touch sent a jolt. "You play well," he spluttered.

"Thank you," she whispered stepping even closer to him. "It was part of my training." The sentence shocked John back into reality and he stepped, jumped really, away from her. He looked at her in hazy shock mixed with anger. "Were you... oh what the fuck is this? Was all this some kind of set up? Some kind of offering for yesterday?"

Nikita recoiled as if slapped, her eyes widening with hurt and confusion. "What? No, John, that's not-"

"Don't lie to me," John growled, his voice low and dangerous. He could feel the anger rising within him, hot and familiar. "Is that what this was all about? The dinner, the candles, the music? Some kind of…" He couldn't bring himself to finish the sentence.

Nikita shook her head vehemently, tears welling in her eyes. "No, John, please. It's not like that at all. I just… I wanted to-"

"To what?" John interrupted, his fists clenching at his sides. "To make me feel something? To manipulate me? To what!?"

The pain in Nikita's eyes was palpable. "I just wanted to thank you," she cried. "I don't know how else, but surely you must be lonely, no? You might not feel anything for me but that doesn't mean I can't be of some comfort"

John was too far gone in his anger to see the hurt. "Damn it, Nikita! Is any of you real? Is any of you not what you were trained for? Every measured word, the cooking, the music, the candles! If it's all your training, then WHO ARE YOU!? I don't want your advances, your affections, your fucked up thank yous, or your bed!" He was shouting now, berating her and at the same time hating himself for it. "You want to know what I want? I want to trust, respect, and to treat you as an equal. And I can't do that if all you ever show me is what you were trained for. I should go. I should go. This was a mistake."

John's words hung in the air, heavy and stabbing. Nikita stood frozen, her face a mask of shock and pain. Tears streamed down her cheeks as she struggled to find her voice. "John, please," she whispered, her voice breaking. "It's not like that. I'm not-"

But John was already moving, striding toward the door with purposeful steps. His hand was on the doorknob when Nikita's voice stopped him. "I lied," she said. "About the lights."

John paused, his back still to her. He didn't turn, but he didn't leave either. Nikita took a shaky breath. "The lights work fine. I just… I thought the candles would be nice. Because that's what I like. Not what

I was trained for, but what I've always enjoyed, eating by candlelight." John stood at the door, his hand on the knob. He could hear the pain in her voice, could feel the weight of his own words hanging in the air. He turned slowly, his anger deflating as he saw her standing there, looking small and vulnerable in the flickering candlelight.

"I appreciated the candles," his voice softer now, exhausted and regretful. "But I should still go. I'm sorry, dinner was delicious, thank you." And without looking at her again, he strode out of the apartment. Closing the door behind him, John's footsteps echoed in the empty hallway as he descended the stairs, each step feeling heavier than the last. The cool night air refreshing as he stepped outside. He paused on the sidewalk, running a hand through his thick black hair, his mind a whirlwind of conflicting emotions.

He hadn't meant to hurt her, but he had found himself too close and reacted poorly. He climbed back in the car knowing he would have to make it up to her somehow. If she gave him the opportunity that is. He ran a hand through his hair again. The liquor store's neon sign flickered in the distance, tempting him with familiar numbness. He sat, angry at himself for his outburst at Nikita, angry that he had got that close to her, felt something for her. He wasn't the type people should get close to; it always ended poorly.

He glanced at the empty seat beside him and groaned as he noticed Nikita's bag. "For fuck's sake." *She'll need that tomorrow.* Especially as he wouldn't see her until the afternoon. *I'll have to go back and return it.* He sighed as he exited the car. John trudged back up the stairs, Nikita's bag clutched in his hand like a lifeline, each step bringing him closer to a confrontation he didn't want to have. He paused outside her door, his hand raised to knock, but hesitated. Through the thin walls he heard it, crying, but also screaming.

12

Chapter Twelve: The full picture

John-

"Please! Stop!" a woman's voice begged; he heard a male voice reply. He dropped the bag and tested the door, it was locked. John's heart raced as he heard another muffled cry from inside. Without hesitation, he stepped back and kicked the door hard near the lock. The wood splintered and the door flew open. Bursting into the apartment, his eyes quickly scanned the scene. What he saw shocked him and he was not a man easily shocked. It broke and remade him, filling him with wild animalistic rage and yet simultaneously turning his blood to ice in his veins, rooting him to the spot. As if his body couldn't quite understand how to feel or react to what he was seeing.

Nikita sobbed again and he spotted her lying in the fetal position on the floor in front of the couch, her face red and contorted in pain, her hand still clutching a wine filled glass. But it was what John saw on the TV facing her that had him transfixed. That's where the screaming and voices were coming from. He took a half step forward with great effort, made almost immobile by the depiction of abuse on screen, searing itself into his brain like a hot brand on livestock. He felt sick, the wine and stroganoff threatening to reappear.

In an instant so many things about Nikita became clear to him. Why she was so afraid of men. Why she always wore long sleeves. Why she thought John, as violent and worthless as he was, was a better, fairer man than most. He knew she was owned and had been mistreated. But this…what was happening to the woman on the TV went beyond mistreatment, it was abuse solely for entertainments sake. Until the day he died John would never forget every detail of what he saw on that screen, never forget the sound of the woman's screams, the rattling of chains as she struggled. Never would he forget, and never would he tell a soul. When absolutely necessary, he could describe in general detail what happened to the woman on screen. But exactly what he saw would go with him to the grave.

"All you have to do to end it is to say 'stop.'" One of the three men on the screen called again.

"STOOPPP!! PLEASE!" the woman wailed. Her pleading met with another heavy slap. "You think anyone cares what you want!?"

The woman's hair flew back as another slap landed, and John saw what he already knew to be true. The woman on the screen, face contorted in pain, drenched in tears, puffy and red from being slapped, was Nikita.

The confirmation of her identity grounded John in reality, jolting him into action. He strode over to the TV searching for a button to make the video stop. He struggled to find it and unable to bear anymore, tugged the power cord from the wall. He turned to face Nikita's curled body as she let out another wail, curling even tighter. The shock and embarrassment at John's presence coupled with the reliving of her abuse overwhelmed her completely as she lay sobbing.

He took a step toward her and stopped. He wanted to hold her, to comfort her, to make her feel safe. But how could he? He paced two steps to the left and back to the right, his hands clenching into fists and releasing repeatedly. How could he approach her let alone touch her after what he had just seen. How could she ever trust another man again? Her sobbing continued and galvanised him into action. John's heart raced as he approached Nikita, his movements slow and deliberate. He knelt beside her, careful not to touch her as he gently removed the wine glass from her grasp, his voice barely above a whisper. "Nikita, it's me. It's John. You're safe." He longed to comfort her but knew his touch could only cause more harm as she lay there exposed and vulnerable. He couldn't comfort her, but he could make her less exposed, give her the privacy to recover.

He stood now, dragging the couch over, pulling the table onto its side and gathering the rest of the furniture until it formed almost a complete circle around the small woman lying on the ground. He then walked into the little room off to the side that Nikita slept in and ripped the comforter off the bed, throwing it over the piled furniture, forming a small, protective room around her.

"I'm right here," he said, settling onto the floor a few feet away. "I won't let anyone hurt you." He faced away from her but let his left hand post at the entrance of the makeshift room. He wasn't going to touch her, but he was here if she needed him. He didn't know what else to do, he wasn't good at this stuff. He was a man of action, to track, to fight, that was where he excelled. He was way out of his depth here.

Long minutes passed in silence, broken only by Nikita's ragged breathing. Slowly, she uncurled slightly, peeking at John through tangled strands of hair. Her eyes were red-rimmed and filled with pain. "I'm sorry, I'm so, so sorry. You… you weren't supposed to see that. Any of it," she whispered.

John swallowed hard, still not looking at her, fighting back his own emotions. "You have nothing to apologise for Nikita."

"Why?" she whispered hoarsely. "Why did you come back?"

"You left your bag in the car, I came to return it, and I heard screaming, so I kicked in the door…."

"You came in to save me," she whimpered "There's nothing left to save." She broke down sobbing again.

John's chest tightened as he listened to Nikita's anguished sobs. He wanted desperately to reach out, to offer some tangible comfort, but he knew he couldn't. Not now. Not after what he'd seen. He closed his eyes, fighting back the searing rage that threatened to consume him. Those three men in the video should be praying to every deity in existence that John never found them. He wanted nothing more than to hunt down the men responsible and tear them completely apart. Yet that wasn't what Nikita needed right now.

"I don't believe that for a second." he said as softly as his rage allowed. "You're in there, I was just too blind to see."

Nikita's crying subsided slightly, replaced by short sharps breaths. "How can you say that? After... after seeing what I let them do to me?"

"You didn't let them do anything," he said firmly. "What happened... that wasn't your fault. Stuff like that is never the lady's fault."

After what felt like hours, Nikita's sobs quieted to soft hiccups and sniffles. John heard her shift behind him, the rustle of fabric as she sat up. He fought the urge to turn and look.

"John?" Her voice was raw, barely audible.

"I'm here," he replied softly.

"May...I have a glass of water?"

Without a word, John rose and made his way to the small kitchenette. He filled a glass with cool water, then hesitated before grabbing a clean washcloth and wetting it with warm water. Returning to the makeshift shelter he placed both items at its entrance. Sitting at the entrance facing away again, his left hand again posted in sight.

"You want to know why I watched it?" she phrased it as a question, but it was a statement.

"You don't owe me any explanation, Nikita," John replied evenly.

Silence stretched between them, broken only by the soft rustle of fabric as she reached for the water. John's shoulders tensed, his jaw clenching as he fought the urge to turn and look at her. He could hear her sipping slowly, the gentle splash of water against the glass.

He remained silent, his calloused hand resting on the ground, a silent offering of support. He could feel the weight of her gaze on his back, could almost taste the hesitation in the air.

"Sometimes…I watch it when I need reminding," she said quietly. An incredulous look came across John's face, and he was thankful Nikita couldn't see it. *Need reminding? Of that?* .

He sat silently, sensing she needed to not have her momentum broken.

"When I mess up, or feel low, or act like I could ever get away or be something, I watch it to remind myself what I am. I'm sorry about tonight, I overstepped. And I'm so sorry you saw that video. You shouldn't have had to. Please, forgive me." And with what must have taken every last remnant of courage and strength she could muster, John felt her reach for his hand and almost imperceptibly, tug on it.

It was all the invitation he needed, crashing through the gathered furniture and folding her into her arms, her head burying itself into his chest. "There is nothing to forgive," John whispered. He held her so tightly, as though if he just held tightly enough, he might be able to weld the pieces of her broken soul back together. "I should be asking your forgiveness. I'm not a good man Nikita. I didn't realise when you lit the candles that you were giving me all you had."

"You're the best man I know," she said quietly. The words stabbing into John as he realised the truth of her statement.

John scoffed, "I am a killer, Nikita," he laughed a bit, but it was a bitter laugh.

She sniffled, her head still on his chest, melting into his arms. Not cruel and restrictive like some men's arms, warm and safe like a weighted blanket. "You told me, but you were attacked, it's not your fault."

"There's more than that one time," came his quiet reply. She looked up at him and John felt her eyes asking a silent question. The same question everyone wanted to know, *how many people have you killed?*

"Eighty-four…. My point being, you owe me nothing, no explanation, no asking for forgiveness." John hated himself for what he was about to ask given the state she was in. But he had to try. "Who did this to you? Who were those men?"

"I don't know. I never saw their faces."

Lie, John thought, though he wouldn't press the matter. Not in her current state. Somehow, he knew before she answered that it would be a lie. Of the three men on that footage two did wear balaclavas, true enough. The third however… John would never forget his face, and he doubted Nikita ever would either.

Nikita opened her eyes again, her gaze resting on his bruised knuckles. A reminder of how he fought for her. He stood up for her that day, and he was here now, in those two things alone he had done more for her than any man she had known. She sank even further into his embrace and utterly exhausted, fell asleep.

13

Chapter Thirteen: Business as usual

Nikita-

Nikita's eyes shot open in a bed she didn't recognise. Panic gripping her chest as she took in the unfamiliar surroundings. The room was dimly lit, with soft morning light filtering through heavy curtains. She sat up abruptly, her heart racing, until the events of the previous night came flooding back. *John. The makeshift shelter. His arms around her.* She exhaled slowly, forcing herself to relax. As her eyes adjusted to the low light, she recognised the room, *John's bedroom*. The space was sparse, utilitarian, much like the man himself. A worn dresser stood against one wall, a single framed photograph perched atop it. She caught sight of a familiar figure slumped in a chair across the room.

John.

Nikita felt her breathing slow. She was safe. Sunlight streamed through half-drawn curtains, illuminating John's sleeping form. His face, usually so guarded, looked almost peaceful in repose. But even in sleep, his brow was furrowed, as if he carried the weight of the world on his shoulders. Nikita's gaze travelled to his hands, resting on the arms of the chair. Those hands that had comforted her, protected her. Hands that, by his own admission, had taken lives. She shuddered, remembering his words from the night before. *Eighty-four lives.* The number hung in the air between them, even now. *Eighty-four people who would never see the sun again, never laugh, never taste food, never do anything again, because of him.* Yet last night, he had held her with such gentleness, such care. He must have carried her to the car then back here. *The rules were different with John,* Nikita reminded herself again.

She peeled the blankets off and swung her legs over the side of the bed, noticing she was still fully clothed. Slowly, she rose from the bed. Her sock covered feet touched the cool, wooden floor, and she padded silently toward John. She studied his face, noting the deep lines etched around his eyes and mouth, the furrows in his forehead even now. *What horrors had he seen? What burdens did he carry?*

Without thinking, she reached out, her fingers hovering just above his cheek. She wanted to touch him, to smooth away the worry lines, to thank him for being there when she needed someone most, when no one else would have bothered. Yet she hesitated, her hand trembling. As if sensing her presence, John stirred. His eyes snapped open, instantly alert. For a moment, confusion clouded his features before recognition dawned.

"Nikita," he said, his voice rough with sleep. "You're awake."

She quickly withdrew her hand, a flush creeping up her neck. "I'm sorry, I didn't mean to wake you," she said softly, taking a step back. John straightened in the chair, wincing slightly as he stretched his stiff muscles.

"It's alright," he replied, his voice still gravelly. "How are you feeling?"

Nikita wrapped her arms around herself, suddenly feeling exposed under his intense gaze. "I'm... okay," she said, though her voice wavered slightly. "Thank you for... for everything."

John nodded, his eyes never leaving her face. "You're safe here," he said simply.

A heavy silence fell between them, filled with unspoken words and lingering questions as John stood. His face was gaunt and he held his head as though it ached. Nikita shifted uncomfortably, unsure of what to say or do next. She glanced around the room, her eyes landing on the framed photograph on the dresser.

"Is this Amy?" she asked. She was grateful for the distraction. Although part of her thought *Oh what a good idea, remind him of his murdered wife. Smart, good segway, idiot.*

"Who else would it be?" came the gruff reply.

"I'll put some coffee on, have a shower. I packed you a bag. We have that meeting in two hours."

"I'm coming to the enclosure meeting?"

"Of course. Shower."

An hour later found them in the car. "I'd like you to stay at my place for at least the next little while" John started. "No funny business, I'll take the couch till I can get another bed in here."

Nikita's heart skipped a beat at his words. She felt a mix of relief and apprehension wash over her. Relief at not having to return to her own apartment, with its haunting memories and loneliness. Apprehension at the thought of sharing a space with John, a man who both comforted and still slightly intimidated her.

"Are you sure?" she asked, her voice barely above a whisper. "I don't want to impose."

John's hands tightened on the steering wheel. "It's not an imposition," he said gruffly. "It's safer this way."

Nikita nodded, understanding the unspoken concern in his words. After last night, he wanted to keep her close, to protect her. *But from what? From herself?*

"One more thing. Two things really. Firstly, I'm sorry about last night, for what I said. When you lit the candles, you weren't trying to be inappropriate. You were being vulnerable and I attacked you. That was wrong of me and I hope you can forgive me."

"Of course I do." Looking at him she continued. "And the second?"

"No matter what, promise me you will never ever watch that again." His voice was calm but firm. Nikita's breath caught in her throat. She turned to look out the window, watching the city blur past as she considered John's words. The weight of his request settled over her like a heavy blanket.

"I…" she began, her voice faltering. She wanted to promise, to assure him she'd never revisit those dark moments. But the truth was more complicated. "I don't know if I can make that promise, John." She felt his gaze on her, intense and questioning. Nikita forced herself to continue, her words barely above a whisper. "It's not that simple. Sometimes…"

John's jaw clenched, his knuckles whitening on the steering wheel. "Nikita," he said, his voice low and intense. "That video… is poison. It is not who you are."

She closed her eyes, fighting back tears. "But what if it is?" she whispered. *What if that's all I'll ever be?*

The car slowed as John pulled over to the side of the road. He turned to face her. "Look at me," he insisted gently. Nikita hesitated, then slowly turned to meet John's gaze. His eyes were intense, filled with an emotion she couldn't quite name. "What happened to you was not okay. It will never happen again. I won't let it. You are strong, you are kind, and you matter."

Nikita felt tears welling up in her eyes. She wanted to believe him, desperately. But years of shame were not erased on a man's say so.

"How can you be so sure?" she whispered, her voice trembling.

John's hand moved toward hers, hesitating for a moment before gently covering it. The warmth of his touch sent a shiver through her.

"Because I see you, Nikita," he said softly. "Now dry your tears. I need you at my side in the meeting."

***

"What seems to be the problem Dima?"

Nikita translated for him. "The caracal isn't taking to the training," she turned to John, "it won't go in the crate. And the male chimp has stopped pressing his head to the ground but now has something going with his left hand." John had assigned Dima to Nikolai's old round.

John sighed, running a calloused hand through his short black hair. "Tell him to try sardines with the caracal and don't be too worried. It's a long process and we have time. As for the chimp, I'll come have a look at him this afternoon."

Nikita relayed the message, her voice soft and assuring. As she spoke Nikita noticed Johns eyes lingering on her, his gaze washing over her. She glanced back at him only for John to avert his eyes.

That afternoon John, Nikita, and Dima stood outside the chimpanzee enclosure. "He sits at the back there holding that right arm" Nikita said.

"Okay, can you ask Dima to call the troop to back of house and we'll see if he can get a closer look at Hondo there," John replied. Nikita translated and Dima moved quickly performing the procedure he had been taught. All the female chimps and the young left. But Hondo still stood at the back. Not even the lure of his favourite food encouraged him to come in.

John frowned, his brow furrowing as he observed the male chimp's stubborn refusal to move. "This isn't normal," he muttered. He turned to Nikita, his eyes meeting hers. "Actually, it's a bit fucked. If he won't move, we might have to dart him. But we can't dart him because the vet isn't back until…till when?"

"Day after tomorrow," Nikita replied. And that was the crux of the matter, she knew. John was not technically a vet, which didn't mean anything in a place like Africa. But here in Russia it meant he couldn't buy or access some veterinary drugs, which meant that he couldn't dart the chimp without a registered vet. Which was fine, except that

Hondo didn't seem like he could wait for another two days.

John let out a long sigh. "Fuck me," he said quietly.

Nikita looked away from him and hid the start of a sly smile. *In another life perhaps,* she thought. *Stop that,* she immediately chastised herself. Although she had to admit John's combined tender compassion coupled with a fierce protectiveness left her feeling all sorts of things. She looked at the chimpanzee again. "Something's wrong," Nikita said softly, her voice laced with concern. "He's in pain, isn't he?"

John gave a curt nod, his jaw clenching. "Looks like it. I need to get a closer look. His left arm or hand is hurting him, but it's interesting. He's not holding it close to his body. It's kinda away from him." Dima returned beside John and Nikita and also studied the chimp.

"It's caught in something" Nikita looking intently. "That's why he's holding it away from himself, why he didn't head inside, he can't."

John looked again. "Are you sure? I can't see properly."

"Pretty sure."

"I need you to be better than pretty sure. I need you to be 'bet your life on it' certain."

Nikita squared her shoulders "I'm certain," she said with more confidence in her voice. "Okay, I trust you," he replied, his voice eerily calm. "Stay here, no matter what."

With that, he unlocked the enclosure.

***

John-

John's heart raced as he stepped inside; his eyes locked on the male chimp. He moved slowly, deliberately, aware that any sudden movement could startle the already distressed animal. The air felt thick with tension, and he could hear Nikita's sharp intake of breath behind him.

"Easy, Hondo," John murmured, his voice low and soothing. "I'm here to help."

As he drew closer, he could see what Nikita had noticed - the chimp's left hand was indeed caught in something. It looked like a piece of frayed rope, probably left over from one of their enrichment activities. The chimp's eyes, usually so full of mischief, now held only of pain and fear.

John inched closer, his muscles taut with anticipation. He knew how dangerous a cornered, injured chimp could be. One wrong move and those powerful arms could lash out, causing serious injury, even death. Five times stronger than a human, there was no way John would ever approach a chimpanzee that was free moving, but he couldn't turn back now.

"That's it, handsome," John coaxed, his voice barely above a whisper. "Just stay calm."

He was close enough now to see the frayed rope wound tightly around Hondo's wrist, cutting into the flesh. The chimp's eyes darted between John and his trapped hand, a low warning growl emanating from his throat.

He reached the trapped animal now, close enough to feel it's hot breath on his face. John lowered his eyes to the ground; his right hand wrapped around his bear claw knife. He took a breath and whispered. "For what I'm about to do, please don't kill me" and with one quick strike, he cut the rope.

Hondo immediately thumped him in the chest, sending John sprawling. He hit the ground hard, the impact knocking the wind out of him. He rolled quickly, instinct taking over as he scrambled to put distance between himself and the now-free chimp. His heart pounded in his ears, adrenaline surging through his veins.

"John!" Nikita's voice cut through the chaos.

He swung out a hand, signalling her to stay back. His eyes never left Hondo as the chimp paced back and forth, alternating between examining his injured wrist and casting wary glances at John.

Yet Hondo didn't pursue. The chimp examined his newly freed hand, before letting out a series of hoots, throwing objects around the enclosure. It was a display of dominance, but also, John realised, one of relief. Hondo's agitation seemed to subside slightly, his movements becoming less frantic.

Slowly, carefully, John got to his feet. His chest ached where Hondo had struck him, and he knew he'd have an impressive bruise come morning. But he was alive, and equally importantly, Hondo was okay.

John took a cautious step backward, then another, slowly working his way toward the door. With less than three meters to do. Hondo locked eyes with John... and charged.

"OPEN!" John screamed as he turned and leapt for the door. Nikita swung it open just in time for John to hurl himself through it. Nikita and Dima slammed it shut, the lock instantly catching a split second before Hondo thudded into it screeching. Nikita turned to John, lying on his back on the cold concrete.

"Are you okay"? Are you hurt?" her hands searching across his chest where the chimp attacked him.

Breathlessly John battered her hands away. "I'm...fine." he managed between gulps of air. Nikita and Dima helped him to his feet. "If I ever have an idea like that again, slap me in the face." The three colleagues fell into laughter as the adrenaline of the moment washed over him.

"Fuck I'm a moron sometime" he said to Nikita as they headed back to his office.

"You are either the dumbest, or the bravest man I know," she laughed in reply.

14

Chapter Fourteen: Sleep

John-

"You should take a few days off," his voice was unsteady. "Do you have parents or family?"

"Just a father, my mother died when I was young. I was an only child," came Nikita's response. "Did you want to visit him for a couple days?" John enquired.

"Not particularly." He glanced at her now, one eyebrow raised in question. "Who do you think sold me in the first place?" she quietly offered.

Fucking hell. A pain shot through John's chest at the thought of a father selling his own bloody daughter.

"May I ask why you're suddenly so interested in me going away for a few days?" Nikita was sitting at the small table in John's apartment, drinking a type of Australian hot chocolate called Milo. John was standing at the kitchen with his own mug.

"I just think it would be best you leave me be for a few days. I can't sleep," John stated quietly.

"Oh?" Nikita replied, "Do you want to switch beds?"

It had been about six weeks since Nikita had moved in. John had given her the larger bed in his room and had purchased a smaller bed he slept on in the living room.

"No, it's not that."

"Well, if you're having falling asleep, we could dim the lights, play some gentle music, could get black out curtains. We co-"

"IT'S NOT THAT I'M NOT TIRED" John shouted, instantly regretting it as Nikita flinched. "I'm sorry, that was uncalled for… Nikita, do the things you've been through ever come to you at night?" he asked quietly.

"Sometimes. Oh… I see."

"Yeah"

"When's the last time you slept?"

"I got about three hours on Monday night."

"John…it's Friday today."

"I KNOW WHAT FUCKING DAY IT IS," he snapped again "Sorry, sorry. Before Monday I hadn't had any sleep since last Friday night."

"You've had three hours sleep in the past week? I'm so sorry. How can I help?" Her voice was gentle; concern etched on her face.

John's grip tightened on his mug, his knuckles turning white. He stared into the dark liquid, avoiding Nikita's gaze. *It is what it is.*

"You can't help," he said, his voice barely above a whisper. The weight of his sleepless nights seemed to press down on him, making his movements slow and deliberate, his eyes distant. "It's not something that gets fixed."

Nikita stood up, her chair softly scraping against the floor. She approached John cautiously, as if he were a wounded animal. "Maybe not," she said, "but you were there for me, allow me to be there for you."

John shook his head, still not looking at her. "It's different. What happened to you… it wasn't your fault. But me? The things I've done…" His voice trailed off, thick with self-loathing. "Those are my fault."

Nikita reached out, her hand hovering near his arm, not quite touching him. "John, look at me," she pleaded.

Reluctantly, he raised his gaze to look at her, his eyes bloodshot and rimmed with dark circles. For a moment, the tough exterior cracked. Nikita gently placed her hand on his arm, feeling the tension in his muscles. "Whatever you've done, whatever haunts you, it doesn't change who you are to me," she said softly. "The man I know, the one who protects me, that's who you are now."

"You have no idea who I am or what I've done," he muttered, his voice hoarse. "The sheer number of lives I've taken, the choices I've made...."

Nikita took a deep breath, steeling herself. "Then tell me," she said, her voice steady despite the fear fluttering in her chest. "Tell me every horrific terrible thing you've done and watch me stay anyway."

John knew there was something important in what she just said. But he was simply too tired to be able to isolate it. "Never," he whispered. "I just want you to go, this will get worse before it gets better. I can't stop it, but I can stop you from having to see it."

Nikita's grip on John's arm tightened slightly. "I'm not going anywhere," she said firmly, her eyes locked on his. "You've seen me at my worst, John. You didn't abandon me then. I will not abandon you now."

John's jaw clenched, a mix of frustration and desperation flashing across his face. "You don't understand, you need to go," he growled, pulling away from her touch. "This isn't just nightmares or bad memories. It's like being back there. I can hear it, smell it..." His voice cracked, and he turned away, bracing himself against the kitchen counter.

Nikita took a step closer, her voice soft but unwavering. "Then let me be your anchor. Let me remind you where you are, that you're safe."

"I KNOW I'M FUCKING SAFE. I just can't fall asleep. And the longer I go without sleep the worse I am to be around. And I'm not easy to be around on a good day. I only have one way to ensure I go to sleep which I don't want to use unless I get desperate. I can't stop this, but I can stop you from getting hurt during it. It just happens sometimes. It's happened before and it'll happen again. I like you. I don't want you to see this." The words tumbled out of him, uncoordinated.

"I didn't want you to see my video…." her quiet voice replied. A gaping silence filled the room. The three seconds of footage replayed in John's mind, knowing she suffered long after filming stopped. You don't ever quite recover from something like that, not fully. On the day to day, she suffered so quietly and so bravely that he sometimes forgot she suffered at all; and hated himself even more for it.

Nikita continued now, "You said before that you have a way to ensure you go you sleep if you're desperate. Three hours in a week sounds desperate to me. Let's do whatever that is."

"Not. While you. Are here," John said firmly, still clutching the mug.

"Can you at least tell me what the plan is?"

"I drink. Heavily. Until I pass out. It's not pretty, and I'm not kind or easy to be around."

"Oh," Nikita said not for the first time tonight. "Does it stop what you see when you sleep, being that drunk?"

"No," came John's terse reply "Just means when it starts, I don't jolt back awake like when I'm sober."

"So, your big plan to overcome the psychosis bought on by sleep deprivation is to drink so heavily that you trap yourself in with your PTSD nightmares? Just so I understand," she stated with a slight tone of disapproval.

"Well, it sounds kinda dumb when you word it like that." A slight chuckle broke through his exhaustion. He pulled a credit card from his wallet and placed it in her hands. "Have a night out, on me. Call a friend, go for dinner, rent a room in the Plaza. Just please don't stay here. Not tonight. When you're around me, I want you to feel safe." He was pleading now. "Just go, please."

Nikita cocked her head to the side slightly, "May I try something before I go? Please? If it doesn't work, I'll go and you can drink yourself into a stupor. But let me try, please?"

John didn't have the heart to deny her. "Try your thing, then call your friends, okay?"

"Deal."

She led him to the couch, a placed a glass of Blantons in his hand. "Just breathe nice and deeply for me. Close your eyes if you want. But just keep breathing."

John bit back a retort along the lines of why would he stop breathing? She was trying to do something nice, and he was going to at least let her try.

Nikita lit several candles and turned off the lights. Taking up her seat at the piano John had retrieved from her apartment, Nikita began to play the same melody she had six weeks ago when she hosted John.

He closed his eyes and smiled in spite himself. Last time he had briefly fallen asleep standing up. He knew where Nikita was going with this. It wouldn't work, but he did genuinely appreciate the effort. He opened his eyes again to watch her as she played. Sipping his bourbon, he marvelled at how the candlelight warmed her porcelain white skin, her blond hair hanging gently over her shoulders, delicate fingers fluttering over the keys. She truly was one of the kindest, most beautiful women he had ever laid eyes on. And God, how she played!

His eyes snapped open to see her still playing, *A micro-sleep* he told himself, *like one gets when driving for too long.* He noticed his glass still in his lap, empty. He'd refill it at the end of the song, no need to disturb her playing. His back was already stiff from sitting. John looked across to where the bottle sat on the small dining table next to two candles burnt so low, now almost to their bases. *Wait what? They had been new not two minutes ago.* He looked around the room. All the other candles were down to their bases too. John turned to gaze at Nikita once more, a slow realisation washing over him.

"Have….have you been playing all this time? Was I asleep?

He saw her shiver just a little as he spoke, obviously not aware he had woken.

"Yes" she replied still not breaking her melody. I went to stop a few times, but every time I did you seemed to stir. So, I continued."

John looked out the window to see the first cold grey streaks of dawn fighting to take hold of a new day. He checked his watch, it read 5:16am. He could have sworn she sat him down on the couch around eight pm. She had sat playing the piano for him for over nine hours through the night so he might get a chance to sleep. Whatever her favourite thing in all of St. Petersburg was, John suddenly had the urge to buy her three of them.

"You mean you played through the night? For me?" he asked in disbelief, even though he already knew the answer. She stopped and stood, stretching her arms up. "It was worth it."

He stood now, striding over to her and enveloping her into a hug. "Thank you," he said gently in her ear. "You are too kind to me. Get some sleep. We have today and tomorrow off. I do need to do some shopping later. And if you could help me select some good Russian vodka to send to a friend, I'd certainly appreciate it."

"Maybe breakfast, too?" She asked hopefully.

"Absolutely, Of course, we'll hit that café you like next to the bookstore."

Nikita beamed at him and headed to bed.

15

Chapter Fifteen: Broken barriers

Nikita-

Nikita watched John stir sugar into his coffee. This was Nikita's favourite café, and oddly enough the only one where John took sugar in his coffee. She warmed her hands on her cappuccino; her happiness at the success of last night and this morning sent warmth throughout her body. She tried and failed to suppress a small smile while watching John. She had felt genuine fear when first introduced to him, how could she not? That day she had not thought him to be particularly attractive. But the more she was around him, the more his rough vulnerability and protective nature won her over. And now it was as though every day together she noticed something new. Whether it was the line of his jaw, his shoulders and back filling out with the regular food and weight training, *and those hands…* hands that she stood nearby, willing them to reach out and touch her. *You're getting carried away, when have you ever willed a man's hands to touch you?*

He seemed to have a soft spot for those everyone else looked over. Hell, he had even made friends with several of the homeless in the area. He was and always would be a killer, she reminded herself. But then again, she was and always would be owned, so she could hardly complain. To everyone he was this fearless, ferocious bear. But he was her bear, in a way his capacity for violence comforted her. She felt, for the first time in a long, long time…. safe. She turned her gaze away from him and back across to a red dress in a display window across the street.

"Are you going to try it on or what?" John's voice punctuated the silence.

"Sorry?"

"You've nothing to apologise for." He said that a lot Nikita noticed, whenever she said 'sorry' out of habit.

"You keep staring at that red dress. Why don't you try it on?" he continued.

The dress was stunning; she had to admit. The colour a deep, rich red that seemed to glow in the sunlight. It was a simple, yet elegant design, hugging the mannequin's curves in all the right places. The fabric was soft and smooth, creating a slight sheen in the sunlight and it seemed to glow from within, beckoning with promises of confidence and romance. Nikita's mouth watered involuntarily as she admired the dress. She could almost taste the luxurious feeling of the silky fabric against her skin. Imagining what it would be like to wear a dress like that, the kind that made you feel special just by wearing it. It was beautiful… and not for the likes of her.

"Wouldn't suit me."

"Course it fucking would. Look at it, it's gorgeous."

Nikita fixed him with a stare, not sure how to proceed.

"Okay it's a gorgeous dress, and it would suit my figure amazingly. But it's not for me. Firstly, where is a person like me going to wear something like that? And secondly, its sleeveless and backless with a plunging neckline. Think about how many of my scars would be on display. Those dresses should make you feel like everyone in the room envies you, and I could never wear it. What's the point of trying it on?

Besides I could never afford something like that."

"Fair," John started. "I didn't think about that, sorry. I just saw a pretty woman looking at a pretty dress that she obviously likes. Didn't put anymore thought into it than that."

"It's alright," she responded. John could be a bit obtuse, but he was a good man, not that he'd ever admit it, and she was determined not to let this mess with the good day they were having.

John drained the last of his coffee. "I'm going to head over the road and put some credit on my phone. Why don't you have a look through the bookshop, I'll meet you there."

***

John-

He walked across the road towards the convenience store next to the dress shop. John had been a little surprised by Nikita's outburst. But also proud of it. There was no way at all she could have spoken to him like that a few months ago. The Nikita that could only speak to him with "yes or no sir" was slowly being replaced by the real thing, and John loved it. As he entered, a man bumped into him. John looked into his face and froze.

"Sorry, friend," the man said as he moved to step past John.

"No worries," he replied. But he was full of worry. The man's face, his long-hook nose, the shoulder length black hair that fell about in ringlets, the scraggly beard, and the tattoo on the inside of the right forearm. John had seen this man before. In a video…. cutting Nikita. John hurried into the convenience store, his mind racing. He purchased his credit voucher, as well as a cheap burner phone and took some cash out of an ATM. He hurried outside. The man was sitting in a car now, and John discreetly took a picture with the burner before placing it and the cash into the small paper bag he had been given. His eyes settled on Dave, a homeless man who he knew often stayed in the area. He approached him, smiling broadly.

"How goes?" he asked.

"It goes," came Dave's response. "Why are you smiling like that?"

John however continued to wear it. "Smile and nod like I'm saying something interesting."

Dave did so, his curiosity obviously peaked.

John continued, "Greasy fucker sitting in the white BMW, to your right."

"I see him."

"See him around here often?"

"Most days, most evenings too in fact."

John laid the paper bag beside Dave, still smiling. "I need to have a talk with him. There's a phone with my number in it, and thirty thousand rubles in that bag. I need you to text me every time you see him around here. Can you do that for me?"

"What you need to talk to him about?" Dave's curiosity getting the better of him.

"He hurt a friend of mine in a way you don't ever recover from."

"The woman you walk with?" It was more statement than question. "I like her, she's kind. I'll be texting you John, I'm sure this man would appreciate the chance to talk with you," Dave smirked.

"Fucking doubt it," John returned. He reached out and shook Dave's hand, "Be hearing from you."

***

Nikita-

John met her in the bookstore and pretended to peruse the isle. It wasn't a great pretence. Nikita knew he couldn't read Russian, just speak it a bit. She noticed he would stay a few metres behind her, picking up and looking at whatever books she seemed interested in. They were mainly books on Africa. On Rwanda and Sudan. Places he'd said he'd been. *Maybe today he'll go through the photos with me.*

"Ready to go?" her voice softly called.

"Ready when you are," came his reply.

The two friends continued their day out. Nikita helped him pick out a good bottle of vodka and some Russian delicacies and souvenirs to send to Kelsey back in Australia.

"She seems like some woman," Nikita probed. In truth, she was in a way jealous of Kelsey. Though she had never met her, Nikita knew that she and John were close in a way that Nikita doubted her and John ever could be. John protected her and appreciated her, she knew that. But he seemed to refer to Kelsey as an equal in a way that Nikita felt she couldn't quite live up to. Kelsey could shoot and fight, they had been through a lot together. The thought was that if he ever were to move on, it would be with someone like Kelsey, not her. In her heart of hearts, Nikita knew that while she enjoyed John's company, cooking with him, going to the café and bookstores, playing house, she knew he was a job, that she would never actually be his. She was owned, and while she could pretend all she wanted, there was no riding off into the sunset with her savage protector. He would leave, eventually, and she would go back in front of a camera. Still the heart wants what the heart wants.

"Yeah, they broke the mould with her. If you're still interested, I'll go through my Africa stuff this afternoon with you; there'll be a few photos of her in there" John mused.

"I'd like that… Can I ask a question?" she put forward tentatively.

"Sure," John said.

"When…Everything happened. Why didn't you go with her back to Australia? You two seem close. Even when you first came to Russia, you could have gone back instead."

John blinked hard and yawned. *Obviously not entirely recovered from his lack of sleep,* Nikita thought.

"Nikita, if you've not noticed, I have all the subtlety of a bull walrus. And I get the feeling that you're not asking what you want to ask, you're just talking around it hoping to get enough information to satisfy yourself," came his reply.

She turned away quickly, still walking beside him. "No, sorry. I didn't mean to pry. Forget I said anything."

John let out a long sigh. "You've nothing to apologise for. When Kels first went back to Australia, I had lost Amy only three days prior. I wasn't thinking straight, and I reasoned that Kels needed to get on with her life. Meet someone, date, fall in love, all that. You're right, we are close, and she did offer for me to live with her. But after what we've been through and how tight that makes us, how would she have a normal life with me there? And as for why I came here instead of going back home, well, Africa was broken for me. Kelsey is the only family I have in Oz, and I just explained that. So why not here?"

He kept walking as he placed an arm around her shoulder, "I could be wildly wrong here, and please… forgive me if I am. But if you're wondering if the reason I turn you away is that I would want a woman like Kelsey and not you, that you wouldn't be good enough — it doesn't work like that. Kels and I, we're like brother and sister. She's remarkable, but it's not about my taste in women, moving on and choosing her over someone like you. I don't know if that answers your question."

John removed his arm as the two passed a street performer playing a handpan drum.

"I shouldn't have questions, I had no right, I'm sorry," she said almost at a whisper.

John stopped and looked at her. "You have nothing to apologise for. You are enough." He paused before adding, "If I was capable of being with someone in any capacity, you would have been enough for me." The last sentence whispered so quietly Nikita wasn't sure he intended for her to hear.

Nikita felt her heart swell with a mixture of emotions as John's words sank in. She blinked away the tears that threatened to roll down her cheeks. "Thank you," she said softly, her voice barely above a whisper.

John nodded, his expression clearly pained and tired still. They continued walking in silence, each lost in their own thoughts. The bustling streets of St. Petersburg was a fitting background as they navigated the complexities of their relationship.

After a few minutes, Nikita spoke again, her voice steadier now. "So, about those photos of Africa... I'd still love to see them, if you're willing to share."

John glanced at her, relief evident in his eyes. "Absolutely. We can look through them when we get back to the apartment."

They continued their shopping, the tension from earlier slowly dissipating. As they browsed through a small shop filled with souvenirs and trinkets, Nikita's hand brushed against a delicate matryoshka doll. She picked it up, examining the intricate designs.

"Kelsey might like this," she said, holding it up for John to see.

He nodded, a small smile tugging at the corners of his mouth. "She would. Good eye."

As they made their way to the checkout, Nikita felt a sudden urge to know more about the woman who meant so much to John. "Tell me something about Kelsey," she said, her voice tinged with curiosity. "Something I won't see in the photos."

John paused, considering her request. His eyes took on a distant look, as if peering into memories from another lifetime. "Kelsey... she's got this uncanny ability to find humour in the darkest situations," he began, his voice low and thoughtful. "There was this one time in Rwanda, we were pinned down, outgunned and outnumbered on the side of this mountain. Things were looking proper fucking grim, right. And there she was, cracking jokes about how she'd always wanted to try skydiving, but this wasn't quite what she had in mind."

A chuckle escaped him, surprising them both. "She just never gives in you know? Didn't matter the situation, even when everything's going to hell, you can always count on Kels. She is the rock that problems break themselves on. "

Nikita nodded, absorbing this new information about the woman she'd only known through John's sparse mentions. It made her both admire the woman and feel a twinge of that familiar inadequacy.

"She sounds… incredible," she finally said.

"So are you, in your own way. Kels is formidable true, and just indomitably loyal. But she's got her own demons too."

***

"I didn't know Africa had deer," Nikita quipped. She was clicking through photos on the TV as John prepared dinner in the kitchen. Tonight they were having chicken filo. A puzzled look was on his face as he came out of the kitchen. "It…doesn't."

"What's that then?"

John poked his head around the corner glancing at the image. "Kudu. Type of antelope."

"What's the difference between antelope and deer, then?" She was enjoying John sharing this part of his life. Plus, if she ever had the opportunity to leave Russia, she would have loved to visit Africa. This would be as close as she would ever get.

"Hang on, let me get this in the oven and I'll be with you."

She continued flicking through the photos for a minute or two before John reappeared beside her with some kind of spirit in his glass, and wine in the other hand for her. He settled on the floor beside her leaning against the couch.

"You know this one?" he asked. Nikita took in the large black and white animal before her admiring the massive horns which curled back from its head. "No, but it's another antelope, isn't it?"

"Yeah, Sable antelope. Prime target for snare poaching. The shape of their horns makes it easy for their head to go through the loop, but they can't get out. Nasty way to go."

"And the difference between deer and antelope?" she prompted.

"Oh, right. Deer have antlers with multiple tines or points." He placed his fingers branching out from his head to demonstrate. "The males grow them every year for the rut, their mating season, and cast them off when it's over. With antelope, they're much more closely related to things like goats or cattle. They have horns as opposed to antlers. They're like bone and are fused to the skull, not cast off. If they get injured or broken, they stay that way."

She continued flicking through picture after picture. So many animals and places, some she knew, some she didn't. John came back with dinner in his hands to find her staring at a picture of himself against a broken wall, a rifle laid against his shoulder. A woman a little shorter than John with thick mousey brown hair, cradled her own rifle across her lap, eating while John appeared asleep. The rubble all around them in stark contrast to the seemly restful moment they found themselves in. Nikita looked at John, "Kelsey?" she asked. He gave an affirming grunt as he sat back on the floor beside her, sliding her the chicken wrapped in pastry.

"Where was this taken?" Nikita continued. "The place looks destroyed. Was this the compound in Sudan?"

"No this was the Congo, the job where I met Kelsey."

Nikita nodded, her eyes lingering on the image. She couldn't help but notice the ease between John and Kelsey, even in such a dire setting. A pang of something—jealousy, perhaps—flickered in her chest. She looked sideways at John, and leaned her shoulder against his. *When did his shoulders get so big? His shirts do him no favours at all.*

"What was the job?" she asked, her voice carefully neutral.

John took a long sip of his drink before answering. "Anti-poaching operation. My team and I were tracking a group that had been hitting the mountain gorilla populations pretty hard." His voice grew quieter.

Nikita sensed the weight behind his words. She reached out, her fingers brushing his arm. "You don't have to talk about it if you don't want to."

He shook his head. "It's fine." He gestured to the screen. "That picture was taken right after we'd had a run-in with them. We'd been tracking them for two days before they backtracked and laid a trap, ambushing us in that village. The fighting was… messy."

John's eyes grew distant, lost in the memory. "Kelsey saved my life that day. I'd gotten pinned down, separated from the rest of the team, I was down to five rounds in a pistol. She came out of nowhere, straight out of the fucking jungle, rifle tucked into her shoulder and just starts dropping folks as she walked." John held up his hands mimicking a rifle's moments as he spoke. "She kept going till she ran out of ammo, let the rifle fall, its sling catching it and drew her pistol. She continued to fire and move toward them." He huffed out a humourless laugh. "I thought she was batshit insane, the risks she took. But that's Kelsey for you." He paused before adding. "You know I never did find out what Kelsey had been doing out there on her own. But I'm glad she was there."

He motioned for Nikita to go to the next image. A burning town met her eyes; collapsed buildings and rubble everywhere. It looked broken, uninhabitable. Nikita's eyes widened as she took in the devastation captured in the photo. She felt a chill run down her spine. She'd seen her share of violence and destruction, but this… this was something else entirely.

"My God," she whispered.

John grunted softly. "Two days later. This was the township we and the vet team were operating out of. The local groups were so furious they had been made to run by a woman that they came to level the town in revenge. They wanted Kelsey, and anyone who knew her. Didn't care who got caught in the crossfire."

"Did everyone get out?" Nikita asked wide eyed.

John took a long sip, draining his glass. "We evacuated the vet and hospital teams, any NGO's, while we held outskirts of the town."

Nikita's breath caught in her throat as she lingered on the devastation captured in the photo. The burning town, the collapsed buildings, the rubble strewn everywhere—a harsh reminder of the brutal realities John had faced before moving to Russia.

"You held the town? That?" she motioned at the rubble.

He nodded again, "My team, plus Kelsey. She was one of the vets that we were trying to evacuate." He laughed bitterly, "but she wouldn't go while people still defended it. Didn't want others doing her fighting for her."

Nikita nodded, her throat tight. She could see it in her mind's eye - John, younger and perhaps less burdened, fighting alongside this fierce woman who'd become such an important part of his life.

"It was chaos. Gunfire everywhere. Buildings collapsing. And in the middle of it all, there was Kelsey. Cool as ice, picking off targets like she was born for it. For three days they came, and for three days we held them off. The town broke, but we didn't, we held. There's some videos of the fighting on that drive somewhere, GoPro footage, but I don't recommend you watch it."

Nikita looked back at him.

"After that," John continued, "we just… clicked. She understood things about me; I understood about her… we became a team. We worked together for years, all over Africa."

Nikita nodded slowly, processing this information. "You two must be close."

"We are," John admitted. "Kelsey… she understands me in a way few people ever have. The things we saw, the things we had to do - it creates a bond."

There was a heaviness in his voice that made Nikita's chest tighten.

She reached out, covering his hand with hers. "John, I-"

He shook his head, cutting her off. "I told you It wasn't like that," John said, his voice low. "Kelsey and I... we were partners, friends, brother and sister. But nothing romantic, ever."

Nikita studied his face, searching for any hint of untruth. "Really? After everything you went through together?" John met her gaze, his eyes intense. "Really. Kelsey... she's family, dearer to me than my own blood. But my heart belonged to Amy as soon as I met her."

At the mention of Amy's name, John's expression clouded over. Nikita squeezed his hand

"Tell me about her," Nikita said softly. "About Amy."

John was quiet for a long moment, his thumb absently tracing patterns on his glass. When he spoke, his voice was thick with emotion.

"Amy was... everything. Kind, brave, stubborn." A ghost of a smile flickered across his face as he paused. He began again, his voice low and pained now. "We met in Botswana, at this little school. Kelsey and I were there doing security work at a nearby reserve. From the moment I saw her, it was like... like coming home. She was this vibrant, passionate teacher who'd come to Africa to make a difference. I was... well, I was lost. Trying to find purpose after leaving the army."

He paused, a ghost of a smile playing on his lips. "She saw right through my bullshit. Called me out on it, actually. Said if I really wanted to help, I should stop feeling sorry for myself and do something about it."

Nikita was listening intently, barely breathing. John rarely spoke about Amy, and never in such detail.

"We fell hard and fast," he continued. "Got married six months later, in this tiny village where she taught. It was... it was good. Really good. For three years. For three years, we had it all," he finally said, his voice barely above a whisper. "We were making a difference, building a life together. I thought... I thought we'd grow old watching sunsets together, you know?"

Nikita stared at the man before her. Feeling guilty at the effect his proximity had on her when even now, Amy held such sway over him.

"You know the rest. It was bound to happen." He spoke barely above a whisper.

She frowned and John caught sight of it. "She was more than I ever could deserve. Men like me, there are no happy endings. I should have known that, should have known that if she hitched herself to my wagon, it would all end horribly."

"I don't think I agree with that," Nikita was calm and measured in her approach. "You said you had three perfect years. Three years against one terrible day. Means it wasn't only harm that came to her, there was a lot of good, too."

"Anyway you spin it," he started as he rose, knees protesting. "Neither of us got what we deserve no matter what way you look at it." He made a motion to move to the next image, effectively ending the conversation. Nikita did so and was greeted with an almost comical picture of forest elephants, a baby wrestling a small tree.

16

Chapter Sixteen: Leg Day

John-

John's legs burned, his breath coming in ragged pants. Sweat dripped from his brow as he bent his left leg, allowing his body, weighed down by a pair of dumbbells, to slowly lower. His right foot rested on a bench behind him. He briefly wondered if Bulgarian split squats did actually originate in Bulgaria, or if whoever named the exercise simply thought it was a cool sounding name. It didn't matter. What mattered was that they, like all good leg exercises, hurt. They burned his legs and whispered against his will. Leg day as much mentally punishing as it was physically; perhaps that's why he liked it. He found solace and peace in the pain. Or maybe it was simply distracting enough to take his mind off her. It had been a week since she played through the night for him.

As John pushed through the burn, his mind inevitably drifted back to Nikita. Her golden hair, her freckled face, the way her eyes crinkled when she smiled. He grunted, forcing himself to focus on the weight, on the strain in his muscles. Anything but her.

But she was always there, lurking at the edges of his consciousness. Even in the gym, his sanctuary, he couldn't escape her presence. John lowered himself into another rep, relishing the searing pain that shot through his quads. It was a welcome distraction from the ache in his chest and the dull, dogging hurt in his head. He finished the set and collapsed on the bench, checking his watch. Ninety seconds, then the next set. His mind wandered back to the small Russian woman and the promises he made to her.

He remembered the day he'd first seen her, introduced as his assistant. How small and fragile she'd seemed, almost broken in a way. He would find out later how broken she actually was. But he also thought about how far she'd come since then, growing stronger, more confident. Even correcting him about the red dress. Ten seconds to go. He collected heavier dumbbells and set his feet in place again. He would be her salvation, that much John was determined to be. But after that, she needed to go. Go far away from him; she would never be free while she stayed. He lowered himself again, his muscles protesting even more for their short rest. As John forced himself through the last excruciating set, his muscles screaming in protest, he couldn't help but think of how Nikita had changed him.

After Sudan, the shock and grief was like a sucking chest wound. A physical pain so bad, it felt like every breath would be his last. In the weeks that followed, it became a gushing wound, the blood seeping life and will from his body. As the months wore on it dimmed slightly to broken ribs, where one knew they would live, yet were in pain with every move, every breath. This constant pain had been what drove him to drink, to engage in reckless, near suicidal behaviour. Now, the pain had become a dull ache, one that came on sometimes, that he was aware would always be there, but was no longer as debilitating. It was as though life might be worth planning for again.

Nikita had been a big part of that. She had wormed her way into his life, pulling him out of his drunken haze. The days simply no longer needing self-medication whenever she was a part of them. She was almost the air in his lungs now; he couldn't imagine a life without her as his constant companion. But he had to. For her sake. He knew she was developing feelings for him, but they couldn't be allowed to take hold. She was only looking at him because although he was a monster, he was a monster on her side. John reasoned, *as long as I'm an option, she'll view me as the only choice. She must go once this is over, she needs to go if she's to be truly free.* And he intended to see her truly free.

The weights clanged as he dropped them into the rack, his breath coming in heavy gasps. He grabbed a towel, wiping the sweat from his face, and caught a glimpse of himself in the mirror. The man staring back at him was a far cry from the broken man who'd first met Nikita. His eyes, once dull with pain and regret, now held a spark of something he couldn't quite name. Hope, maybe. Or fear. Physically he had changed too. He was stronger, fuller. He ate more, drank less…

John shook his head, trying to dispel the thoughts. He couldn't afford to hold those them. They weren't helpful. He turned and saw the weighted sled in the corner. *Perfect…that'll hurt.*

***

It wasn't for another forty-five minutes until John finally limped back into his apartment. Nikita was laying on the couch, her book in hand and a glass of wine on the small table beside her. She looked up as John entered, her eyes flicking over his sweat-soaked form. Noticing the way his clothes clung to him, highlighting his changing physicality and leaving little to the imagination. His shoulders looked like two boulders on top of a granite torso; thick muscled arms extended from those boulders. His legs were now like tree trunks, solid and dependable. The whole physique gave an impression of rugged capability — if you were into that sort of thing. And Nikita was realising with each passing day that she was. The more she knew him, the more attractive she found him.

"Rough workout?" she asked, her voice carefully neutral.

"Good workout," John replied, more cheerful than he felt.

He headed straight for the kitchen. He needed water. As he gulped it down, he could feel her eyes on him, studying him. Her concern, her care for him, it was all too much. He couldn't bear it, couldn't allow himself to get used to it. John sank onto a chair by the dining table, his muscles protesting every movement.

"What book you reading?" At John's encouragement, Nikita had recently joined a book club to meet new people and have something outside of John and the zoo. He even built a bookcase for her room. The book he could see, but the title was in Russian. Of course it was. Nikita set it down, "It's a bit hard going so far. I'm only a few chapters in. It's the story of a half dog, half wolf pup."

A thinking frown crossed John's face. "Not White Fang?"

"Yes, have you read it?"

"Yeah. It's one of my favourites. Written by Jack London in like 1906. Interesting your group is reading it, most of his works were banned in this part of the world for a long time."

"Is it worth finishing? It's pretty rough so far."

"Well, I think it is, obviously. In my opinion it's a beautiful story of surviving and human kindness in the face of overwhelming brutality. Worth it in the end."

She took in the sight of him again and stood, "Shall I run you a hot bath?"

John was about to retort that he could run his own bath but as he went to stand, he realised he could barely do that. "That would be nice, thank you."

As Nikita disappeared into the bathroom. He heard the water running, imagining Nikita's delicate hands testing the temperature. The thought made his chest tighten. *Oh Cut that out for fuck's sake.*

He limped towards the bathroom, pausing at the doorway. Nikita was perched on the edge of the tub, testing the water temperature with her hand. The sight of her there, so domestic and caring, sent a pang through his chest.

"Water's ready," she said, looking up at him. Her eyes held a softness that made John want to look away.

"Thanks," he managed, his voice gruff. He stepped into the bathroom, careful not to brush against her as she stood to leave.

But Nikita hesitated at the door, her hand lingering on the doorframe. She turned back to John, her eyes searching his face. "John," she asked softly, "are you okay?"

The question caught him off guard. He was used to her quiet concern, but this direct inquiry felt different. Dangerous. He forced a smile that didn't quite reach his eyes. "Just sore. Nothing a hot bath won't fix."

Nikita didn't look convinced. She took a step closer, her brow furrowed. "You've been… different lately."

John felt his defences rising. He couldn't let her in, couldn't let her see the turmoil inside him. "I'm fine," he said, his voice coming out harsher than he intended.

Nikita flinched slightly at his tone, and John immediately regretted it. He softened his voice. "Really, I'm okay. Just tired, sore, and crabby." He did his best to flash a smile, and winced as he struggled to remove his sweat-soaked shirt, his muscles no longer obeying him.

"Do you need a hand with that?" Nikita asked quietly. John looked her in the eye.

That would be courting temptation too much. "No, thank you." he said firmly but smiling, and closed the door.

17

Chapter Seventeen: Eighty-Five

Nikita-

Two weeks later, Nikita was laying in her bed in John's apartment, staring at the ceiling, unable to sleep. The past few weeks had been wonderful. They'd been shopping, having lunch out, and she and John had gone through thousands of photos and hundreds of stories. He been sleeping well again. Everything was perfect. And that was a problem. It was too perfect, her growing feelings for John only made more intense by the good times they'd shared. Which in turn only made the pain of knowing she could never have a life like this equally more intense. Nikita knew what she was, and with tears in her eyes she felt that familiar terrifying pull of despair.

She tried to blink her welling tears away, willing the urge to go away with them, but it persisted, gnawing at her like a hungry beast. Her fingers twitched, longing to reach for her phone, to pull up those dark videos that reminded her of her place in the world.

Nikita squeezed her eyes shut, trying to block out the invasive thoughts. But the darkness only strengthened the horrifying, irresistible urge that tore at her like terrifying shadowy fingers.

With trembling hands, she reached for her phone on the nightstand.

The screen's harsh glow illuminated her tear-streaked face as she navigated to the hidden folder. *Just one video*, she told herself. *One reminder of who she really was, to shatter this beautiful illusion.*

But before she could press play, a muffled sound from the living room caught her attention. Nikita froze, listening intently. Without thinking, she slipped out of bed, padding silently across the cool floorboards, stopping at the doorway.

"John?" she quietly asked.

Silence met her, and she peeked around the corner to see his bed empty; she noticed his gym bag and shoes gone too. He did sometimes have the habit of sleeping for a few hours, going to the gym and sleeping again. Like he was allergic to getting uninterrupted sleep. Unless Nikita was playing the piano, of course.

She must have heard him leaving Nikita realised, and in doing so, it had broken her silent battle, allowing her to resist the urge to look at her abuse. By leaving the apartment he had saved her yet again. She let out a long pent-up sigh. Perhaps a small walk in the brisk air outside might be good for her. Certainly, better than heading back to bed. She quickly dressed and put her shoes on. She could have her walk, calm down, and be back by the time John came home.

Bouncing down the stairs she opened the main door and was greeted with the crisp cold air. Suddenly she was very, very, awake. The still night quieted her thoughts. *This was a good idea* she told herself. And almost as if the universe was rewarding her for her good choice, she noticed a single white speck gracefully falling from the sky before coming to rest on the pavement. Then another, and another, until the first snowfall of the season was happening all around her. She twirled, smiling broadly as she took in the beauty, and stopped dead in her tracks. Her eyes fell on a man walking toward her.

He hadn't seemed to have noticed her yet. But the black hair in ringlets, crooked nose and scraggly beard…her blood ran cold. *She knew this man.* Nikita hugged her arms tight to herself, her fingers subconsciously brushing over her the deep scars he had left on her upper arms after a particularly brutal session.

Nikita's heart raced as she stood frozen, unable to move or breathe. The man's footsteps echoed in the quiet night, each one bringing him closer to her. She wanted to run, to scream, to hide, but her body refused to obey. The snowflakes continued to fall, oblivious to the terror unfolding beneath them.

As he drew nearer, recognition flickered across his face. His eyes narrowed, a cruel smile twisting his lips. "Well, well," he drawled, his voice sending shivers down her spine. "If it isn't my favourite little songbird. Fancy seeing you here."

Her mind screamed at her to run, to flee back into the safety of John's apartment, but her body refused to obey. She stood frozen, rooted to the spot as the man drew nearer. The falling snow, moments ago so beautiful, now felt suffocating. Each flake that touched her skin burned like acid, a cruel reminder of her vulnerability.

Just then a white windowless van screeched to a stop beside the man. He leapt back as the door slid open only for someone to sprint from behind an alley wall, slamming into the man and knocking him into the van. The assailant's head was covered in a black woolly mask, but there was something familiar about the way he moved. The man took a brief look at Nikita, who still unable to move.

"Go home, girl," the masked man commanded, in the worst attempt at a Russian accent she had ever heard. "Run."

Nikita needed no further invitation, all thoughts of a nice walk in the snowfall gone. She turned, and ran as the van pulled away.

***

John -Thirty minutes earlier.

John slid out of his bed almost silently as the phone vibrated. He had been waiting for this message. Dave had been astute in his duties, letting him know whenever the man with the forearm tattoo was in the area.

Yesterday, John had rented a windowless van. Dave knew of a few other homeless that would be willing to assist, for a nominal fee, of course. But a small price to pay John thought, for the answers he was going to get. Tonight was the night he was sure of it. He opened his phone to see the message. "Entered diner," it said simply. John pulled his shoes on, picked up his gym bag, and headed for the door. He paused for a second as he passed the framed picture of him and Amy on their wedding day. "I know what I am. I'm sorry," he whispered before placing the frame picture side down and left.

He positively froze now as he stood waiting, his back leaning against a wall. The shoes were a poor choice; he should have worn boots, but he had hoped that the fact his shoes and gym bag were gone would convince Nikita he had gone to the gym if she woke. He wished the man would hurry up; John was getting impatient. His phone buzzed again. "100m," the message read. John prepared himself, pulling his balaclava down over his face.

As the man walked past the alley John was hiding in, he could hear him talking to someone. *Maybe he was on the phone?* John couldn't hear any other voices in response. Right on time, the van pulled up, the door opening. The man jumped back but John shoved him with all his might, causing him to fall into the waiting arms of Dave and another man who quickly moved to bind and gag him. John went to jump in the van too, but was stopped cold catching sight of an obviously shocked Nikita. His face covered, *She can't see you* he told himself. "Go home girl," he mustered his best Russian accent. "Run," before he too stepped into the van and it pulled away.

An hour later John surveyed the man in front of him. Bound to a chair and gagged, he looked almost pitiful. *He hadn't looked pitiful torturing Nikita.* And now John was going to get every question he had answered. They had taken him to an abandoned warehouse in a now derelict industrial park. The air reeked of musty mould and rust, the scent of neglect and decay lingering in every corner. It had been a bit of a drive to get here, but this was exactly the kind of place John needed. He could taste the grit and dust in his mouth as he breathed in the stale air of the warehouse; he could feel the adrenaline coursing through his body as he prepared to do what needed to be done.

Somewhere deep inside him, a small flame flickered to life as John stood behind the bound object of his attention. He allowed his hands to fall on the man's shoulders. The man flinched, and then quickly composed himself. The warehouse's dim light cast long shadows across the concrete floor, amplifying the tension in the air, silent save for the muffled whimpers coming from behind the gag. John savoured the fear in the man's eyes, remembering the cruel indifference he'd shown Nikita. *No, not indifference. The pleasure on this animal's face as he cut into her.* John could almost feel his heart harden with anticipation of what was to come. He walked around to the front of his target.

"The woman you were talking to when we grabbed you. You were in a video with her. I saw what you did."

Leaning in close, John locked eyes with his captive. "You're going to tell me everything. Every name, every location, every sick little detail about every question I ask. I'm not going to believe you in the beginning, I'm going to think you're not being honest with me, I'm going to be…. upset by your dishonesty. But believe me, by the time we're done, I will trust your word like you were my own brother."

John reached out, roughly yanking the gag from the man's mouth. "Start talking."

The man spat, a mixture of saliva and blood hitting the floor. "I don't know anything," he rasped, his eyes darting around the room.

John's fist connected with the man's jaw, the impact echoing through the empty space as the small flame took hold and grew. "Wrong answer," he snarled. "I know what you did to her. I saw the video, saw your face." John let another short, sharp punch go. *Not too hard, you can't get good answers from someone with a head injury.* "The other two wore masks. I want their names."

The man's head lolled to the side, a trickle of blood running from the corner of his mouth. He let out a harsh laugh. "You have no idea who you're messing with."

John's eyes narrowed behind his balaclava. He reached into his gym bag, pulling out a claw hammer. The metal glinted in the dim light as he held it up as a question before laying it on an old, unsteady work bench. He did the same with several other tools; some straight nose pliers, a small pry bar and lastly, a pair of woodworking clamps. "I've seen your work," John started slowly, "I know you like to cut. I personally feel like that's too much clean up. So, we're going to start by bending something. Something that was not meant to bend. Then I think we'll crush a few things. Finally, we'll break a few things, by that time I will trust whatever you say."

Fear flickered in the man's eyes, but he quickly masked it with bravado. "All this to say she's yours now? Fuck you, bitch! And that thing I was talking to before? You wait till I get my hands on her again, I'll make last time seem like a day at the spa."

John shoved the man's gag back. "That's… disappointing, although a part of me was hoping you'd say something like that."

He slowly reached for the hammer, knuckles turning white as he gripped it. "She is her own. You…are mine." The fire inside him was well and truly alight now.

***

Three hours later, John stumbled back into his apartment, utterly exhausted. He had changed his clothes and burnt his old ones. He had taken his time, trying to repaint the pain he had seen on Nikita's face on that of her tormentor. But regardless of how he had tried, it didn't feel like enough. By the end he had good information. Aliases for the other two men *Ghost and Bear* plus a location for where a hard drive containing the originals of Nikita's films was kept. *The Red Dragon.* Good information, though not as much as he'd like.

Shower then, John looked at his watch, *about two hours sleep. It's going to be a long day.* He turned the tap and let the hot water cascade over his body. John closed his eyes, begging the water to wash away more than just the physical evidence of the night's events. The adrenaline wore off, leaving him feeling hollow and heavy. He'd gotten the information he needed, but at what cost? The memory of the man's screams echoed in his mind, mingling with the sound of the running water. He kept as quiet as possible, trying not to wake Nikita.

A pang of guilt twisted in his gut. Not for his actions tonight, but for Nikita. Hopefully she hadn't recognised him. She had no idea what he'd done tonight, what he was capable of. And if everything went according to plan, she never would.

"John?" a soft voice called out.

John froze, his hand hovering over the shower knob. He hadn't heard her approach. Quickly composing himself, he called back, "Yeah, it's me. Sorry if I woke you."

"It's okay. I was already awake. Are you alright? You were gone a long time."

John's mind raced, searching for a plausible excuse. "Yeah, I'm fine. Just… couldn't sleep. Went for a long gym session to clear my head."

There was a moment of silence, and John held his breath, praying she wouldn't push further. Finally, Nikita spoke again, her voice laced with concern. "Okay. If you want to talk about anything, I'm here."

"Thanks," John managed, his throat tight. "I'll be out in a minute."

As he stepped out of the shower and began to dry off, John caught sight of himself in the mirror. His face was hollow and hate filled, his knuckles were raw and bruised, betraying the violence he'd unleashed earlier. He quickly wrapped a towel around his waist, slipped out of the bathroom, and found himself face to face with Nikita.

Nikita's eyes widened as she took in John's appearance. Her gaze lingered on his bruised knuckles before meeting his eyes, a mixture of concern and suspicion clouding her features.

"John," she said softly, reaching out to touch his arm. "What did you do?"

He flinched involuntarily at her touch, guilt and shame washing over him. "It's nothing," he muttered, avoiding her gaze. "Just got a bit carried away at the gym." He attempted to move past her, but she blocked him.

Nikita's hand dropped to her side, her concern growing. "Don't lie to me," she said, her voice barely above a whisper. "I saw you earlier. In the alley."

18

Chapter Eighteen: Aftermath

Nikita-

Nikita stood in the doorway, blocking John's exit.

"I woke up and you were gone. I couldn't sleep so I went for a walk. I saw you take him. You know I saw you. Why would someone tell me to run in English, with a Russian accent? They would just say it in Russian."

John took a step back, crossing his arms as if trying to put a barrier between them. "Nikita, I…" he started without looking at her, but she cut him off.

"Why?" she asked, her eyes searching his face. "Why on earth would you put yourself in this?"

John's jaw clenched, a war of emotions played out across his face.

"He hurt you," he said finally, his voice dripping venom. "I couldn't… I just could not walk past that."

Nikita's eyes widened, a wild mix of emotions flashing across her face and her eyes filled with tears. Her voice was barely above a whisper. "You did this… for me?"

John nodded, still unwilling to meet her gaze. "I had to know who they were, where to find them. And how to stop them. I promised no one would ever hurt you again, and I keep my word."

The rules were different with John. Nikita took a step closer, her hand reaching out to gently touch his bruised knuckles. "I… I don't know what to say." Her touch was soft against his battered skin. But he pulled away, as though her touch burned him, unable to even look at her.

When he did finally look up, his eyes met hers again. "You don't have to say anything. I know it was wrong, but I'd do it again in a heartbeat if it meant keeping you safe. This is who I am, all I'm good for. I am not a good man, but for you, I would be the worst."

Nikita's eyes welled with tears as she gazed up at John, she reached for him again, her fingers attempting to intertwine with his. He grimaced as though her hand was like acid on his skin. "You're good for so much more than you realise," she whispered, her voice thick with emotion. "But this…"

"I'm good with what I am. What happened to you was not okay. I can't undo it, but I promise it will never happen again. I will free you." He spoke softly, almost tenderly, as if he was not someone that was capable of the abject violence he had obviously spent hours inflicting.

"Don't, I'm not worth the price you'll pay," she could barely muster a whisper.

"Whatever the price is, you are absolutely worth it."

Nikita pulled back slightly, her tear-streaked face tilted up to meet his gaze. "At what cost to you, John? To your soul?" Her hand came up to rest on his cheek, her touch gentle. He went to pull away again, but not so much that her hand left his face. "I can't bear the thought of you becoming…" her voice trailed off, unsure how to voice her concern.

"My soul? That worthless thing? Gave it away ages ago." John let go with that bitter laugh again. "I'm good with what I am," he repeated, "and if this is all it takes to protect you, then I count it as cheap."

Nikita's eyes traced the lines of worry etched on his face. "And who protects you, John? Who saves you from the darkness?"

For a moment, John was silent, his eyes searching Nikita's face. Then, almost whispering, he spoke. "Who says you don't. Who says you aren't enough?"

I do, I say it Nikita thought, as her breath caught in her throat at John's words. For a moment, they stood frozen, the weight of his admission hanging between them. Then, with a gentleness that belied his earlier violence, John reached up and covered Nikita's hand with his own, pressing it more firmly against his cheek. Finally, Nikita spoke in a whisper. "John, I…" She trailed off, struggling to find the right words. "I'm not worth this… I'm broken. You know I'm broken."

John's hand rested on her face, his calloused fingers rough against her skin as he wiped away a single tear rolling down her cheek. "What, and I'm not?" He smiled sadly.

"Before you, I was lost in darkness. And I deserve to be there, after everything I've done. But you…" He swallowed hard. "You give me a reason to bother waking up every morning."

Nikita went to speak but he cut her off gently, pressing his forehead against hers. "I know I'm not a good man, Nikita. I have done… terrible things…"

The air fled Nikita's lungs, her eyes searching his face. Slowly, hesitantly, she leaned in, her lips brushing against his in a feather-light kiss. John froze for a moment, as if overwhelmed by the tenderness of her touch, so at odds with the violence that had consumed him earlier.

Nikita felt John's arms tightened around her, pulling her closer as he deepened the kiss. All the pent-up emotions - the fear, the sorrow, the desperate need to be near him - poured out as her lips moved against his. For a moment, the world fell away, and there was only this - the warmth of his body against her, the softness of her lips, the gentle strength of his arms.

When they finally broke apart, both breathless, John rested his forehead against hers. "Nikita," he whispered, his voice hoarse with emotion. "I…"

She placed a finger gently on his lips, silencing him. "I know," she said softly. "I know, John."

"I… we shouldn't…"

She silenced him with another quick kiss. "Don't," she said softly. "Don't push me away. Not now."

John closed his eyes, "You deserve better than me," he said, his voice barely above a whisper.

"Better than a man who would risk everything to keep me safe? Who sees me as more than an object?" She shook her head, a sad smile playing on her lips. "John, you're the best man I've ever known."

John kept his eyes closed, as if to hold her gaze would be the end of him. Nikita knew he wanted to argue, to tell her all the reasons why she was supposedly wrong about him. That he was a killer, that was no good, barely human, that he was not a thing to be wanted or cared about. Simply used and discarded, told where to go and what to do. Hating himself for it all. All the things he raged against when she said them about herself. He drew in breath to speak but the words died on his lips as she pressed herself closer, her body warm against his exposed torso, hands resting on his muscular chest.

John's eyes opened, meeting hers with a mixture of disbelief and longing. "You can't mean that. After what I've done tonight…"

"What you did," She took a deep breath, her next words coming out in a rush. "If you think that changes how I feel about you, you're wrong."

Nikita thought she could actually hear Johns heart thud in his chest. "How… how do you feel?" He asked hesitantly, as if he was unsure whether he really wanted the answer. "About me."

Nikita's eyes softened. "I feel… safe with you, John. Protected. But it's more than that." She took a shaky breath, her fingers tracing the line of his jaw. "When I'm with you, I feel seen. Not as a victim, not as damaged goods, but as me. Just me." She pressed on, her voice gaining strength. "I feel alive when I'm with you. Like maybe there's a future worth thinking about, hoping for." Her eyes searched his face, a flicker of uncertainty crossing her features. "And I think… I think I'm falling in love with you."

The look on John's face…as though this was everything he both wanted and feared to hear. Then, slowly, he brought his hand up to cup her cheek, his thumb gently wiping away a stray tear. "Can't be love Nikita. God wouldn't let you love something like me," he said softly. *There it was again. 'Something' not 'someone' as though he thought so little of himself he didn't even consider himself human, let alone someone who could be loved.*

"I know who you are, John." she kissed him deeply again. "And I choose you."

She felt John's resolve crumbled as her lips met his once more. He pulled her closer, one hand tangling in her hair as he deepened the kiss. The world fell away, leaving only the two of them, broken but somehow whole in each other's arms.

***

John-

When they finally broke apart, John searched her face, seeking any sign of doubt or hesitation, or disgust. He found only warmth and acceptance in her gaze.

Nikita traced the contours of John's muscled form. Her fingers trembled slightly as she did.

"John," she whispered, her voice barely audible.

He held her hands in his, his battered ones in stark contrast to her soft skin. "Don't do this…I— I will not use you…" he started, then faltered. Words had never been his strong suit.

"You're not using me, I choose this, I choose you. That is a major difference."

With her permission, something broke free in John. He knew it would come, this wave of testosterone. *There's nothing like a fight to put you in the mood for a woman, and there's nothing like a woman to clear your head before the next fight.* His lips crashed into hers in a fervent kiss, filled with energy and the promise of escalation. His arms wrapped around her slim body, pressing the small, willing Russian against him.

Nikita responded with equal fervour, her hands gripping John's shoulders as she melted into his embrace. The heat between them intensified, months of pent-up desire finally finding release. John's calloused fingers tangled in her hair, tilting her head back as he deepened the kiss.

For a moment, the ghosts of his past receded. The weight of guilt and self-loathing lifted, replaced by a primal need that consumed him. He backed her against the wall, his muscular frame caging her in. Nikita gasped, her nails raking down his back coming to rest on the towel around his waist.

"John," she breathed, her accent thicker with arousal. She looked into his eyes, the intensity and fire in them created a heat in her. Her fingers lingered on the edge of his towel in a silent question.

John's breath caught in his throat as he gazed down at Nikita, her eyes burning with desire. For a fleeting moment, doubt crept in, reminding him of his unworthiness. But the feel of her body against his, the warmth of her skin, drove those thoughts away.

"Nikita," he growled, his voice rough with need. "Are you sure?"

She answered by staring directly into his eyes, and tugging at his towel, letting it fall to the floor.

John held his breath as the towel fell away. He watched as Nikita's eyes roamed over his body, taking in every tattoo, every scar, every imperfection. But he saw no judgement in her gaze, only acceptance and desire.

"You're beautiful," she whispered, her fingers tracing a long scar on his abdomen.

John shuddered at her touch, overwhelmed by the tenderness in her voice. "That's like Usain Bolt calling a four-year-old fast," he laughed softly. He captured her lips in another searing kiss, his hands slipping under her shirt to caress the soft skin of her back. Nikita arched into him, a soft moan escaping her. John could feel his blood rise, if they didn't stop soon…he would be all she could handle. He looked at her now; she didn't seem to want to stop.

With trembling fingers, Johns hands drifted down, his fingers under the hem of her shirt pausing to give her a chance to change her mind. "Leave the shirt on," she whispered. John realised that to Nikita, his scars were battle won, hers were a tapestry of shame. He hesitated for a second before Nikita took his hands, and slipped them under her waistband. *She was willing to remove those,* John thought.

She pressed closer now, her hands exploring his body with growing confidence, leaning up to kiss him again, silently willing him to continue. John slid her pants down, melting into her embrace. His fingers caught at the end of her underwear, giving her a last chance to decline the oncoming storm. She looked in his eyes, almost as if asking when he would get the damn message. She wanted the storm.

Nikita answered his unspoken question not with permission, but by sliding her underwear off herself, as clear a message as she could send. Only her socks and shirt remained. She leaned into his ear, almost knowing that John was the kind of man that would require a verbal confirmation. Barely audible she whispered two words, "take me," and with that John broke free.

Nikita gasped as John lifted her effortlessly, her legs wrapping around him as he carried her to the dining table as easily as one might carry a plate. He set her down; his eyes filled with desire. John pressed another kiss to her lips, against her neck, even over her grey long-sleeved shirt as he trailed kisses against her chest, abdomen…her inner thigh. A pent-up breath escaped Nikita as he tasted her…

Thirty minutes later, John slowly lowered Nikita to her feet, his arms still wrapped around her to steady her shaky legs. He brushed a strand of hair from her face, his touch impossibly gentle for hands that had seen so much violence. He watched as she gingerly made her way to the couch, collapsing there panting and exhausted. And as John looked down, with the clarity that so often comes with release, on her half-naked, crumpled, exhausted body, shame, like a tidal wave, crashed down on him anew.

She had been bought in for his use, and used her he had after promising he would never. John gently pulled away, his mind reeling with conflicting emotions. The euphoria of their encounter quickly gave way to a crushing sense of guilt and self-loathing. He had sworn to protect Nikita, to be different from those who had exploited her in the past. Yet here he was, having given in to his basest desires. He took in the room around them, its scattered destruction emphasising the frenzied nature of their activities. The couch was off centre, there was a broken dining chair, a coffee mug had been smashed on the kitchen floor having been knocked from the bench, the dining table sat in disarray. Each piece of disrupted furniture was an accusing reminder of his testosterone fuelled failure.

Nikita gave a contented sigh and John reassessed the situation. She didn't seem to look like someone that had been used. *Then again, would she?* Remorse flooded him anew. Tomorrow they could talk about this, but right now aftercare was the least he could do. John gently gathered Nikita into his arms, cradling her against his chest as he carried her to the bedroom. She nuzzled into his neck, her breath warm against his skin. As he laid her on the bed, Nikita's eyes fluttered open, a soft smile playing on her lips.

"I'll be right back," he said quietly. He ducked into the kitchen and boiled the kettle, steeping a tea Kelsey had sent from Australia made with ashwagandha and chamomile to help him sleep. He placed the tea on the small table beside Nikita's bed, his bed really. He remembered a few weeks ago when he invited her to stay. "No funny business," he had said. *Fucking idiot.*

"Stay with me," she murmured, reaching for him.

Hesitating for a moment, John nodded, hating himself and unable to deny her request. He slid into bed beside her, pulling the covers over them both. Nikita immediately curled into his side, her head resting on his chest. John's arm wrapped around her instinctively, his fingers tracing soothing patterns on her skin. The silence stretched between them, filled only by the sound of their breathing. John's mind raced, torn between the comfort of holding Nikita and the crushing weight of his perceived transgression. The intimacy of the moment could not be more different from the passionate frenzy of earlier.

Finally, John lifted his head, his eyes searching Nikita's face. Gently, she cupped his cheek, her thumb tracing the stubble along his jaw.

"I don't deserve this, or you," she said

John's eyes darkened at her words, a storm of emotion brewing behind them. He pushed himself up on his elbows, his gaze never leaving hers. "Don't say that."

Nikita's breath caught in her throat at the fierceness in his tone. She tried to look away, but John's hand came up to cradle her face, forcing her to meet his eyes.

"You deserve everything," he said, each word deliberate and heavy with meaning. "Everything good in this world, Nikita. I will free you, and I will take you with me when I go, if you want."

She turned her face away, as if unable to bear the weight of his conviction.

"John, I—"

He silenced her with a gentle kiss, pouring all his unspoken feelings into the gesture.

John closed his eyes, leaning into her touch. The weight of his past still lingered, but for the first time in nearly two years, it felt bearable. Nikita's presence was a balm to his wounded soul, a promise of redemption he'd long since abandoned hope of finding. And he hated himself even more for it.

19

Chapter Nineteen: An invitation

John-

Nikita lay curled against him, her blonde hair fanned out across his chest, her breathing deep and even. John allowed himself a moment to study her face, relaxed in sleep, free from the guarded expression she so often wore. His fingers itched to trace the constellations of freckles across her cheeks, but he held back, not wanting to wake her.

He slid from the bed and headed to the shower, the events of last night running through his mind.

The hot water cascaded over John's tense muscles, but it did little to ease the turmoil in his mind. Last night had been… unexpected. Nikita's vulnerability, her trust in him, it was both exhilarating and terrifying. He braced his hands against the shower wall, letting his head hang low as the water pounded against his neck.

He didn't deserve this. Didn't deserve her, he should not have taken advantage of her feelings for him. The ghosts of his past whispered in his ear, reminding him of his failures, of the look on Amy's face. He clenched his jaw, fighting back the wave of self-loathing that threatened to overwhelm him.

When he emerged from the bathroom, a towel slung low on his hips,

Nikita was awake. She sat up in bed, the sheet pulled to her chest, her eyes wary.

"John," she said softly, her voice barely above a whisper. Her eyes searched his face, looking for any sign of regret or rejection.

He stood frozen, water droplets still clinging to his skin. The air between them felt charged, heavy with unspoken words and lingering doubts. John's throat tightened; his usual terse demeanour amplified by the emotional weight of the moment.

"You, okay?" he managed to ask, his voice gruffer than he intended.

Nikita nodded slowly, but her fingers twisted in the sheet, betraying her nervousness. "Are you?" she countered, her gaze steady despite the vulnerability in her posture. John moved to the dresser, pulling out clothes with mechanical efficiency. He needed the distraction, needed to put some distance between himself and the raw intimacy of the previous night.

"Fine," he grunted, not meeting her eyes.

Nikita's voice was soft, hesitant. "John, about last night—"

He tensed, his back to her. "It was a mistake," he said sharply, pulling on a shirt with pointed, angry movements. "It won't happen again."

The silence that followed was heavy. When Nikita finally spoke, her voice was carefully controlled. "Is that what you really want?"

John turned. The vulnerability he saw there made his chest ache. He wanted to go to her, to take her in his arms and never let go. But he couldn't. He didn't have the right. He was angry at himself, not her. He was the one that had fucked up, that had made the mistake.

"What I want doesn't come into it," he said finally.

"Does what I want come into it?" the return of her measured cadence letting John know he had wounded her.

"What do you want Nikita?" he asked. If you think your freedom depends on you tying yourself to me, it doesn't. That's not freedom. I'll take you with me regardless. Tell me, what do you want?"

Nikita's eyes flashed with a mixture of hurt and determination. She rose from the bed, wrapping the sheet around her body like armour. "What I want," she said, her voice low and intense, "is for you to stop making decisions for both of us based on your guilt and self-loathing."

John flinched as if she'd slapped him, but Nikita pressed on. "You think you're protecting me by pushing me away?"

"You don't understand," John growled, his fists clenching at his sides. "I'm not good for you. I'll only bring you pain."

"You think I haven't known pain?" Nikita challenged. "You think I can't make my own choices about what's good for me?"

She took a step toward him, her gaze unwavering. "Last night wasn't because I feel obligated or because I think my freedom depends on you. I chose it. Because despite everything, despite all the pain and darkness we've both been through, I see you. And I know you see me. I started last night fighting the urge to look at that video again. That's why I was awake, that's why I was out walking last night."

John went to speak and found no words.

"That's how I started last night, and I ended it held in the arms of a man that had shown me such kindness and care, that had accepted every part of me and who I had thought understood I accept every part of him." Tears welled in her eyes now. "And now you wake up and allow your self-hatred and guilt to take that away from me? Why?" What gives you that right?" Angry tears began to fall.

John's jaw clenched, his emotions warring within him. The raw honesty in Nikita's words cut through his defences, leaving him exposed. He turned away, unable to meet her gaze, his hands gripping the edge of the dresser.

"I don't have the right," he said, his voice rough with suppressed emotion. "That's the point. I've taken so much from you already. Your freedom, your choices—"

"No," Nikita interrupted, her voice firm. "I'm freer now than I ever have been before, thanks to you."

She moved closer, close enough that he could feel the warmth radiating from her body. "John, look at me. Last night wasn't because it was expected of me, or to repay you. It was because I was able to choose. And I chose you. What do I want?" she repeated, her voice low and intense. "I want you to stop pushing me away, John. I want you to see yourself the way I see you. And I want to allow yourself to be chosen, and maybe, one day if I'm really lucky, you'll choose me back. But if you're not ready to choose me, then at least don't regret last night, don't take from me the first time I got to choose."

John turned back toward her, "I'm sorry." he said softly. "I'm so sorry. I never wanted to hurt you."

***

At two o'clock that afternoon, John was sitting in his office, the door closed on the phone to Kelsey.

"I fucked up and I don't know how to fix it," he said quickly.

"John, tell me exactly what happened. Spare no details," her concerned voice replied.

"I slept with her last night, with Nikita. And this morning I handled it poorly."

"Oh no, you slept with a gorgeous woman that's into you." Kelsey responded with mock apprehension. "Wait a second, I'll get some wine then I really am going to need every detail."

"Kelsey!" John hissed. "Not helpful, and how do you know she's gorgeous anyway?"

"So, she is gorgeous," Kelsey squealed. John had walked right into that one. He looked through the office window at Nikita sitting at her desk, typing away. He knew he hurt her this morning and regretted it immensely.

"Will you stop that and help me?" he hissed again.

"Not sure I understand the problem to be honest with you."

John sighed heavily, pinching the bridge of his nose. "The problem is I'm not… I can't… She deserves better than me, Kels."

"Oh, for Christ's sake, John," Kelsey groaned. "Not this shit again. When are you going to realise that you're not the monster you make yourself out to be? We've hunted monsters John, we know what they are. Men more beast than human. Argument could be made that you and I are bad people fair enough, but we are far from those savages. Every bad thing you've done, I've done too. But I doubt you'd stop me from finding comfort or love. You'd tell me I deserve it. In fact, if I recall correctly, one of the reasons you didn't come with me to Oz was so that I had a chance to meet someone. So spare me the 'oh no, a hot Russian woman wants to ride me like an unbroken colt, this is terrible,' bullshit, okay?"

John sighed heavily, pinching the bridge of his nose. His voice dropped to a whisper. "I don't know how to do this after Amy…"

He trailed off, the weight of past sins pressing down on him. Through the window, he watched Nikita tuck a strand of golden hair behind her ear, her brow furrowed in concentration.

The sight of her made his chest ache.

"This morning… the look on her face…" John's voice cracked. "I hurt her, Kels. Just like I hurt everyone else."

Kelsey's voice softened on the other end of the line. "John, listen to me. You're not hurting everyone. I know I don't quite understand the dynamic here, but from what you told me. Being around you is safer for her, no?" Kelsey paused before continuing, "Part of the reason she's your assistant?"

John's jaw clenched. "That's different. It's my job."

"Bullshit," Kelsey snapped. "You're just a zookeeper now. You went above and beyond for her, just like you always do. And now she sees you for who you really are – a good man, a hard man willing to do what it takes."

John's eyes never left Nikita as she worked, her fingers flying across the keyboard. He remembered the feel of those fingers on his skin last night, gentle and urgent.

"I can't give her what she needs," he muttered.

"And what's that?" Kelsey challenged.

"A future. Hope. Someone whole."

Kelsey's voice hardened. "Johnathon, you listen to me right now. You are whole. Scarred, yes. Damaged, most definitely. But whole. And you have more hope to offer than you realise."

There was a long pause before Kelsey's exasperated sigh crackled through the phone. "John, you thick-headed moron. Did you ever stop to think that maybe she doesn't want some perfect, shining knight? That maybe she wants your therapy needing arse, scars and all?"

John's grip tightened on the phone. "Who gives a fuck what she thinks she wants?"

"Excuse the fuck out of me!?" Kelsey shouted down the phone "You want to try rewording that?"

John took a long slow breath, "She doesn't know what she's asking for."

"I think she's the only one who can make that assertion."

"You don't understand—"

"No, you don't understand," Kelsey cut him off. "I don't know shit about her, but I know enough to know that woman has been through hell, just like you. She's not looking for some fairy tale prince. She wants someone who gets it, who's walked through the fire too."

John's gaze drifted back to Nikita. She looked up, catching his eye through the window. For a moment, her carefully composed expression faltered, revealing a flash of hurt before she quickly looked away.

"How do I fix this?" he asked into the phone.

Kelsey's tone softened, a rarity for the typically sharp-tongued woman. "I don't know, but you've been carrying this guilt for far too long. What happened with Amy… it wasn't your fault. You can't keep punishing yourself forever. I don't know how we fix this but we're going to figure it out. Amy isn't coming back, and she wouldn't have wanted you to spend the last year and a half trying to kill yourself."

"Maybe she would."

"That's not true John." There was no venom in Kelsey's voice. "For God's sake man, get out of your own way, 'coz this, 'I don't deserve this,' bullshit has gone far enough. Fix this." She paused again, "But first, details. I haven't got any in months and I know you haven't."

"You're the worst," John chuckled despite himself. "Once again, thank you for nothing."

"Fix this, John." she said again as he hung up. He looked out across the bullpen again. Nikita no longer sat there, but a plan starting to form. He wasn't sure how, but he was going to set things right.

There was a knock on his door. He opened it and his heart sank at the sight of her. The professional mask she had so often wore when they first met now firmly back in place. "Director Aleski would like to see you in his office, Mr. Wilson."

Kelsey was right, he was going to have to fix this. "Thank you, Nikita, it's still just John though."

She nodded silently, and left. John pinched the bridge of his nose and sighed as he walked down the hall. He should have never let her in last night, yet a part of him didn't regret it. It was the closest he had felt to being whole in a long time. He stepped through the open door of Aleski's office. The curator was reading a paper, his brow furrowed.

"Everything alright?" John enquired. Aleski continued studying the newspaper, seeming not to notice. "Hmm?" he looked up, "Oh nothing. Actually wait, what do you know about bears?"

An odd question.

"Not a lot," John admitted. "There's none in Africa. Can't say I've worked with them outside of a zoo. Why?"

"A friend of mine," he waved the paper "was found this morning dead in the forest. About three hours from here. They're saying it was a bear attack. He was damn near completely torn apart and most of his bones were broken."

"I'm sorry to hear that. Was he an outdoorsy fella?"

"Not really, no one seems to know why he was out there."

The two men sat in silence for a moment, Aleski still distracted. He looked back at John who in turn arched his eyebrows in a question.

"Of course, I didn't ask you in here to talk about bears. There is a dinner being held at the Hermitage Museum in a few weeks. You have been invited."

John looked, puzzled at the envelope placed in front of him. "I'm so confused. Who invited me? And why?"

Alseki waved a dismissive hand. "It's all in there."

John walked out of the room, opening the envelope as he did so. Inside were what seemed like two red tickets, and a small letter, all of which were in Russian. *Of course they were,* "For fuck's sake." He muttered under his breath.

***

That afternoon the car ride home was thick with silence, the morning's charged conversation still weighing on both John and Nikita. He had been in the wrong, he knew that. He just wasn't sure how to broach the subject.

"Should I stay at my own place from now on?" her soft whisper shattered the silence.

John's grip tightened on the steering wheel, his knuckles turning white. The thought of Nikita leaving, even temporarily, sent a jolt of panic through his chest. He swallowed hard, trying to find the right words.

"No," he said gruffly, his eyes fixed on the road ahead. "That's not… necessary."

Nikita turned to look at him, her green eyes searching his face for any sign of emotion. "What did I do wrong?" she asked.

"Nothing Nikita. You did nothing wrong. This morning was my fault." he looked her in the eyes now. "I am genuinely sorry. I know I hurt you, it was uncalled for."

John swallowed hard before continuing. "I swore that I would not lay a hand on you, that I wouldn't use you…" His voice off for a few seconds. "I don't regret last night." he said quietly. "And in a way I'm angry at myself for that fact. That's not your fault at all."

He took a deep breath, forcing himself to continue. "I got scared," he admitted, the words feeling foreign on his tongue. "Waking up next to you, feeling… happy. I panicked. That's not your fault. This morning's conversation wasn't because you did anything wrong."

John heard Nikita's breath catch, as though she were feeling the weight of John's confession. He watched as tears welled in her eyes before she blinked them back, determined not to show weakness in this tough conversation. He knew she understood all too well the fear of happiness, the instinct to push away what felt good before it could be taken away and hurting all the more.

"I can understand that," she said softly, her fingers absently tracing patterns on the car door.

John's shoulders sagged slightly, the tension in his body easing just a fraction as he nodded.

"I have thought and hoped about my freedom before," she said in a voice barely above a whisper.

The car slowed as they approached a red light, and John turned to face her fully for the first time since they had left work.

"This, with you. I know it cannot last, I know it is not real. But I also know," she paused to gather her thoughts. The light turned green, but John didn't move, his gaze still locked on Nikita. A horn blared behind them, startling them both. John cursed under his breath and put the car back in motion.

"Continue, please?" he spoke.

"It is as close as I will ever come. To freedom, to love, any of it."

He wanted to rage against the statement, but knew he must be silent. *You caused this you fucking moron, the least you can do is hear her out.*

"Last night was the first time where I got to choose. That is more freedom and hope than I have ever had. And much better than what I though was going to happen when I met you."

Nikita's words tumbled out of her.

"I know what I did wrong, and I do not mean to replace Amy. This, us. You are a killer, and I am owned. I will never be free, really free. But this is as close as I can get, this and dreaming. People like us don't get happy endings; you said that yourself. But I don't regret last night, and I am glad you don't either. I chose you, and that matters to me."

John sat still in the car as he parked. The weight of her words sat upon him like heavy bricks.

"I should count myself lucky that you chose me," he said quietly. "I don't know if I'm capable of love, Nikita. But I know you deserve it. Whatever hope you feel when we are together, feel it. No one will ever harm you again or force you to do anything you don't want to do. I promise."

John's eyes flickered to Nikita, an uncertainty in them that betrayed the depth of emotion roiling beneath his stoic exterior. They exited the car, walking to the apartment in silence, both acutely aware of the shift that had occurred.

John found himself stealing glances at Nikita's profile, noticing the lines of tension around her eyes, the set of her jaw. He realised how much effort it had taken for her to open, to admit her fears.

"Nikita," he said softly, his hand hovering uncertainly before settling on her shoulder. "Thank you. For being honest with me." She smiled that sad sweet smile at him again, the one that killed him. Like deep down she believed that one day she would be back in front of the camera again and she was simply trying to enjoy the time she had left with him.

He unlocked the door, holding it open for Nikita to walk in first. "I'll make us some coffee," he said gruffly, breaking the silence.

Inside, Nikita perched on the edge of the worn sofa, watching John move about the kitchen. The familiar scent of brewing coffee filled the air, providing a comforting backdrop to the tension between them.

John returned, two mismatched steaming mugs in hand. He handed one to Nikita, their fingers brushing briefly. The contact sent a jolt through them both, a reminder of the connection they shared despite the turmoil of the day.

John settled into the armchair across from her, his mug cradled in his calloused hands. He stared into the dark liquid, as though he might find the right words in its depths. "Aleski gave me this today, I'm told it's an invitation to a dinner of some kind. But obviously it's in Russian."

Nikita glanced over the invitations and letter. "It is an invitation to a state function dinner. The president himself has invited you. Seems he holds a special fascination with African animals and is interested in the update at the zoo." She looked up, wide eyed as she understood. "The president of Russia wants to meet you."

"Meet us, you mean. There are two tickets in there and I'm certainly not going alone."

Nikita was shocked now, "No" she said "I can't go to something like that. It's..it's..I just can't!"

"Well then I'm not either," John said flatly and moved to placed his mug on the small table beside him.

"But you have to," Nikita cried out.

"I wish you'd make up your mind. I can't go if you won't."

Nikita opened her mouth as if to say something, then closed it. She repeated the action twice more before eventually replying, "I don't have a dress."

"We'll both have to go clothes shopping," John admitted. "I doubt my keeper's uniform would be sufficient."

20

Chapter Twenty: Nikita and Kelsey

Nikita-

The next three weeks seemed to pass in awkward normalcy. John unsure what to do and Nikita was unwilling to push him. *He was hers,* she sometimes thought to herself, *he just didn't know it yet,* and she wasn't sure she wanted him to pay the price it would take. They made dinner, they drank and talked and laughed — well Nikita laughed. *John,* she thought *may as well be allergic to it.* The comfort and ease they enjoyed with each other was strained now, but still there.

The State dinner was to be on Saturday the 11th of December.

On Wednesday the 8th of December, John and Nikita entered his apartment at the end of another workday.

"You shower first; I'll get dinner started," Nikita said not entirely selflessly. They might not be where they were a few weeks ago, *but a girl shouldn't deny herself life's simple pleasures, right?* John would always exit the bathroom with a that towel slung low across his hips, leaving his upper body exposed for her to take in. The outline of abs, leading up to the massive chest, the raised scar on his right breast, as if left by a brand, words tattooed in Swahili — *at least I think it's Swahili,* under the scar. His boulder shoulders, descending into meaty, muscular arms, the veins along his forearms. Forearms that couldn't be more different from one another. The left, heavily scared by leopard, with part of a tattoo still there. *Maybe a battle axe of some kind?* The right forearm was hard muscled and perfect. Both arms ended in those comforting, strong, gentle hands. Hands that touched her far too little these days.

John grabbed her by the arm, ripping her from the daydream. His right pointer finger was on his lips, a silent warning to be quiet. His eyes locked on the small dining table. A bottle of Singlton scotch was braced by two cigars, the green bands marking them out as H. Upmann the banker cigars.

"Show yourself," John commanded, pulling Nikita behind him. "Now you slimy fuck."

A man emerged from behind the kitchenette. At least six feet tall, his frame was thin and wiry. Long limbs stretched out from his body, his fingers appearing almost bony. His face was angular, with sharp cheekbones and a pointed chin hidden by the beginnings of a scraggly beard. His jaw length black hair was messy and unkempt, adding to his dishevelled appearance.

His hands spread out in a placating gesture.

"Jean-Paul De Smet," John issued.

"What gave me away?" Jean-Paul smiled, a distinct French lilt coming through.

"How can you be so fucking conceited?" John nodded at the table. "My favourite scotch and your favourite cigars. Means you want something."

"Maybe I just want to talk to an old friend." He smiled.

John lunged at De Smet, pinning him to the wall. "You don't have friends, and you always want something. Open a window Nikita, our guest is about to leave."

Nikita didn't dare move or speak. Jean-Paul's eyes moved across to her and Nikita felt her skin prickle under his gaze.

"Cold blood isn't your style, John." De Smet still had his hands spread out.

"For you I'll make an exception," John growled.

"I told you this was a dumb idea," a second voice, female, punctuated the stand-off.

"He hasn't tossed me yet," Jean-Paul offered.

"Give him time," the woman's voice replied before coming in view.

Even having never met her before. Nikita knew instantly that this woman before her was the mythical Kelsey. Her brown hair was tied back in a tight ponytail, an almost smug smile sat on her face, and her eyes darted between John and Jean-Paul. She moved with a fluid grace and ease that betrayed her readiness for action.

"Nice to see that old habits die hard John," Kelsey said, a hint of amusement in her voice. "Though I can't say I blame you with this one around." She jerked her thumb towards Jean-Paul.

John looked at Kelsey, then back to Jean-Paul. "What. Do you. Want?" he slowly questioned through gritted teeth, his eyes never leaving Jean-Paul.

The Frenchman sighed dramatically and coughed. "Always so direct. Can we not catch up first? Maybe Ariela can take your friend out to dinner while you and I share a drink?" He gestured towards the bottle on the table. Kelsey and John exchanged a glance before both starred daggers into the Frenchmen. John pulled De Smet from the wall and slammed him back into it, denting the plasterboard.

"TALK!" he yelled, his patience wearing thin. "And if I find you dragged Kelsey into something…"

Jean-Paul coughed as his demeanour shifted, the playful smile no longer there as the air stilled.

"Boys!" Kelsey gave an exasperated sigh. "I take it you're Nikita. John said you were beautiful. He very much undersold it."

Nikita's cheeks flushed at the unexpected compliment, but she remained cautious, her eyes darting between the newcomers and John. "Thank you," she said. "You must be Kelsey. I have heard so much about you."

"All bad, I hope" Kelsey laughed back. "Why don't you get changed and then maybe you can escort me to a restaurant? I'm starving and these two idiots need to have a long talk."

The two men stared at each other, as though talking was the last thing on their mind.

John unhanded the Frenchman yet looked ready to resume hostilities at moment's notice. "Kelsey," he said, his voice low and with a warning tone.

"Oh, fucking relax," Kelsey replied, rolling her eyes. "We're all friends here. Or at least, we're not enemies… Yet. And you, I haven't seen you in well over a year, and not so much as a hug?" John's stance softened. "Caught me unawares is all, breaking into my home with no head's up."

He stared at her for a brief second before they both broke out in broad smiles and embraced. "I wish it had been under better circumstances, but it is good to see you brother."

"You too."

Nikita came back from the bedroom now changed. She couldn't help but feel a twinge of sadness, or was it jealousy? John had never looked at her like that.

"What kind of food are you in the mood for?" she asked Kelsey.

"Surprise me. I'm sure you have good recommendations. "You two play nice." She issued to the men.

***

Twenty minutes later had Kelsey and Nikita sat waiting for their food, wine in hand.

"Who's Ariela?" Nikita asked. There had only been the four of them in the room. John, Nikita, Kelsey and Jean-Paul, no Ariela.

"Someone the three of us used to know. Happens to everyone, occasionally calling a friend by a different friends name." Kelsey then changed the subject, "What do you think of our John? Can't imagine he's been wonderful company these past few months."

Nikita squirmed in her seat. She had a million questions to ask Kelsey, but in truth she was a bit intimidated by the other woman and her reputation. And they had only just met.

Nikita took a small sip of her wine, buying herself a moment to collect her thoughts. Her eyes darted around the dimly lit restaurant, avoiding Kelsey's piercing gaze.

"John is… complex," Nikita said carefully, her fingers tracing the stem of her wine glass.

Kelsey let out a short, humourless laugh. "That's putting it mildly. He's got more baggage than an international airport."

"I'm not-" Nikita started as her fingers tightened around her wine glass. She felt a sudden urge to defend John, but held back, unsure of where she stood with Kelsey.

Kelsey leaned forward, her brown eyes intense. "Look, I've known John for years. He's a good man, but he is his own worst enemy. He's been through hell, repeatedly, and sometimes I think he believes he deserves to stay there."

Nikita nodded slowly, her mind flashing back to moments when she'd caught glimpses of the turmoil behind John's stoic facade.

"I've seen that," she admitted softly. "There are times when he looks… lost maybe? Like he's carrying the weight of the world on his shoulders. Like all its evil is for him alone to solve."

Kelsey's expression softened slightly. "That's John, alright. Always trying to atone for sins that weren't even his to begin with."

Nikita felt a chill run down her spine, but she forced herself to meet Kelsey's gaze. "I'm not afraid of it though," she said, surprising herself with the firmness in her voice.

Kelsey raised an eyebrow, "Maybe you're tougher than you look," she mused. "But John is not an easy man to love."

The word 'love' hung in the air between them, heavy and loaded. Nikita felt her cheeks flush, and she took another sip of wine to hide her reaction.

"I'm not…" she began, but Kelsey cut her off with a wave of her hand. "I don't mean to say you're in love with him. You haven't even met the man."

A waitress appeared with their food. Stroganoff for Kelsey-on Nikita's recommendation; lamb shashlik for herself. As they began to eat, Nikita found herself warming to Kelsey's blunt honesty.

"Can I ask you something?" Nikita ventured, her curiosity finally overcoming her hesitation.

Kelsey arched her eyebrows. "As long as I get to ask you something. A question for a question. Sound fair?"

"John and I once played a similar game it was ah…. unnerving."

Kelsey stared directly at her. "He'd never harm you."

"I know that now, I did not know it that night."

The air stilled between them as Nikita felt Kelsey study her. "What was your question?"

Nikita paused for a second, she had so many. But could she trust Kelsey? She was the person closest to John. *Surely this entire conversation would be relayed to him.* Kelsey's eyes pierced hers, as though reading her mind. "I like you," she said with a laugh. "You're as untrusting as I am." She fished inside her shirt collar for her necklace, drawing her fingers down to the centre and exposing a ring. "I was engaged in Australia, briefly. He drank. I told myself that was fine. I drink. Then he punched holes in the wall. Told myself that was fine, he'd never lay a hand on me. Till one night he did… I got a plate in my left cheekbone, two surgeries on my right hand and a few broken ribs. Now, you know John just a little. If he knew, would he have stayed in

Russia?"

"No," Nikita had to admit. "More likely he would have travelled all the way to Australia to bury him in a drum or something."

"Ha," Kelsey laughed. "You do know him. Point being, I can keep a secret, even from John. And you have been good for him. I don't know if you knew that; and I'm grateful. Ask whatever your questions are, and we'll go one for one."

Nikita took another sip of wine as she thought what to ask, "You said before that I haven't met John, what did you mean?"

"That?" Kelsey said, jerking her thumb in the direction of Johns apartment. "Not him. He died in Sudan, no one can tell me otherwise. I heard it happen."

"John told me. Said you saved his life then, repeatedly. He said you were death itself that day."

"It wasn't enough. And I was only repaying the times he saved my life."

"Such as?"

But Kelsey was already shaking her head. "It's one for one. My turn. "How did you come to be his assistant?"

Nikita drew in a long breath; unsure how fair she could trust Kelsey.

"I'll know if you lie," Kelsey added, as if she could read Nikita's inner turmoil. "With the exception of Amy, John seems to have penchant for cripples, bastards, and broken things. Which are you?"

Nikita stiffened at the implied insult, "Broken. And you?"

"Oh, definitely broken," Kelsey raised her glass in slight salute, "You'll find no judgement here, girly," she said. "Again, how did you come to be his assistant?"

"I have…experience assisting certain types of men. When they were trying to get John to accept the position here, they knew he'd need an assistant and who better than someone that could fill his every need and tolerate his every inclination." If Kelsey was half the person Nikita thought, she'd read between the lines.

Kelsey took a long breath and slowly nodded. "And how do you feel about that?" She inquired.

Nikita's eyes flickered with a mix of pain and defiance. She took a deep breath, her fingers tracing invisible patterns on the table between them, her eyes down.

"At first, I felt… used. Like always," she said, her voice barely above a whisper. "John… well frankly I was terrified of him. Doesn't take much to realise he's a dangerous man. And if they were bringing him me…" She trailed off as Kelsey watched her.

"John is a dangerous man, yes. He is a killer, and I think he's tortured people," Nikita continued "But he was different. He never touched me wrongly, never even looked at me that way. It was like he saw through all the layers they had put on me. That they had made me. Saw straight to who I really was. Or at least who I think I want to be."

Kelsey leaned forward, her sharp gaze softening slightly. "He's a bit of a morally grey fella, our John. Kind in his way but not afraid to get his hands dirty." She admitted. "And how do you feel about him now? Seeing as though it's just us girls talking."

Nikita met her eyes, a small, sad smile playing on her lips. "Now I don't know what I feel. It is all tangled up inside me." Kelsey arched her eyebrows in question.

"Oh no, you are several questions ahead of me." Nikita waved down a waitress and spoke in Russian. The server disappeared briefly before returning with more wine, refilling Nikita's glass. Nikita pointed to Kelsey's glass also empty, an unspoken question on her lips. "I'm hesitant to ask, lest you count it toward my questions," she finally said.

Kelsey let out a laugh, "Oh I do like you, fucking paranoid like the rest of us. Have her leave the bottle. I think tonight will be fun. Your questions, you have three?" Nikita waited until the waitress had left.

"You and John, you are awfully close. You never had anything happen between you, romantically?"

Kelsey leaned back in her chair and kissed her teeth. "You know, you really would think that huh? Expect it to be honest. But no, never. We are closer to each other than our own blood family. But it is and always has been purely platonic. We are as fierce as brother and sister, and as unlikely to sleep together."

Nikita was glad to hear it but honestly wasn't sure why. John, she knew, would never be hers, not really. Three weeks ago would be the closest she would ever come. He hadn't touched her since. Still, it bought her some level of comfort to know he and this larger-than-life woman had never been an item.

Kelsey swilled the wine in her glass. "Next?"

"That Jean-Paul guy. John hates him. Why?"

"Oh, wonderful question. We're getting to the good shit now." She leaned forward and took a breadstick from the table, using it to mop up some of the left-over sauce from her meal. "This was delicious, by the way. Alright so, Jean-Paul. Where does one fucking start? He is the head of a group which protects national parks in the Congo. The Democratic Republic of Congo, not the Republic of Congo. They're different places. John was working for him went we met."

Nikita's eyes widened at the mention of the Congo.

"John told you stories, I see."

"Pictures too," Nikita added. "It looked like a war zone."

"Yeah, it was pretty fucked. But that's not why John hates De Smet," Kelsey continued. "You see, some men are singularly focused on their goals. Billionaires want more billions, property developers want more properties, you get my drift. Jean-Paul is one of those singularly focused men. His only goal is to ensure the safety of the mountain gorillas in his park. No small feat mind you." She lifted her glass slightly as she spoke. "And he is willing to use anyone, do anything, to further that goal. You can trust Jean-Paul entirely, as long as you trust him to use you. And John, you may have noticed, hates users."

Nikita nodded slowly, absorbing the information. She could see why John would despise someone like that. His own moral code was grey and complex, but unyielding all the same; and the idea of using people as pawns would be abhorrent to him.

"What happened?" she pressed, leaning in closer.

Kelsey's eyes darkened and she took a long sip of wine before continuing. "De Smet used John's skills to further his cause. But when things went south…" She trailed off, her gaze distant. "Let's just say Jean-Paul's priorities weren't exactly aligned with saving lives. Human lives, that is."

Nikita felt a chill run down her spine. "You mean he—"

"He left them to die," Kelsey finished bluntly. "John, myself, the other volunteers. All expendable in the grand scheme of protecting his precious gorillas."

Nikita's hand moved to cover her mouth. "That's… that's monstrous."

Kelsey nodded grimly. "Yeah, well, welcome to the fucking jungle, right? John never forgave him for it. Not just for himself, but…" She trailed off, seeming to catch herself. "Well, a lot of the villagers lost their lives too."

"Makes more sense now, the stories. Why you and John held the town so long."

Kelsey nodded grimly. "Yeah, it was a fucking nightmare. But you know what? John still managed to save most of us. Dragged us out of that hellhole, patched us up, got us to safety. All while Jean-Paul was probably sipping champagne in some fancy hotel, congratulating himself on a job well done."

Nikita's mind was reeling. She thought of John, his stoic demeanor. How he reacted so aggressively this evening. It all made more sense now.

"And your third question?" Kelsey prompted, refilling both their glasses.

Nikita hesitated, weighing her words carefully. "John… he seems so… broken. Is there any way to help him? To reach him?"

Kelsey's expression softened, a mix of fondness and sadness crossing her features. "Oh, honey. That's the million-dollar question, isn't it?" She sighed, running a hand through her hair. "When you do what we do, you do bad things. And to reconcile that with yourself you must be able to say, 'I do bad things, but I'm not a bad person because xyz.' John lost his xyz. I think he's always viewed himself as some kind of protector, getting his hands dirty to for people or animals that can't stand up for themselves."

"Makes sense."

"He lost that in Sudan, crossed a line he didn't think himself capable of. Forfeited a piece of his soul and still lost the woman he loved. He's been through hell, seen things most people couldn't imagine."

So have you, Nikita thought to herself. For nearly all the things John had dealt with in Africa, Kelsey had been by his side, dealing with them too. She wondered how the woman in front of her seemed so unaffected, when John was clearly battered by his experiences.

"But that's not why he's broken. I think if he crossed that line but hadn't lost Amy; he'd still forfeit that piece of him, but he'd deal with it. And I think if Amy left, but John hadn't done what he'd done, he'd grieve, of course. But he wouldn't be broken and damned like this." Kelsey continued. "But now, I don't know if he can ever be remade or put back together." Then, unexpectedly, she smiled. "You know, I think you might have a chance. John's walls are high, but I saw how protective he was over you. And I know you have feelings for him."

Nikita took a long sip of her wine. Kelsey, it seemed, saw through her as easily as John did. "It does not matter. It…cannot be like that, even if I wanted it to be."

Kelsey pretended not to catch the full weight of those words. "Listen and listen good. John's not an easy man to love. Platonically or romantically. He's got demons, and they don't play nice."

Nikita nodded solemnly, her fingers tracing the rim of her wine glass. "I understand. I've got my own demons, you know. Maybe that's why I feel drawn to him."

Kelsey's expression softened. "Yeah, I figured as much. Takes one to know one, right?" She reached across the table, placing her hand over Nikita's. "Look, I'm not gonna sugarcoat it. Loving John Wilson is like trying to tame a wounded lion. He'll push you away, he'll snarl and snap, but deep down he's just scared."

Nikita laughed, *John? Scared? John doesn't even understand what fear is.* Her laughter died taking in Kelsey's expression, noting it seriousness. "Of what?' Nikita continued.

Kelsey studied her for a moment, as if wondering if what she was about to say was a betrayal of sorts. "Of the same thing you are." Nikita's head picked up as Kelsey continued. "Of being seen, of being ripped open and laid bare before someone. And once having been seen, of being found unsightly. So, we armour ourselves in the wrong we've done. We lead with the things we hate most about ourselves. Do our best to drive people off before they can leave. Because if they leave, it cements the belief we already have, that we are not worth staying for. That's how Amy got him so bad."

Nikita felt tears well in her eyes. That, she understood. She remembered the fear and horror and shame that slammed through her body as she lay crying the night John came back for her. The fear that he had seen, really seen her. And that it would disgust him.

"Yeah, you know what I'm talking about. That's why I said you have a chance." Kelsey finished.

"I already told you. It does not matter." Nikita looked up and saw Kelsey's eyes on her, soft and compassionate, her silence beckoning

Nikita to explain. "John once said, happy endings are not possible for people like him, well they aren't possible for me either. I like John, I do. But three weeks ago is as close to perfect as I can ever hope. And I don't know that John will ever get over Amy's death. He feels he failed her."

Kelsey pulled her head back, confusion covering her features. "What the fuck are you talking about? Amy isn't dead."

21

Chapter Twenty-One: Amy

Nikita-

Nikita froze, her wineglass halfway to her lips. "What do you mean, she's not dead? John told me—"

"Amy is very much alive," Kelsey said, her eyes narrowing. "What exactly did John tell you?"

Nikita's mind raced, trying to reconcile this new information with everything she thought she knew. "He said… he said he lost her. The camp was under attack. Amy and the two boys were cornered by child soldiers. John… well he fought them."

"Killed them," Kelsey interrupted. "Don't sugar coat things on my account. I was there."

"Killed them," Nikita corrected herself. "He said he turned, and he could tell from the look on Amy's face that she was gone."

Kelsey let out a long, slow breath. "Fuck me sideways. That's what he's been telling people?" She ran a hand through her hair, eyes closed momentarily as if processing this revelation.

"That's not what happened?" Nikita asked.

Kelsey's laugh was bitter.

John laughs like that, Nikita thought.

"Jesus Christ. Yes and no," Kelsey said before draining her wine glass and immediately refilling it, her movements sharp and agitated. "Amy didn't die, Nikita. She left, divorced him. Packed her bags after the attack and flew back to England."

The words hit Nikita like a physical blow. She set her wineglass down with trembling fingers. "She... what?"

"She fucking left him. But not before she made sure John knew exactly what she thought of him." Kelsey's voice turned cold, her protective instincts for John evident in every word. "She was horrified by what he'd done, even though he'd done it to save her life and the lives of those boys she was protecting.

She told him he was a monster, only good for killing, beyond redemption. That she could never look at him the same way. Never mind that those 'boys' would have raped and murdered her if he hadn't been there. Never mind he broke himself to get her safe, then put all that to the side, walked out that cottage and turned the tide to save the rest of us. Bet he didn't tell you that part?"

Nikita stared at Kelsey, her mind reeling. "But John said—"

"John said she was gone because she is. He says he lost her because he did."

Nikita traced the rim of her glass, the pieces clicking into place with devastating clarity. The way John had pulled away after their night together, the self-deprecating comments, the walls he'd built around himself, the self-loathing and guilt. It all made more sense now.

Now it was her turn to be angry. "Do you know how messed up he is about that? How much he hates himself? All I hear is that he's worthless, a monster, that he doesn't matter, all this nonsense. And then he has the AUDACITY to say 'I'm good with what I am.' I mean what even is that? He doesn't even say 'who' he says 'what' He's put in this impossible, horrendous position, breaks a piece of himself to save her and she leaves!?"

Kelsey nodded, a grim satisfaction in her eyes at Nikita's reaction. "I think some women, with all good intentions mind you, have this romanticised idea of wanting a man that would do anything for them. Who would find a way, no matter what, to get to her."

I want a man like that. No, I want him. You didn't have to break him; I'd have taken him. Now I'll never have the chance.

Kelsey went on, "But you can't have the protector without the predator; and I don't think Amy understood that, not really. In her defence, it must have been a hard thing to see and would have been pretty traumatic. I can't blame her too much for reacting badly. But she should have stayed, and she shouldn't have said what she did. But she said it, and John believed her."

"That's insane," Nikita whispered, her accent thickening with emotion. "He saved her life."

"Yeah, well. John has this warped sense of morality. Always has. He thinks because he was capable of that level of violence, that Amy was right—that he is just a killer at heart. He always said she was all the best in him, when she left it was like she took his sense of self with her."

Nikita felt anger rise in her chest, hot and fierce. "She destroyed him," she said quietly, her voice trembling with suppressed rage. "She took a man who sacrificed a piece of his soul for her and she told him he was worthless."

Kelsey's fingers tightened around her glass. "After that he just fell apart. Not in the crying, emotional breakdown way—John's not built like that. He just… hardened. Took more risks. Stopped caring if he made it back from jobs." She shook her head. "I thought I was going to lose him."

Nikita's hands trembled as she reached for her wine. "So, what do I do?"

"Honestly? I don't know. But like I said if anyone has a chance of putting him back together it's you. You… you've seen darkness, haven't you? You understand what it takes to survive."

Nikita met Kelsey's gaze, something raw and vulnerable flickering in her eyes. "Yeah," she said quietly. "I understand what it's like to do things… to become things. To have pieces of yourself carved away until you're not sure what's left."

Kelsey leaned forward, her voice gentling. "Then you understand why he's so fucking scared. Amy was his anchor to who he thought he was—the protector, the good man doing necessary work. When she left, she took his entire sense of self with her."

"But he is good," Nikita said fiercely. "Damaged, yes. Dangerous, absolutely. But good. He could have taken advantage of my situation a hundred times over and never did. He sees me as a person, not a… not what they made me into."

Nikita clenched her fists. "Three weeks ago is as close as I'll ever get." She said it under her breath, yet Kelsey heard it all the same.

"What happened three weeks ago?" Kelsey asked quietly, her voice losing its earlier sharpness.

Nikita's face flushed, and she looked down at her hands. "We… John and I…" She trailed off, unable to find the words.

"Ah," Kelsey said, understanding dawning in her eyes. "And then he pulled away?"

"Like to touch me was to hold hot coals," Nikita whispered. "The next morning it was like it never happened. Worse than that—he became so careful around me. He's been treating me like fragile glass ever since, walking on eggshells, keeping his distance. Like he was afraid to even look at me."

Kelsey cursed under her breath. "Fucking idiot. He probably convinced himself he'd taken advantage of you, hadn't he?"

Nikita nodded miserably. "He said it was a mistake. That it shouldn't have happened, and the worst part is, I can see it eating at him. The guilt, the self-hatred. He thinks he's protecting me from himself, but he's just…"

Nikita felt Kelsey's eyes on her for long seconds. "You love him," Kelsey said quietly. It wasn't a question.

Nikita's breath caught. "It doesn't matter—"

"Bullshit." Kelsey's voice was sharp. "It's the only thing that matters; the rest is semantics. Do you love him or not?"

Nikita's composure finally broke. Tears spilled over her cheeks as she pressed her palms against the table, her whole body trembling. "Yes," she whispered, the word torn from somewhere deep inside her. "God help me, yes. I love him so much it terrifies me."

Kelsey reached across the table and gripped Nikita's wrist. "Then fight for him."

"You don't understand," Nikita said, her voice breaking. "I can't…I'm not… People like me don't get happy endings either, Kelsey. We don't get to keep good things. I was made to be used and discarded. That's all I know how to be."

Kelsey laughed. She rested her elbows on the table, hands rubbing her temples like she was trying to get rid of a tension headache. "Jesus Christ. I get it now."

"Get what?" Nikita asked, wiping at her eyes with the back of her hand.

"You're both doing the same fucking thing," Kelsey said, exasperation written in every line of her face. "You're both so convinced you're broken that you can't see what's right in front of you."

Nikita stared at her, confusion replacing some of the pain in her expression.

"John thinks he's a monster who destroys everything he touches. You think you're damaged goods who doesn't deserve love. Meanwhile, you're sitting here telling me how good he is while he's probably back at that flat right now thinking about how he doesn't deserve you.

You're both furious at what hurt the other, while talking about how you don't care yourselves" Kelsey shook her head. "It's like watching two people drowning while refusing to grab the life raft because they think they don't deserve to be saved." Kelsey laughed again, "There's fucking two of you. This is exhausting."

Nikita sat back in her chair, processing. "I don't know how to do this," she finally said.

"That's fine, John doesn't either. You're on equal footing." Kelsey checked her watch. "We have about another hour until we should head back. "Now, about what happened three weeks ago…"

"Oh, I can't tell you that." Nikita was suddenly flustered in her reply. Kelsey studied her for a second before breaking out squealed laughter, kicking her feet. She picked up the empty bottle and waved it grinning at the waitress, clear communication in any language. "Oh, yes, you can," said Kelsey. "And spare no details, I'm in a spell drier than the dessert."

"Do you think John will do want Jean-Paul wants?"

"Yeah, he'll act like he won't. But he'll cave, he'll do it. I just hope he negotiates good payment. Because whatever this is that's got De Smet coming all the way to Russia to ask for John's help? It's got to be biblical, I mean just gloriously fucked."

The new bottle arrived, and Kelsey popped the cork, refilling both glasses. "Alright girly, details. Let's go."

22

Chapter Twenty-Two: Life breaks everyone

John-

It was almost midnight by the time Nikita and Kelsey walked back into the apartment, both obviously tipsy at least. John sat alone at his table, the scotch half empty, the last of a cigar on his lips.

"See you two had fun, how worried should I be?" he said half smiling.

Nikita moved off to shower; she hadn't had the chance when Kelsey and Jean-Paul arrived. Kelsey watched her walk in the bathroom before turning to John. Her eyes narrowed as she studied John's face. She sank into the chair opposite him, her movements slightly uncoordinated.

"Worried? About us? Please," she scoffed, reaching for his glass and taking a swig before he could protest. "You should be more concerned about yourself, sitting here in the dark like some brooding hero from a bad romance novel."

John's jaw tightened, but he remained silent, his gaze fixed on the closed bathroom door.

Kelsey leaned forward, her voice dropping to a whisper. "She's not Amy, you know."

John's eyes snapped back to Kelsey. *Oh, we're going to fight.* He thought, *it's going to be that kind of night.* "You're out of line," he growled, his voice low and dangerous.

Kelsey didn't flinch. *She never flinched,* John thought. She was probably the only person in the world that could stand and argue with him as an equal. *What are brothers and sisters for anyway?*

"Am I? Because from where I'm sitting, you're the one who's out of line. Pushing her away, drowning yourself in guilt and scotch. She deserves better than that, John."

The silence stretched between them, broken only by the muffled sound of the shower. John's hand tightened around his glass, knuckles turning white. "You don't know what you're talking about," he said finally, his words clipped and terse.

"Of course I do," Kelsey challenged. "I know you better than anyone alive." She blinked hard and grimaced, "Tell you what, your girl can hold her liquor, but I'm out of practice."

John's eyes shot at the mention of Nikita. He took a long drag from his cigar, exhaling slowly before responding. "She's not my girl."

Kelsey leaned forward, her voice dropping to a conspiratorial whisper. "Maybe she should be. You two dance around each other like… like…" She waved her hand, searching for the right words. "Like two porcupines trying to mate."

"Porcupines? That's what you're going with?" John replied, a trace of a smile on his lips.

Kelsey smirked, her eyes gleaming with mischief despite her inebriated state. "Hey, I'm drunk. Cut me some slack on the metaphors."

John shook his head, a hint of amusement breaking through his stoic facade. But it vanished as quickly as it appeared, replaced by a haunted look that Kelsey knew all too well.

"It's not that simple," he muttered, his gaze drifting back to the bathroom door.

Kelsey leaned back in her chair, her expression softening. "Nothing ever fucking is with you, is it?"

The shower stopped, and they both fell silent. John's posture stiffened; his eyes fixed on the bathroom door to his right.

Kelsey drew in breath to speak but the bathroom door opened, killing off her words. Nikita emerged, wrapped in a towel, her damp hair clinging to her shoulders. She paused, sensing the charged atmosphere in the room.

"Everything okay out here?" she inquired.

"Just friends catching up," Kelsey responded cheerily. She winked at Nikita. *What's that about?* John wondered.

"We'll try not be too loud" he offered apologetically. "Get some sleep Nikita."

Nikita bid her farewells and went to the bedroom. Kelsey turned back to John, "Get some sleep Nikita," she said mockingly. "Pathetic."

"What do you want me to say?" he asked.

Kelsey leaned back, the alcohol making her even bolder than usual. "I want you to say what you feel for once, instead of hiding behind that stoic, brooding bullshit you wear like armour. And honestly, would it kill you to call her something other than Nikita? Love, Sweetie, Darl, a fucking nickname — something."

A part of John broke at that. For reasons he couldn't tell Kelsey, he referred to Nikita solely by her name on purpose.

"You think I'm hiding? That's rich, coming from you," was all he could muster.

"Don't deflect. This isn't about me." Kelsey's eyes narrowed. "I've seen the way you look at her. Like she's water and you've been lost in the desert."

"Kels," he started through gritted teeth. "It's not that simple. But I'm working on it."

"Explain it to me, like I'm five." She lifted the glass in her hand.

"You'll need a new one by the way, I'm keeping this."

John sighed and walked to the kitchenette to retrieve a glass. Pouring some more, he sat opposite Kelsey again. "You and I, we're bad people. We're dangerous and destructive to say the least."

"And someone has hurt her before. I'm not stupid," Kelsey interjected.

John nodded grimly, taking a long sip from his glass. "You have no idea. She's been through enough. The last thing she needs is someone like me complicating her life."

Kelsey leaned forward; her eyes intense despite the alcohol clouding her system. "And what if that's exactly what she wants? What she needs?"

"There's more to it than that," he began again.

"Oh, spare me the self-flagellation," Kelsey snapped, her patience wearing thin. "We've all got our demons. But you know what? That girl is strong. Stronger than you give her credit for."

John's eyes flashed in anger and pain. "You think I don't know that? Christ, Kels, that's part of the problem. She's strong enough to handle anything, including me. But that doesn't mean she should have to."

Kelsey rolled her eyes. "Oh, here we go again with the martyr act. Has it ever occurred to you that maybe, just maybe, she wants to handle you? That she sees something in you worth fighting for?"

"Shut up and let me finish," John growled. "Someone didn't hurt her. Three people did, they filmed it, and they distributed it. Did she tell you she was 'bought in' to be my assistant? She's fucking owned. And what they did to her? You and I have seen some shit, done some things. I saw three seconds of footage and I will never fucking forget it. So, you'll forgive me if I'm careful as to my next move, no matter how badly I want to be curled up in that bed with my arms around her."

Kelsey's face fell, the sharp retort dying on her lips. The gravity of John's words hung heavy in the air, suffocating any trace of her earlier sarcasm. She swallowed hard, her eyes darting to the closed bedroom door where the woman in question slept.

"Christ, John," she whispered, her voice barely audible. "I had no idea."

John's shoulders sagged, the anger draining from him as quickly as it had flared. He ran a calloused hand over his face, suddenly looking every bit his age and then some.

"Yeah, well," he muttered, "now you do."

Silence stretched between them, thick and uncomfortable. Kelsey fidgeted with the hem of her shirt, her mind clearly racing to process this new information. When she finally spoke, her voice was almost red with anticipatory violence.

"What's your plan then? We could-"

"We...are going to do nothing tonight." John cut her off gently. *Typical Kels, in for a penny in for a pound right off the bat.* "Not while we're drunk. I'll explain in the morning. But I've promised her that she will be free, with me or without. There's nothing to talk about with her until she's free. Understood?"

"Sleep then? We'll regroup in the morning." She rose up and took the cushions off the couch, bringing them over to the small bed with a devious smile. "I'm sleeping here tonight. Guess you're going to have to use another bed. Go and curl up with her in your arms, you both want it. We'll sort the rest tomorrow."

John bent over and kissed Kelsey's forehead, "You're the worst. Goodnight." He walked to the bedroom.

John stood in the doorway; his eyes fixed on Nikita's sleeping form. Her golden hair splayed across the pillow, catching the faint moonlight that filtered through the curtains. For a moment, he allowed himself to drink in the sight of her, peaceful and unguarded in sleep.

With a deep breath, he moved quietly into the room, aiming for the chair beside her bed. As if sensing his presence Nikita stirred slightly, her brow furrowing. John froze, torn between his desire and the fear of crossing the line again.

"John?" Nikita's voice was thick with sleep, her eyes fluttering open.

"I'm here," he whispered, his voice gruff with emotion. "Go back to sleep."

Instead of closing her eyes, Nikita reached out, her fingers brushing against his arm. "Stay?"

The single word hung in the air, laden with vulnerability and hope. John felt his resolve crumbling.

"Are you sure?" he asked, his voice barely above a whisper.

Nikita nodded, her eyes shimmering in the dim light. "Please."

With a barely controlled breath, John eased himself onto the bed, keeping a respectful distance between them. Nikita, however, had other ideas. She inched closer, nestling herself against his side, her head finding the crook of his shoulder.

John's body tensed at first, unused to such intimate contact. But as Nikita's warmth seeped into him, he felt himself relaxing, his arm instinctively wrapping around her slender frame.

"Is this okay?" Nikita murmured, her breath tickling his neck.

John's voice was hoarse, thick with emotion. "Yeah, it's okay."

They lay there in silence, the rhythm of their breathing slowly synchronising. John's mind raced, a war between his desire to protect Nikita and his growing feelings for her. He could feel the softness of her hair against his chin, smell the faint scent of her shampoo. It was intoxicating and terrifying.

Nikita's hand found his in the darkness, her fingers intertwining with his. The simple gesture sent a jolt through John's body.

"John?" Nikita's voice was barely a whisper.

"Hmm?"

"Thank you. For everything."

John swallowed hard, fighting against the lump in his throat. "I haven't done anything."

"Don't do what he wants, don't take that job."

"It's okay," John breathed deeply. "I got the right price." He was asleep before Nikita's silent tear hit his chest. She knew she would lose him and go back to her previous life. But she had hoped to keep him a while longer. "No price is worth losing you." She whispered to his now sleeping form.

***

"RIGHT SIDE! RIGHT SIDE!" The urgent screams pierced John's consciousness, wrenching his eyes open. A heartbeat later he collided with Nikita. The force of his body pushing her off the bed, and he landed atop her with a heavy thud. In a swift motion, he shoved her beneath the bed, draping the bed sheets over her like a protective shield, before turning his attention toward the living room.

He could hear the rapid, urgent patter of Kelsey's footsteps approaching, her voice raw and strained with panic.

"They're coming! Multiple hostiles, heavily armed!" she yelled, her words tumbling out in a breathless rush.

Kelsey burst into the bedroom, her entrance punctuated by the door slamming shut behind her with a resounding bang. She dropped into a low crouch on the right side of the door frame, clutching what appeared to be a rifle with a determined grip. Ready to withstand the oncoming assault.

Wait, what? John wondered, blinking in confusion. *Where did she get the rifle?* As his vision adjusted to the dim light, it became clear that Kels was not wielding a rifle at all but rather his trusty broomstick. The absence of any sounds of approaching assailants struck him, and he relaxed slightly, his posture softening as he realised what this was and motioned for Nikita to emerge from her hiding spot beneath the bed.

Nikita emerged cautiously, her blonde hair dishevelled and eyes wide with confusion. John's gaze darted between her and Kelsey, who remained frozen in her defensive stance, knuckles white around the broomstick.

"Kelsey," John said, his voice low and steady. "There's no one out there. You're safe."

Kelsey's eyes snapped to John's face, fear and disbelief etched across her features. "You are with me, John. We're in St. Petersburg Russia. Nikita is here too" John continued. She blinked rapidly, her grip on the broomstick loosening slightly but she seemed unconvinced.

"No. I heard them… I saw…You have to get ready. They're coming." Her voice trailed off as reality began to seep back in.

Nikita approached slowly, crouching on her haunches, her movements careful and measured. "It's okay, Kelsey. Just a dream. You are here with us. With Nikita and John."

John watched as Kelsey's shoulders sagged, the adrenaline still coursing through her body.

"I broke again, didn't I?" She asserted, her eyes clearer now, even as tears welled, "Christ John, you should just shoot me. I'm no better than a sick dog. Don't make me suffer anymore."

John's jaw clenched, pain at her words evident on his face. He moved towards Kelsey; his steps deliberate and calm. "No," his voice firm but gentle. "You are not broken, Kels. You're surviving the best you can, like everyone else."

John carefully pried the broomstick from Kelsey's hands, setting it aside. His arms gently wrapped around Kelsey's trembling form, anchoring her to the present.

"We've all got our demons. But we face them together, and we'll get better together." John may hate himself, but his friend didn't deserve this; she needed help.

Kelsey's breath hitched, a sob threatening to break free. She looked up at John, her eyes searching his face for any sign of disappointment or disgust. Finding none, finding only understanding and love she slumped forward, her forehead resting against his chest as he held her.

Nikita moved closer, her hand hovering near Kelsey's shoulder, as if uncertain whether the touch would be welcome before John extended his arm, bringing her into the embrace of his old friend. "You're not broken, Kelsey. You're healing, just like the rest of us." Nikita offered.

"What part of this looks like I'm fucking healing?" Kelsey's eyes darted between them, her breath coming in short, sharp gasps. She slumped against the wall, sliding down until she was sitting on the floor. She threw her head back, smacking it into the wall behind her with a dull thud. "I thought… I was so sure…" Her voice trailed off, thick with emotion.

John crouched down beside her, hoping his presence was solid and reassuring. "What did you see?" he said quietly, his voice a low rumble that seemed to steady Kelsey's trembling hands.

Kelsey took a shaky breath as she recalled the vivid nightmare. "We were back home," she began, her voice barely above a whisper. "The streets were burning, and I could hear screaming…" She squeezed her eyes shut, trying to block out the memories.

Nikita settled on the floor beside them, forming a protective circle around Kelsey. Her hand found Kelsey's, offering a gentle squeeze of support.

"Go on," John encouraged, his eyes never leaving Kelsey's face.

"There were shadows everywhere," Kelsey continued, her voice gaining strength. "I couldn't tell who was friend or foe. And then I saw them," Kelsey continued, her voice cracking. "Kids from school. They were running towards me, screaming for help. But I couldn't move. I couldn't protect them."

John's jaw clenched. He knew all too well the weight of those you couldn't save. He placed his arm around Kelsey, his hand resting on her shoulder.

"It wasn't real, Kels," he said softly. "You're here with us now."

Kelsey shook her head, her eyes haunted. "But it was real once. And I failed them."

Nikita leaned in, her voice gentle. "You did everything you could. You can't save everyone."

Kelsey's eyes flashed with in anger. "But I should have saved THEM! I was trained for this. I should have been better, faster, stronger."

John shook his head, his own demons stirring at her words. He went to speak and then closed his mouth. No words changed the way he felt during his struggles. He knew nothing he could say to her would reach her now. He put his forehead against hers willing for whatever strength he had to quell the pain inside her.

"It's happening more often" Kelsey sobbed. "I can't stop it. Promise me you'll let me go?

John's jaw tightened, He gripped Kelsey's shoulders firmly, forcing her to meet his gaze.

"Listen to me, Kels," he said, his voice low and intense. "I'm not letting you go. Not now, not ever. You hear me?"

Kelsey's tears streaming freely down her face. She opened her mouth to protest, but Nikita cut her off, her voice soft and calm. "You're family, Kelsey. We don't abandon family."

'You've known me for one evening. And this," she gestured to herself in frustration. "Is what you got."

"And my life is better for having known you this one evening," Nikita smiled. Kelsey studied the small Russians face, as if searching for any signs of deceit or mockery but found none. Kelsey looked from Nikita to John; her eyes locking with her old friend. A silent conversation passed between them. John realised that Kelsey understood now. The small Russian woman was kind, understanding, and soothing without deception or bitterness despite her suffering. John knew in that silent conversation that he was no longer alone in his quest. As self-loathing as he was, and as worthless as he knew Kelsey felt, they were both going to free Nikita, whatever the cost.

John smiled, his expression soft for a man so frequently angry. "Kels, you've had my back more times than I can count. Now it's my turn to have yours."

He took her into his arms, and Kelsey turned her face away from Nikita. "We've got to help her, John," she whispered. "She's too good for us."

"I'll tell you in the morning. Time for sleep." He gently escorted her back to the small bed in the living room. Kelsey's breath hitched, a sob threatening to break free again. "I don't know if I can do this much longer," she whispered.

"We'll go hunting tomorrow, you'll feel better then."

***

A while later, once Kelsey was asleep again, John walked back into the bedroom to find Nikita back in bed. She was sitting up, waiting for him.

John paused at the doorway, his eyes meeting Nikita's in the dim light. He moved toward the bed, his steps slow and measured, giving the woman time to change her mind about his presence.

"Is she okay?" Nikita asked softly as John settled onto the edge of the bed.

He ran a hand through his hair, exhaling deeply. "As okay as any of us are, I suppose."

Nikita nodded. She reached out, her fingers lightly brushing against his arm. "And you? Are you okay?"

John's jaw clenched, his gaze fixed on a point beyond the bedroom wall. "I'm fine," he said, his voice gruff.

Nikita's hand stilled on his arm. "John," she said.

"I should have seen it coming," he said in a whisper. "It's always more likely to happen when she drinks. She'll be better in the morning."

"What happened back home? Wherever home is for Kelsey…" Nikita asked.

"Dunno, never been."

"But Kelsey said we-"

"It's a psychotic break, Nikita. She mixes events, mixes things that never happened with things that have. Kelsey has been through a lot, she suffered, even as a child. And although she hides it with her wit or sarcasm, she struggles."

He paused for a few seconds, "Don't think less of her. Life breaks everyone, Nikita. The very good, the very strong, the very kind and the very tough."

***

The tailor continued to take John's measurements.

"Evening or day?"

"Evening," came John's terse reply.

"Formal or social?"

"Formal."

Kelsey walked in. "It's a pretty dress, they said it would be ready tomorrow afternoon by three. I'll slip out and pick it up. And everything is set for Nikki this evening. Which means I guess you and I are going hunting. If you ever tell me the fucking plan." She flopped herself into a leather upholstered armchair, admiring the supple texture. "Very nice."

Neither of them would bring up last night's break, John knew that. It had always been that way.

"A moment?" John asked of the older man taking his measurements. The tailor nodded his head and left.

"De Smet is the one who orchestrated my appointment to the zoo for his insane project. He didn't arrange for Nikita to be my assistant, but he does know who holds her papers, whatever the fuck that means," John explained.

Kelsey leaned forward, her elbows resting on her knees. "And pray tell, what exactly is this 'stupid insane project' of his?"

"He didn't tell you?"

"I know St. Petersburg Zoo and Monarto are doing a deal for us to take your chimp troop. And he did say how it was very important that you took the job here. But that is the extent of it."

John sighed. He wasn't sure how Kelsey would take what De Smet had proposed to him last night. "Don't fucking lie to me." Kelsey put in, "I can see you thinking how to. Why would Jean-Paul, a man that only cares about his park, organise a job in Russia for a man that fifty/fifty would kill him on sight?"

John grimaced, he never had been able to lie to Kelsey. The DRC is imploding a little as you may know. Open war is a very real possibility. Rebel groups have been specifically targeting gorilla and Jean-Paul's down to fifteen or so gorilla left. He's certain they won't survive if war does break out. Which is a fair guess."

"Okay…"

"He's got two options, let them go extinct. Or try something wacky."

"Which is where you come in," Kelsey interjected. "De Smet would try anything rather than let them go, but it's not like he would actually be the one doing it. What's the something wacky?"

"He huh, he wants to dart and relocate as many gorillas out of the country as he can before war starts."

"Fucking hell. That is crazy." Kelsey said quietly. "Still don't see how you being in Russia comes into it?"

John looked at his old friend.

"Oh, what the fuck!? Here? He wants to smuggle mountain gorilla out of Africa and bring them here? Why on earth would he do that?"

"He thinks they'll be safe here. We've been expanding the African wing of the zoo with new purpose-built enclosures. As Monarto is taking our chimp troop, we now have an empty primate enclosure ready and waiting. De Smet thinks Russia is the kind of place to say, 'no mountain gorilla here, that would be illegal' and then unveil their mountain gorilla enclosure two days later."

"The backlash would be insane."

"This is the country that took Georgia in five days, and the world just fucking watched. I think of all the stupidity in De Smet's idea, that bit actually makes sense."

"So. You have to open doors here in Russia, track and dart gorilla in the DRC, and smuggle them out of a war zone? It's a walk in the park, hey?"

"Light work," John replied.

"They'll all die. There's a reason there's none in a zoo anywhere in the world."

"Yeah, I'm working on it."

"This is suicide," Kelsey offered her friend.

"Yeah, well… funny thing is if he bought this to me eighteen months ago, I was so messed up I'd have probably done it for a can of Coke and a meat pie."

"What are we getting paid for on this one?"

John's eyes flashed towards her; he knew she'd try insert herself in this. "This one is just me. My price is Nikita. De Smet helps me get her out free and clear, passport and passage to wherever so she can start fresh. That and helping me get to the people that did that to her."

Kelsey gave him a hard stare and John knew what that meant. They had followed each other into every stupid idea so far, it wasn't going to stop now. *Great. Now not only do I have to do this stupid plan, but I also need to find a way to keep Kels out of it.* He watched as Kelsey raised her sleeve to scratch her left shoulder, revealing the same burned scaring he had on his chest, the same Swahili words under it. *Going to be damn near impossible to keep her away.*

"Jean-Paul De Smet," Kelsey chided. "Always been a devious fuck. Where do I fit in tonight?"

John turned away, staring out the window at the bustling streets below. His shoulders sagged slightly as he took a big breath. "Tonight, while De Smet and I do our thing, I need you to break into an office. Well, into a safe in an office."

Kelsey arched an eyebrow, although John couldn't see. "Do I dare ask?"

"Find the hard drive containing the originals of Nikita's films."

A surprised frown etched onto Kelsey's brow, and she leaned forward, her voice dropping to a whisper. "Fuck, John. You're really going all in on this, aren't you?"

John's jaw tightened, his gaze still fixed on the window. "It's the only way to truly set her free. Completely."

"And what about you?" Kelsey pushed, her tone softening. "What's your endgame in all this?"

John turned back, his face trying and failing to hide the pain he felt. "My endgame? To make things right. To give her a chance at a life she deserves."

Kelsey stood up. Her voice gentle but firm. "You deserve a life too, you know."

"This was my price. De Smet helps me, I help him. You don't have to be a part of it if you don't want."

A heavy silence fell between them, broken only by the distant sounds of traffic filtering through the window. Kelsey crossed the room, leaning against John. Her shoulder against his, her touch conveying more than words ever could.

"Alright," she said softly. "I'm in. What's the location?"

John turned to face her and laughed. "You'll hate it. We're going clubbing."

23

Chapter Twenty-Three: The Red Dragon

John-

John, Kelsey, and De Smet stood on the small sidewalk across the road from the Red Dragon. "We look proper scrubbed up," Kelsey chuckled. "Shame it's not under better circumstances."

"You don't have to come," John reminded her. "This is between him and me," he motioned to Jean-Paul.

"I'm staying. We're getting what you're owed. And we're getting Nikita's life back."

The red neon light of the club cast a hazy glow over the trio, accentuating their features and clothing. The worn brick of the industrial estate provided a gritty backdrop, its cracks and stains adding to the overall atmosphere. The air was heavy with the smell of sweat and alcohol, mixed with a hint of cigarette smoke wafting from passing patrons. A sharp metallic scent lingered from the nearby factory, a reminder of the club's location in the former industrial estate.

"I must admit John. I didn't blink when they said they had someone to sweeten the deal for you. I thought, maybe John would like some comfort after all that time alone, and at least you would be nicer to her than whomever her current men were. But I did not expect this," De Smet stated before coughing.

"Did you know what they did to her?" John shot.

"I assumed what men like them do to women like her. And knew you would treat her better than that, so I saw no harm."

"Remember, your entire plan for your gorilla hinge on me doing what you need. I don't do shit until she is free. Do not fuck up tonight," John voice dripped with implied threats. De Smet seemed unperturbed.

"I will draw out the one who holds her papers, your director. He often has a friend with him; they call him ghost. I don't know much about him. But I will draw them out so you can see their faces."

John stiffened at the mention of ghost, and the confirmation of Bear's identity. Nikita hadn't lied, she never stated that no one at the zoo knew of her videos, only that not everyone knew. He wondered if Aleski was the big bad that Nikita had tried to shield him from. She needn't have bothered. He turned to Kelsey. "Remember your part in this?" he asked. "Nothing else matters if we can't get into that safe."

Kelsey nodded, her eyes narrowing with determination. "Don't worry, I've got it covered. I'll slip away once we're inside. You just focus on keeping those bastards distracted."

John grunted in acknowledgement, his jaw clenching as he stared at the pulsing neon sign of the Red Dragon. The bass from the club's music throbbed in his chest, matching the quickening of his heartbeat.

De Smet cleared his throat, breaking the tension. "Shall we, then?" he asked, gesturing toward the club's entrance with a flourish that seemed out of place in the gritty surroundings.

The three of them crossed the street, the pulsing bass from the club growing louder with each step. As they approached the entrance, a burly bouncer eyed them suspiciously, his gaze lingering on John's muscular frame.

De Smet stepped forward, flashing a charming smile and producing a sleek black card from his pocket. The bouncer's demeanour instantly changed, and he ushered them inside with a respectful nod.

They were met inside with a cacophony of sights and sounds. Strobe lights cut through the smoky air, illuminating writhing bodies on the dance floor. John's eyes scanned the room, searching for familiar faces among the crowd. His mind raced with images of Nikita - her smile, her silent tears, the haunted look in her eyes when she spoke of her past. He pushed the thoughts aside, forcing himself to focus on the task at hand. They had one shot at this, and he would not fail.

As they made their way through the pulsing crowd, De Smet led them towards a secluded VIP area cordoned off by velvet ropes. A svelte hostess approached, her eyes darting between the three of them before settling on De Smet's confident smile.

"Mr. De Smet, welcome back," she purred, unhooking the rope. "Your table is ready."

John felt a prickle of unease at how easily De Smet navigated this world of luxury and vice. He wondered, not for the first time, just how deep the conservationist's connections ran in this world. As they settled into the plush leather booth, John's eyes continued to scan the club, hyperaware of every movement and face in the crowded space.

"Relax, John," De Smet murmured through barely moving lips. "You're drawing attention. We must appear as nothing more than wealthy patrons enjoying a night out."

John forced his shoulders to loosen. Kelsey draped an arm over his shoulder and her legs across his, adding more to the façade.

De Smet signalled to a waiter, ordering a bottle of expensive champagne with practiced ease. "Now, we wait," he said, his voice low and controlled. "Our friends should be making an appearance soon."

Not my fucking friends, John thought to himself. His fingers drummed against Kelsey's leg, the only outward sign of his growing tension. His mind raced through the plan, considering every possible outcome, every potential complication. The weight of Nikita's future pressed down on him, fuelling his determination to see this through. As the champagne arrived, John took a glass, pretending to sip while his eyes never stopped scanning the crowd.

Suddenly, De Smet's posture changed, his eyes fixed on a point across the club. "There," he murmured, tilting his head subtly. "By the bar."

John followed his gaze, his heart rate quickening as he spotted two men standing near the ornate bar. One was unmistakably Aleski, his curator's uniform replaced by an expensive suit that did little to hide his bear-like build. The other man was lean and pale, with close-cropped white hair that seemed to glow under the club's lights. *Ghost*, John presumed, feeling a chill run down his spine.

Kelsey shifted in his lap; her lips close to his ear. "That's our cue," she whispered. Then speaking louder. "Darling you're too tense. Don't you think he's tense Jean? Dance with me, Luke." She grabbed John's hand, pretending to try pulling him to his feet and out to the dance floor. "I want to dance," she continued as the two slipped in among the crowded floor.

Watching them until he was satisfied they were hidden well enough, De Smet beckoned his server again, ordered two drinks to be sent to the pair at the bar, courtesy of the man in the booth. John and Kelsey watched on as they pretended to dance and saw the men receive their drinks and notice Jean-Paul. They made their way to his booth.

"Is that who you thought?" Kelsey yelled above the music.

"Big one is. He's my boss at the zoo. Small one I never saw before. I mean, they were both in the video with Nikita. But they were wearing masks, so I never saw their faces. The third one didn't, he had his face showing, that's how I found him"

"What did they do to her?" Kelsey asked. John had known she was curious, that she had held back the question since last night. But here, about to break into a safe and maybe hurt some people, John felt like maybe she should know why.

"Tell you when we get out. We should go, no telling how long De Smet keeps them occupied."

Kelsey nodded, her expression hardening as she registered the urgency in John's voice. They weaved through the gyrating bodies, making their way toward the back of the club. John's eyes darted around, watching for any sign they were being followed or observed.

As they reached a dimly lit hallway marked, 'Tol'ko Sotrudniki' they slipped inside, finding themselves in a narrow corridor lined with storage rooms and offices. John's heart pounded in his ears as they moved silently down the hall. "Okay, up two flights, then second door on the right," Kelsey rehearsed to herself.

The room was exactly what the man John captured had described. John had been fairly certain of his information; a man under that much torture had few secrets. But it had still been a question in his mind.

An art piece hung on the wall behind the desk. "There, behind that," John pointed. Kelsey found the painting able to swing on its hinges. She stared at the safe behind it. "Fuck. It's old school. Key only," she hissed.

"Can you pick it?" he whispered urgently.

"I can try. It would have been easier to crack with a combination lock or keypad." She tore a lining in her clutch where she kept some small instruments.

"You never cease to amaze me," John whispered. "How long?"

"I'll be as fast as I can," she replied. Just then both their hearts froze as the door swung open, and the man they called Ghost walked in the room. A little taller than John, he was painfully thin.

"Be faster," John hissed and stepped towards the newcomer.

Ghost's pale eyes locked onto John, a cold fury. "Well, well," he said, his voice soft but menacing. "What have we here?"

John's muscles tensed, ready to spring into action. He positioned himself between Ghost and Kelsey, buying her precious seconds. "Just looking for the restroom," John said, forcing a casual tone. "Got a bit turned around."

Ghost's thin lips curled into a cold smile. "Is that so? And I suppose your lovely companion is simply powdering her nose behind that painting?"

John knew the charade was pointless. *Had Ghost had been tipped off? Perhaps by hidden cameras or an alert system they had missed, or maybe De Smet had double crossed him.* Whatever the reason it didn't matter. He had found them regardless. He glanced back at Kelsey, saw the determination in her eyes as her fingers worked furiously at the lock.

"Look," John began, taking a step toward Ghost.

"You are a fucking idiot," Kelsey cackled. Ghost and John looked at her utterly bewildered by the outburst.

"The key is around his neck John," and before anyone had time to react John sent the most savage, short punch he had thrown in his life at the man's chin, dropping him like a sack of potatoes. He had the key off in a flash, tossing it to Kelsey while he wondered what to do with the unconscious form in front of him.

"Got it," Kelsey confirmed, holding up a hard drive. "What else is in there?" John inquired.

"Drugs, it seems, mostly. Some cash, papers."

"Give me the key and go."

"What about him? He's seen us."

"Go, I don't want you seeing this."

Kelsey scoffed in reply.

"I'm serous Kels. You've seen me kill a lot of people. But never murder one. Get out of here. This is on me."

"I'll keep an eye out in the hallways. Be quick."

Kelsey left and John quickly set to work closing the safe and returning the key around Ghost's neck. The man reeked of alcohol. Good. He dragged him onto a balcony outside as he stirred. John clamped a rough hand over his mouth. "Look at me. I saw what you did to her, to Nikita."

A confused look came over his face. "Jesus, fuck. You don't even know her name, do you? She was just a thing to you! Well, I saw what you did, and I am so very sorry you were filled with such remorse that you took your own life." The man's eyes widened and he went to protest. John's hand came away from his mouth. But before he could shout out, the Australian's elbow crashed into his jaw dazing him a split second before John tossed him over the balcony. He fell, wordlessly for what seemed like forever but for what was actually only one or two seconds before colliding violently with a security fence, its points impaling his chest. A passerby rushed to his side, but it was too late. Within seconds he was gone, and so was John.

Regrouping with Kelsey, the pair made their way back out onto the dance floor. Using the cover of the dancing crowd and obnoxiously loud techno music to separate themselves, they exited the club at different times. John checked to see Aleski still talking to De Smet in the booth. *Two down, one to go* he thought to himself. *Your time will come.* He winked at De Smet and left, walking alone back to his apartment.

He walked in, relived to see Kelsey there. She had a glass of the Singleton Scotch for each of them. "Your girl still isn't back," she said grinning. They had bought Nikita and a friend of hers, Anya from the book club, a VIP package to see the ballet tonight, keeping her away from the night's operation.

"Again, she's not my girl," John said as he took the glass, draining it in one long sip. "Fuck, that was needed." He reached to pour another.

"Semantics," Kelsey replied dismissively. "Especially now we have this," she waved the hard drive.

John sank into the worn armchair, the weight of the night's events settling heavily on his shoulders. He swirled the amber liquid in his glass, watching as it caught the dim light of the apartment.

"You know," Kelsey said, her voice softer than usual, "what you did tonight… it was necessary."

John shrugged.

Kelsey leaned forward, her eyes searching his face. "John, that man was a monster. What he did to Nikita, to probably countless others… He deserved what he got. In fact, he got off lightly."

"Maybe," John muttered, draining his glass. "But it doesn't make it any easier. And you don't even know what they did or what's on that drive."

"You did say you'd tell me, or should I see for myself?"

"Don't fucking watch it," he growled with an intensity that caused Kelsey to flinch. "You'll never get it out of your head. And she doesn't need anyone else seeing."

"What did they do, John?" Kelsey asked quietly, "It's eating you alive and after tonight I'm in for a penny, in for a pound anyway."

John sighed, took another long sip and hauled his mind back to the small amount of footage he'd seen, shuddering as he did so. "It's torture porn," John's voice was barely above a whisper as he continued, his eyes fixed on a floorboard, unable to look at his longtime friend. "They broke her down piece by piece, body and mind. They filmed everything. Every scream, every plea for mercy. And they…" John's voice cracked, his knuckles white around the glass. "They made her watch it back as they did it. Repeatedly. Until she couldn't distinguish between the pain and the memory of it."

Kelsey moved to sit on the arm of John's chair, placing a gentle hand around his shoulder. "That's why you only ever refer to her by name. They tried to take her humanity; you're trying to give some of it back. Jesus, John. I had no idea."

"Neither did I, not really. Not until I saw it with my own eyes." He looked up at Kelsey. "The three of them, took turns on her as the other two cut and burned and whipped her. Those scars on her arms and back? Her feet? That's how she got them. That's why I can barely touch her no matter how badly either of us want me too. How can I?" The rim of the glass shattered under John's grip, slicing into a finger. He ignored the blood slowly dripping down the glass.

Kelsey's grip on John's shoulder tightened, her own eyes glistening with welling tears. Not just of sadness, but of righteous fury and indignation.

"John, you are not those men. You could never be them."

"Kelsey I've-."

"I know what you've done, most times I've been right beside you as you did it. You don't do those things for your own enjoyment; you do it to protect people you care about. Without those men gone, and this," she waved the hard drive, "in our hands, she would never be safe, never be free." Kelsey's voice was firm, unwavering. "And Nikita trusts you. She feels safe with you."

John shook his head, a bitter laugh escaping his lips. "Safe? I am a killer, Kelsey. A monster in my own right. I'm the dog you let off the leash, not the one you have around your family."

"You know I fucking hate when you do that? Heap sin and shame upon yourself. You think my big flaw is paranoia, well yours was taking the blame for wrongs that are NOT YOURS TO BEAR! We are both killers. South Sudan, Botswana, The Congo, Rwanda. We both have lifetimes of sin and savagery to our names. But you only ever say, 'I,' like you can absolve everyone else by taking the shame upon yourself. Well stop it, I'm good with what I am!"

Kelsey held up a finger, forestalling John's response as she regained her breath. "Now of course she feels safe with you, you're giving that girl a chance at a life without fear. Without constantly looking over her shoulder. And you do love her, I know you do. You just won't admit it to yourself. Not till she's free."

John was about to argue when he heard the soft click of a key in the lock.

***

Nikita-

The door swung open, admitting Nikita, her face flushed with excitement from the ballet. Her smile faltered as she took in the tense atmosphere of the room.

"Is everything alright?" she asked, her voice tinged with concern.

John quickly composed himself, forcing a smile. "Of course. How was the ballet?"

Nikita's eyes darted between John and Kelsey. "It was beautiful," she said softly. "Something's wrong. Something's happened. I can feel it."

Kelsey stood up, giving John's shoulder a final squeeze. "Nothing's wrong, love. Just some heavy conversation. You know how John gets after a few drinks."

Nikita stepped closer, her gaze fixed on John. "You're lying," she said, her voice barely above a whisper.

John's forced smile faltered under Nikita's piercing gaze. He set his glass down and leaned forward, elbows on his knees. "Nikita, I—"

"Don't," she interrupted, her voice trembling. "Don't lie to me. Please." She moved closer, her focus never leaving John's face. "I can see it in your eyes. Something's changed, and you're bleeding."

Kelsey glanced between them, "I should go," she said quietly. Nikita shook her head. "Stay. I want to know what's going on."

John gave her a sad smile. "I promise you that nothing is wrong. I negotiated a hefty fee for helping De Smet. Kels was just making sure I got what I was owed before signing on while telling me how stupid I was for agreeing. That is why it's tense. Nothing is wrong. We are all

199

okay. I promise."

He took the job after all.

Nikita looked back between the pair. As thick as thieves they were, there would be no use in trying to press them further. She changed the subject. "I had never been to the ballet before, neither had Anya. Thank you."

"I'm glad you had a good time," John said, he was beaming now. He really meant it, she realised. A part of her felt wrong for the way she had accused him earlier. He really was good to her. "Are you staying the night again Kelsey? You are welcome, we enjoy having you here."

"If that's okay?" she looked back at John. He smiled back at her, "Wherever I am in the world, you have a place to stay. Don't even ask." Nikita realised that just a few days ago her heart would have hurt seeing John look at Kelsey like that, talk to her like that, but not now. John left the two ladies chatting to each other as he headed for the shower, mumbling something to himself.

Nikita busied herself making tea, her movements precise and controlled, not betraying the turmoil beneath her calm exterior.

"He's not okay, is he?" Nikita finally asked, her voice barely audible over the boiling kettle.

Kelsey pulled a face and took another sip. "To be honest with you, I think he's getting better. You're good for him, you know. Even if you think nothing will come of it."

Nikita turned, her eyes shimmering. "I've seen him like this before. A few weeks ago." A frown crossed Kelsey's features. "He...found someone who, well who wronged me. And John... he hurt him." She was not about to tell John's closest friend that he had in fact tortured and killed a man that had violently tortured her; Kelsey didn't need to know that.

"Nikki? Look at me. I have been with John all night, De Smet has too. I promise you he hasn't done anything bad tonight." It wasn't a lie, because Kelsey believed it.

Nikita nodded, trying to find comfort in Kelsey's words, but the knot in her stomach simply would not unravel. She brought the steaming mug of tea to the coffee table and sat down, her fingers tracing the rim of her cup.

"I want to believe you," she said softly. "It's just… there's something in his eyes. Like he's carrying the weight of the world on his shoulders."

Kelsey leaned forward, her gaze intense. "John's always been like that, Nikki. He takes on everyone else's burdens. It's what makes him… him."

The sound of the shower shutting off echoed through the apartment. Nikita's eyes darted toward the hallway, her heart rate quickening. She wanted to believe everything was fine, that John was just being his usual brooding self. But something nagged at her, a persistent whisper that she knew better than what she was told. She had come to know John quite well the last few months, and he had never been particularly hard to read.

But whatever had happened tonight, it seemed the two friends were determined for her not to know. There was no point pushing. She switched now. "I know you took all the couch cushions and slept on the bed out here so John would have to sleep in my bed last night," she said with a sly smile. "Thank you for that."

Kelsey's cheeks flushed slightly, and she let out a small chuckle. "Well, someone had to give him a little push."

"He just held me, but it was nice," Nikita's smile faltered, her eyes dropping to her tea. "I don't know, Kels. It's complicated. Like I said the other night, happy endings aren't pos-"

The bathroom door creaked open, and John emerged, a towel wrapped around his waist. His muscular frame was still damp from the shower, droplets of water trailing down his broad back. His face was tense, brow furrowed, as he made his way to the bedroom.

Nikita's breath caught in her throat, her eyes following him. She couldn't help but notice the way his shoulders seemed to sag, as if carrying an invisible load.

Kelsey reached across, taking Nikita's hand in hers. "None of us know what tomorrow brings and I believe one needs to take their happy endings wherever they may find them." She flashed that devious grin again and added, "and you best believe I'll be stealing the cushions again tonight." With that, Kelsey rose and headed for the now vacant bathroom.

Nikita sat frozen, her tea growing cold in her hands. The weight of Kelsey's words hung in the air, mingling with the lingering steam from John's shower. She could hear him moving about in the bedroom, the soft rustle of clothing and the occasional creak of floorboards.

Her mind raced, torn between the desire to go to him and the fear of what might happen if she did. John's words from earlier echoed in her head: 'People like us don't get happy endings.' *But hadn't they both suffered enough? Didn't they deserve a chance at happiness, even if it was fleeting?*

With a deep breath, Nikita set down her mug and stood up. Her socked feet padded softly across the floor as she made her way to the bedroom door. She hesitated for a moment, her hand hovering over the doorknob, before she summoned the courage to knock gently.

"John?" she called softly, her voice barely above a whisper.

There was a pause, then a gruff, "Come in."

Nikita pushed the door open slowly, her heart pounding in her chest. John stood by the window, his back to her, now dressed in a simple t-shirt and sweatpants. The moonlight cast a silvery glow on his silhouette, highlighting the tension in those massive shoulders.

She took a tentative step into the room. "Are you okay?"

John didn't turn around; his gaze fixed on the night sky beyond the glass. "For the twentieth time tonight, I'm fine. Nothing is wrong," he said, his voice low and gravelly.

"You cut your hand" Nikita pressed. The blood evident again.

"Leave it, it's fine." He never allowed Nikita to treat his injuries, nor did he ever seem to tend them himself. She knew it was a dead end.

Nikita moved closer, stopping a few feet behind him. She could see his reflection in the window, the tired, strained look in his eyes that he was trying so hard to hide. "Kelsey is sleeping out in the living room again. Will you stay here, with me again tonight?"

The reflection in the window tensed, his jaw clenching visibly. For a long moment, John remained silent, the weight of unspoken words hanging heavy in the air between them.

Finally, he turned to face her, his eyes dark and conflicted. "Nikita," he began, his voice rough with emotion, "I don't know if that's a good idea."

Nikita took another step closer, her heart racing. "Why not?" she asked softly, searching his face for answers.

John ran a hand through his damp hair; frustration etched in every line of his face. "Because…" His frustration grew as he failed to find the words.

She took another step closer, close enough now to feel the warmth radiating from John's body. "Just stay tonight, please?"

She saw his resolve break and knew he could not deny her.

As they climbed into bed, she lay her head on his chest as she had the previous night, recounting her time at the ballet until John fell asleep. Then alone, yet with the man she loved, Nikita's silent tears rolled down her face, wetting John's shirt. *He took the job after all. He's leaving, and this is ending.*

She held him all the harder, as though it might be the last time, until she too, fell asleep.

$$24$$

Chapter Twenty-Four: Last days

John-

John's stare bore into Aleski. This was the third time this morning Aleski had yelled at John's staff. Evidently the man was in a foul mood. John wasn't sure exactly what was being said but he picked up enough to know Aleski was angry at some kind of betrayal. A business partner had taken something from him and hid it before committing suicide. What it was he wouldn't say, but his interactions with John were steely to say the least and he seemed to stare venom into Nikita whenever he saw her. John made sure to keep her close that day. His plan was so near completion that he could burst with desperation. In less than forty-eight hours he would gain her freedom — if he didn't fuck up at the dinner, and De Smet didn't fuck up his part. He couldn't shake the weight of his plans. The constant thrum of anxiety in his chest intensified as he thought about what lay ahead. *Two more days.* Just two more days and Nikita would be free. Then he would have to go and fulfil his end of the bargain.

John's jaw clenched as he watched Aleski's eyes narrow at Nikita from across the offices. He starred back. John didn't place any stock in the idea of telepathy, the idea that people could communicate through thought alone. But as he locked eyes with Aleski, he willed it to be so.

Yeah. I fucking did it, and you're next.

Aleski's face twitched and John smirked as he reasoned the curator got the message. The bear of a man bore so furiously into John that for a second, he thought they might handle things here and now.

You want to go to war with me, you sick piece of shit?

But then, after what felt like eons, Aleski's gaze slid away, his shoulders almost seeming to slump in defeat.

Nikita, sensing the tension, pressed closer to John's side. Her warmth seeped through his shirt, a reminder of all he stood to gain—and lose. He fought the urge to wrap an arm around her, to shield her from Aleski's venomous stare and the weight of his own scheming. Instead, he guided her away from the seething man's line of sight.

"Stay close to me today," he murmured.

Nikita nodded, her body language betraying her unease. "Something's wrong, isn't it?" she whispered. "He's angry."

John shook his head slightly. It wasn't time to come clean yet, to explain the intricate web between him and Jean-Paul, how Aleski fit into it, how John needed to be perfect on Saturday night, and how it was all for her.

"Best not to ask. He's been going through a lot lately. Let's focus on how these guys are doing training their critters." There were two months to go until the move to new enclosures and John had to keep track on how the staff were preparing them.

As they walked, John's mind raced. The plan had to work; it simply must. Every detail, every word exchanged at the upcoming dinner would be crucial. One misstep over the next few days and it would all crumble.

He glanced at her and instantly felt his chest tighten. He would not fail. His phone vibrated; it was Kelsey letting him know that she had picked up Nikita's dress, complete with John's alterations. So far so good.

"Fucking good job," John beamed, slapping Dima on the back. The tricky caracal was now entering and staying in the crate. "Tell him Nikita; he's done excellent work." The small cat had been the real concern and so had the cheetah. They weren't ready for transportation yet. But the keepers had come a long way over the past few months — as had the animals' training. A testament to both John's instruction and the keepers' dedication.

"I can't wait to see them all in new enclosures. These ones now are so sad," Nikita said with a smile on her face.

"Me neither, but we can't replicate the wild," John said. "We can certainly do better than this, and we will." He smiled at her now. "We could not have done this without you."

Nikita's face lit up in a way that made John's chest ache.

25

Chapter Twenty- Five: Turning the tide

Kelsey-

Two days later, on Saturday, Kelsey was walking the streets of St. Petersburg, a slightly exasperated Nikita in tow. "You still have not told me where we are going. And I do need to get ready for the dinner."

Kelsey had asked Nikita for her help with an errand, and John had told his assistant that he would meet her at the Hermitage. John was doing what needed to be done. Kelsey was on bodyguard duty. With John's plans so close to completion, they both felt Nikita should never be out of sight until it was done. Kelsey smiled to herself; she'd had much worse assignments than today. She liked Nikita. The small woman had reached John in a way that Kelsey had been unable to. No, today would be special.

"You'll see in a moment; I wouldn't have asked you here if it wasn't important. In here," Kelsey replied and opened the door to a salon. It was the kind of place Nikita could never afford. Kelsey produced a letter written in Russian when they were greeted. John had one of his staff, Mikhail, write it for him. The lady read it and smiled, guiding them to a pair of seats before briefly disappearing only to return with two flutes of champagne. "A gift from your crabby roommate," Kelsey explained to her friend.

"I've never had my hair and makeup done before," Nikita smiled. "Well, the president wants to meet John which means you're meeting the president too." Kelsey added.

Nikita's eyes widened. "I'm not ready for that."

Kelsey's lips curved into a knowing smile. "That's why we're here. John's arranged everything. Trust me, by the time you arrive tonight, you'll feel like you belong among all those hoity toities."

As the stylist began working on Nikita's hair, Kelsey looked around the room. So many beautiful women, the scent of competing perfumes caught her nose, the benches filled with brushes and applicators of every kind, most of which Kelsey had never seen before, let alone used. "Why didn't John tell me himself?" Nikita asked, tearing Kelsey from her observations.

She snorted, taking a sip from her flute. "You know how he is. Man of few words and all that. Plus, I think he wanted it to be a surprise." She looked back around the room. Kelsey never had trouble attracting a man. Attracting the right one was another story. She was pretty and fit, but not beautiful the way these women were. Her hands weren't as soft as theirs, she bore scars she was certain they didn't. For a small moment a twinge of inadequacy washed over her. Nikita fit in here, Kelsey did not. Then the inadequacy vanished as Kelsey smiled to herself, realising not one of these women could fight. She could trounce every single person in this room if she needed to. Her watchful gaze returned to Nikita.

"You're smiling," Kelsey observed, her tone teasing. "Thinking about our grumpy bear?"

Nikita's cheeks flushed, and she averted her gaze. "I am just… grateful. For all of this."

Kelsey's expression softened. "He cares about you, you know. Even if he's too emotionally constipated to voice it properly."

The words hung in the air, heavy with implication. Nikita swallowed hard, her voice barely above a whisper. "I know. I'm going to miss him when he goes with Jean-Paul." Kelsey squeezed her hand. "Then we have to make tonight count," she smiled.

"Kesley?" Nikita asked without turning her head.

"Hmm?"

"Will you tell me what John did in Sudan? You said he turned the tide?"

"John never told you? Didn't expect he would to be honest. Some men tell you only of their success, John speaks only of his failures." She closed her eyes briefly, memories washing over her of that fateful, horrendous day. She turned to face Nikita.

"Okay, so I heard the shots, and then silence…

***

Kelsey- Jabori Wildlife Reserve, South Sudan, twenty-three months ago.

"John," Kelsey choked, looking at Thimba's body beside her.

"Thimba is down, Amana's wounded. I'm out of ammo and more are headed your way. I'm coming to you, but you must get out of there or dig in"

Silence was her reply.

"JOHN!! How copy?"

"Solid copy," John replied. The words were flat and robotic to her ear.

She made her way off the roof, sliding down the ladder as quickly as she could without injuring herself.

She saw John emerge from behind the cottage, revolver in hand. He looked to her as if operating on autopilot. The revolver in his hand had a mind of its own, taking life wherever it saw opportunity.

Realising John was headed for the front gate, Kelsey made a beeline for where a wounded Amana was resting beside the upturned troopie. The main gates had been breached again when the men had left it to respond to the group attacking B side. Only Amana had stayed, and paid the price.

John reached Amana a second or two before her. Wounds leaked blood from the big man's chest and left arm; he'd caught a round in the left thigh, too.

"He's here, out front, off to the right. We can end this now." He tried to rise, and spluttered, coughing blood and fell back down.

"Stay here," John said, his voice devoid of emotion as he reloaded his sidearm, glancing at the bodies and weapons all around him.

Kelsey dropped beside the giant who had been her protector through so much of her time here. Tears loosed themselves at the sight of her strong, proud friend reduced to this broken mess before her.

"I go out …the way I choose. And I choose on my feet," he coughed again.

Kelsey surveyed the compound. B and D side were back under control, albeit with fierce fighting continuing on B side. But the compound wouldn't be safe as long as the front gates remained open and the enemy could just stream in.

"The three of us, together," Kelsey started, "we'll cut straight for Lord, we can break them here or kill him hopefully." She looked into Amana's eyes, they were losing their colour, he didn't have much left. "Are you sure you want this?" she asked.

He nodded emphatically. "Point me at the enemy," and Kelsey helped him to his feet one last time.

"Let's do this," she turned to John.

"Stay here." was all he said to her.

"John, we're coming with you," Kelsey insisted checking her rifle; she had left the Dragonov on the roof but kept her M4.

John turned to her, his eyes vacant and cold. "Not for this.

Concentrate everyone's fire on the centre when they converge. Thank you for everything, sister."

Kelsey's jaw clenched, "I'm coming with you" she growled. She watched as John cocked his head slightly and gave her a wane smile. "You need to let me have this, I'm sorry." Without further warning he sprang forward shoving Kelsey in the chest. The force sent her stumbling back into Amana. The giant's mighty arm wrapped around her, pinning Kelsey in place against his torso, and with that, John turned and stepped out from behind the vehicle.

"No!" Kelsey screamed, struggling against Amana's grip. "Let me go!"

But the giant's arm, even in his weakened state, was an iron band around her. Blood from his wounds soaked into her shirt as she thrashed against him.

John didn't look back. His figure cut a stark silhouette against the chaotic landscape of the compound—smoke rising from burning vehicles, bodies strewn across the dirt, the metallic smell of blood and gunpowder hanging in the air. His movements were mechanical, precise, like a man who had already accepted his fate.

"He has chosen his path," Amana whispered, his voice a ragged breath against her ear. "Honour it."

"It's suicide," Kelsey hissed, tears streaming down her face as she fought in vain to free herself from her friend's grip. She watched as John moved with terrible purpose toward the open gates, watched as he holstered his revolver, watched as he picked up a PK machine gun from a fallen rebel, it's bipod swinging uselessly as John held it like a normal rifle."

The weapon looked enormous in his hands, but he carried it with the practiced ease of a man who'd spent too many years holding death in his palms. Kelsey's throat burned with unspoken pleas as John checked the belt feed with mechanical efficiency.

"John stop!" she screamed uselessly, her voice breaking as she bucked against Amana's grip once more. "Fucking... let me go!"

Amana's grip loosened slightly as he slumped against her, his breathing growing more laboured.

Through the haze of dust and smoke, Kelsey could make out Lord's men regrouping beyond the gates, their shadows converging like vultures. John walked forward alone, a solitary challenge against the reserve group surrounding Lord. He moved with an eerie calm, as though death couldn't touch him, as though he didn't care if it did.

Kelsey felt Amana sliding down behind her, his massive frame beginning to crumple. She caught him as best she could, easing his descent while keeping her eyes fixed on John's receding form.

"Not like this," she whispered, torn between her dying friend and John seeming to walk deliberately toward his end. Amana's eyes found hers and she could see his consciousness fading. "Sorry, lioness. He wanted me to keep you safe." She smiled sadly at the pet name, Amana one of the few who could call her that.

"I know," Kelsey choked out, gently lowering Amana to the ground. His eyes fluttered, struggling to stay focused on her face. "Save your strength."

But there was no saving him now—they both knew it. His massive chest heaved with the effort of each breath, the front of his shirt now a dark crimson canvas. He sat against the upturned troopie, his head lolling to the side as he looked through the guardhouse doorway at Sefu's body. "It was enough to have stood with friends." He whispered, before his grip finally went slack.

"Stay with me," Kelsey whispered, but his eyes had already gone glassy, staring past her toward some distant horizon only he could see.

Her fingers trembled as she gently closed his eyelids before resting her forehead against his. The space of a heartbeat was all she allowed herself for grief before snatched up her weapon and scrambling to her feet.

The world narrowed to a tunnel of sound and fury as she searched for John. Gunfire erupted ahead—the unmistakable heavy chatter of the PK machine gun interspersed with shouts and screams. She pushed herself harder, lungs burning, legs pumping.

When she cleared the corner of the guardhouse, the scene before her froze her blood. John moved like an invincible juggernaut, firing methodically at any rebel who appeared in his path. Not running, not hiding—just walking forward as if death couldn't touch him. As if he didn't care if it did.

The machine gun bucked in his hands as he walked across the open field, and Kelsey could see rebels scrambling to reposition themselves. John didn't take cover—he stood in the open, methodically firing at the reserve group surrounding Lord.

Bodies dropped before him like wheat before a scythe.

He's lost his fucking mind! Kelsey thought as she levelled her own rifle at the group.

"Lord!" John's voice carried above the din. "Come finish what you started, coward!"

A bullet caught John in the shoulder, spinning him slightly, but he kept walking. Another passed through his thigh. Still, he pressed forward, mechanical and relentless. Kelsey realised with growing horror that he wasn't trying to survive this—he was trying to end it. Then, as it happened, she understood exactly what he had planned. The group attacking the B side stopped and turned, reacting to the threat against their leader. The remnants of the group which attacked the D side did the same; and in their haste the three disorganised groups converged on John, who was still walking toward Lord.

A chorus of panicked shouts erupted as friendly fire tore through the rebel ranks. John's gambit had worked—he'd created chaos in their formation, turning their numbers against them. Blood sprayed as misaimed shots found unintended targets, rebels dropping to friendly bullets in the confusion.

Lord screamed commands that went unheeded in the mayhem. His men, caught in their own crossfire, couldn't coordinate. John kept walking, the machine gun barking in controlled bursts, his body a silhouette of cold determination even as another bullet found its mark in his back, knocking him forward. His shirt darkened with spreading crimson, still he walked.

He's going to get himself killed! Kelsey looked around at the rangers who had ceased firing now. "ON ME!" She raised her rifle, and twenty-three more joined hers.

John was a hundred odd meters away and surrounded by enemy. "I am so, so sorry," Kelsey cried as she fired, every man able to fight joining her. The concentrated fire devastated the disorganised group. With cohesion entirely lost, Lords forces broke and ran.

Kelsey watched as the rebels scattered, fleeing into the brush, she could make out John's silhouette still standing amid the carnage, a solitary figure surrounded by the dead. Even from this distance, she could see his shoulders heaving with laboured breath, the machine gun finally slipping from his grasp, John fell to his knees. Kelsey was already running before his knees hit the ground, her boots pounding against the hard-packed earth as she sprinted toward John leaving her empty rifle behind her. She could hear the rangers shouting orders, securing the perimeter, but their voices seemed distant and muffled.

Leaving her now empty useless rifle she broke into a sprint toward the gates, boots slipping in mud turned crimson. The stench of cordite and copper filled her nostrils as she navigated the battlefield. Bodies lay contorted in death, some rebels, some friends—all reduced to the same quiet stillness. The world narrowed only to this, this maddening dash to her friend, her brother. She ran as if racing time itself, as if she were running against death, straining to reach John before it did.

One hundred meters. A tall man, well dressed in quasi-military clothing had stopped his retreat and was now stalking toward John's kneeling form, a chrome plated pistol in one hand, machete in the other. *Lord himself.*

He was only twenty metres from John, Kelsey still ninety. Her Sig Sauer begged to be drawn, *too far for a clean shot.* "JOHN!"

Her warning echoed across the killing field, but John didn't move, still kneeling, head bowed, like a sinner awaiting judgement. With horror Kelsey realised that was exactly what this was. Her lungs burned as she pushed harder, her boots finding purchase on the blood-slicked earth.

Sixty metres. Fifty.

On the other side of John twenty metres became fifteen as Lord stalked toward the downed prey.

"JOHN!" she shouted again as Lord reached him, levelling the pistol at John's forehead. Kelsey could see Lord's mouth moving, but didn't hear the words.

Thirty metres, *too far but it's now or never.* Her hand flew to her thigh holster, fingers closing around her sidearm. Withdrawing it with muscle memory trained into her since childhood as she ran.

And then the strangest thing happened, Lord hesitated… It was though he couldn't decide who to kill first. Execute John and then turn his attention to Kelsey? Or kill John's would be rescuer as one final wound before dealing with the upstart who had broken his forces?

Lord's smile was predatory as he swivelled back toward John, confident in his advantage. "Watch her die first," he snarled, raising his weapon toward Kelsey.

Twenty-five meters—too far for reliable pistol accuracy with her hands shaking from exertion and fear- Kelsey squeezed her trigger first.

The shot cracked across the battlefield, barely missing Lord as he jerked sideways, returning fire. His bullet whined past her ear, wide but not by much. Still Kelsey closed the distance.

Twenty meters apart, Kelsey and Lord levelled weapons at each other.

A single boom echoed across the field.

Lord staggered backward, the chrome pistol tumbling from his grasp. Blood blossomed across his chest as he looked down in stunned disbelief. John's arm was extended, his revolver—which Kelsey hadn't even seen him draw—smoking in his unsteady hand.

"You can't. Have. Her" John whispered, his voice barely audible as Lord collapsed to his knees, mirroring John's own posture. "You…" Lord gurgled, blood bubbling at the corner of his mouth as he tried to raise his machete. Kelsey fired rapidly as she closed the remaining distance at a crouched run, not stopping until her magazine ran empty. She was beside John in seconds, sliding to her knees as he slumped forward. She caught him before he hit the ground, cradling his body against hers. Blood soaked through her clothes where they pressed together.

"Knew it was you… When he turned his head, knew it was you who'd come."

Kelsey dropped to her knees beside him, her hands hovering uncertainly over his wounds. Blood pulsed through his fingers where he clutched his side, and she could see the exit wound in his shoulder had torn through muscle and sinew. "Of course I came, you stupid bastard," she whispered, pressing her hands against the worst of the bleeding. "You absolute fucking idiot, what were you thinking?"

"Had to end it." John's voice was barely audible, each word a struggle. "Couldn't let him… couldn't let you…"

***

Kelsey- Present day.

Kelsey's voice broke as she finished the story. "John's armour took the worst of it, but he did have a through-and-through wound in his shoulder and another in his leg, so he'd still lost a lot of blood. We got Amana and a few others to the hospital in Juba. The camp closed a few days later. Most of the other rangers were transferred to other reserves. Amy came to his hospital bed, ripped into him, announced her intention to divorce and left. A week later he walked out and took the first contract offered him. Eighteen months later, he came here."

Nikita sat frozen, her hand pressed to her mouth. "He could have died."

"Think that was the point, sweetie," Kelsey said quietly. "I've never seen anyone like that—like he'd already died inside, and his body just hadn't caught up yet." She shook herself slightly. "He didn't talk for weeks after. When he did, he was… different. Like something fundamental had broken inside him. I begged him to come with me you know, several times. But it was like he wasn't in there anymore."

"Do you blame him? For those kids I mean. Do you think he was wrong?"

Kelsey frowned, "How can I? I was at the same battle, do you think those four were the only children in Lord's army?"

Nikita turned sorrowful eyes on her friend as she realised what Kelsey was saying.

"My heart aches for them, they shouldn't have been there. We buried twelve of our own and close to two hundred of theirs. Probably half should have been at school. But I wasn't so different once. Where, and with whom, I grew up — my father taught me how to use a rifle and what it was to hate. The children two kilometres away on the other side of the border were taught by their fathers how to set bombs and what it was to hate. I had my first kill before I had my first kiss.

So yeah, I hurt for those children. But make no mistake they were soldiers, just as I was at that age. That situation was only going to end in blood; either John and Amy's, or theirs," Kelsey explained. Her expression was sombre and quiet.

"At least you two got Lord."

Kelsey shook her head, "His cousin unfortunately. We'd never seen Lord before, so we assumed at the time. Lord was further east with the rest of his forces, apparently didn't think the camp was problem enough to warrant his presence. He's got a good reward out for John and I though, we can never go back."

The lady doing Nikita's hair spoke some in Russian, her tone factual. Nikita laughed, blinking away the tears that had welled in her eyes during the conversation.

"What did she say?" Kelsey bristled.

"She said I have to stop my crying before they do my make up or I'll ruin it."

26

Chapter Twenty-Six: I'm beautiful

Kelsey-

An hour later they were back at the apartment; John was already gone. "Sit here and close your eyes," Kelsey instructed and checked that Nikita's eyes were closed before laying out a gorgeous red dress on her bed. The dress she'd organised on John's behalf while he was at the tailor. She fetched another glass of champagne, placing it on the small table beside Nikita. Although Nikita didn't know it yet, this was a very special night for her.

"Okay, open."

"Oh, he didn't!?" Nikita whispered in disbelief as she rose from her seat. "The dress from the shop across from our café? It's gorgeous, but I cannot wear it…. he knows I can't." The last part added sadly.

"He did say something about that." Kelsey explained. "Apparently there's two parts to it. The dress is the first bit, once the whole thing is on your concerns should be accounted for, whatever the fuck that means." She exited the room so Nikita could get changed in privacy.

Kelsey returned a few minutes later, another bag in hand to find Nikita standing with her back to Kelsey, looking at herself in the mirror, tears welling in her eyes. As she approached, Kelsey could see the now exposed scars on Nikita's back and arms.

Kelsey's breath turned to ash in her mouth as she took in the sight of Nikita's markings. *Christ almighty, what did they do to her?* John had told her about them of course, but it was different seeing this brutal, everlasting reminder of the pain her friend had endured, carved into her skin. For a moment, silence hung between them. Kelsey understanding more now what was driving John's single-minded plans.

"Nikita," Kelsey said softly, her usual sharp tone replaced by gentle concern. "You look beautiful."

Nikita turned, "It's gorgeous, but… I cannot go out like this." she sobbed. "Everyone will see."

Kelsey stepped forward, placing a reassuring hand on Nikita's shoulder. "Stop crying. You're going to ruin your makeup." She gently dabbed away the tears as they formed, careful not to compromise the stylist's earlier work. "We're not done yet. I've got the second piece here," she said, holding up the bag she'd brought. "John thought of everything. He called it a shawl. I'm not sure what it is, but shawl is the wrong term."

From the bag, Kelsey produced a delicate red lace overlay that matched the dress perfectly. With careful movements, she draped it around her friend, attaching it to the dress in various places. It covered part of her chest and her back meeting around her neck, elegant patterns trailed down each arm anchored to her hands by small loops on each ring finger.

Nikita looked at herself in the mirror and spun around trying to see her back. She looked at Kelsey, "I'm beautiful," she said simply, her voice barely audible.

Kelsey's eyes softened as she watched Nikita's transformation, not just in appearance, but in spirit. "You've always been beautiful," she said, her own voice catching. "Now you see yourself as we see you."

Kelsey watched as Nikita turned back to the mirror. The shawl was perfect, covering her scars while seamlessly blending with the dress. It was as if John had known exactly what his woman needed to feel beautiful. *She is his, whether he wants to say it or not.* Nikita's fingers traced the intricate lace patterns, her eyes still wide with wonder. "I never thought… I mean, I always tried to hide them."

"Well, not anymore," Kelsey declared, her usual bravado returning. "Tonight, you're going to walk into that museum like you own the fucking place. And when John sees you? He's going to forget how to breathe."

A small, shy smile tugged at Nikita's lips. "You think so?"

"I know so," Kelsey affirmed, giving Nikita's shoulder a squeeze. "Now, let's finish getting you ready."

A comfortable silence fell between them as Kelsey helped Nikita with the final touches – a pair of elegant heels and a small clutch purse. As Nikita slipped into her heels both she and Kelsey started at the burn scars on her feet. "Do you think people will notice?" she asked. Kelsey heard it in her voice, her spirit wavering. Like she had felt so beautiful not two minutes ago, yet here she was reminded again of what she was. "Step out of them for a second," Kelsey said. "I've got an idea." She rummaged into her bag, bringing out her own make up kit.

Kelsey knelt, carefully applying concealer and powder to Nikita's feet. Her touch was gentle, almost reverent, as she worked to blend the makeup seamlessly over the scars — the last visible remnant of the life Nikita had endured. It was one Kelsey knew she would leave behind for good by the end of tonight, even if Nikita didn't yet know it herself.

The small woman had been good for her old friend, reaching him in his depths in a way Kelsey had not been able to. She had rapidly warmed to Nikita and was proud to be a part of tonight.

"There," Kelsey said, sitting back on her heels to admire her handiwork. "Now no one will notice unless they're staring directly at your feet all night, which would be weird and creepy."

Nikita slipped the heels back on, twisting her ankle to examine Kelsey's work. "Thank you," she whispered, her voice thick with emotion.

Kelsey stood, brushing off her knees. "Don't mention it. That's what friends are for, right?"

For a moment, they stood in silence. Then Kelsey cleared her throat, her normal abrupt mannerisms returning. "Alright, enough of this, we need to get you to the Hermitage before John thinks you stood him up. He's going to stick out like a sore thumb there." She laughed.

Nikita's eyes welled up again, the emotions of the evening threatening to overwhelm her once more. "You have GOT to stop that" Kelsey chided, fetching tissues again.

They made their way down to the waiting car, "Remember," Kelsey said, as she held open the door, "you belong there just as much as anyone else."

Nikita nodded, her fingers nervously twisting the delicate lace of her shawl. "I just hope I don't embarrass John. Or myself."

Kelsey snorted. "Trust me, the only one at risk of embarrassing himself is our dear Mr. Wilson. I'd pay good money to see him try to make small talk with the president." Kelsey opened the door for her friend as she entered the car. "I'll see you later," she said. "Remind John to breathe when he sees you."

"Thank you for everything," Nikita replied for possibly the twentieth time that evening.

"Thank you, Nikita, for everything."

Kelsey closed the door.

27

Chapter Twenty-Seven: Eighty-Seven

John-Two hours earlier.

John waited. His elbows resting on his knees, waiting for De Smet to bring the final piece of the puzzle. Kelsey was taking Nikita to get her hair and makeup done, then help her get ready for the Hermitage. He looked over to where he had hung his suit bag, with the shoes in a box underneath. Two very different spheres of the night, each equally necessary, and equally dangerous.

"Thank you for meeting me," John heard De Smet's voice. "I thought here would be the most convenient."

"It does let us talk in private" Aleski's voice replied, "But this needs to be short. I am a busy man."

It will be short, John thought to himself. *I don't have the time for you.*

De Smet and Aleski stopped by the back of house area of the chimpanzee exhibit. No cameras, just as Jean-Paul and John had planned. "What was so important you needed to come speak to me right away?" Aleski asked.

"I think you know what," John stepped out of the darkness.

Aleski's eyes narrowed in recognition. "Wilson," Aleski spat, his face betraying his anger. "What is the meaning of this?"

De Smet stepped back, his role in organising this confrontation complete. John's gaze never wavered from Aleski, his lips curled into a humourless smile almost baring his teeth like a feral animal as he said one word. "Nikita."

At the mention of her name, Aleski's face contorted with rage. "That little bi-"

"Choose your next words carefully," John seethed as the flame took hold.

"You think you can threaten me?" Aleski snarled, "Do you have any idea who I am, what I'm capable of?"

John's eyes bore into his target, his voice low and dangerous. "I saw exactly what you're capable of. That's why I'm here." The fire spread, the familiar heat radiating through his body.

De Smet shifted nervously, glancing between the two men. John shot him a warning look, and he retreated further, melting into the shadows.

"You're a coward who preys on people unable to fight back. A monster who thinks he's untouchable." John continued, his words dripping with contempt. "I saw the video. I saw WHAT YOU DID TO HER!" His rage threatened to boil over. This wasn't a fact-finding mission. He had all the information, this was solely about retribution. Aleski took a step forward, closing the distance between them. The air crackled with tension, both men coiled tight like springs ready to snap.

"You would judge me, Wilson?" The massive man growled. "A child killer would sit in judgement of me over some whore? Do not pretend you are some noble hero." He spat on the ground. "What do I care? Have the bitch… what's left of her."

The fire took over completely. John lunged at the curator. His fists rained down on the larger man's face, each impact fuelled with pent-up rage and guilt. Aleski fought back, landing a few solid hits of his own to his ribs, but John was relentless. This was not the same man who had struggled with Nikolai.

Aleski laughed, a wet, gurgling sound through the blood in his mouth. "Hit a nerve, did I? Face it, Wilson. You're just a broken man playing hero." He shoved the furious Australian away. "You're lucky Jean-Paul needs you for whatever reason. Otherwise, I'd make you watch while we played with her. Make whatever you saw seem like a day at the spa, then make her watch as we killed you."

John circled to his right. Aleski's arrogance was suffocating. *Guess that's what comes with being so untouchable for so long,* John reasoned. De Smet hung in the background, by a door, right where he needed to be. The Russian's voice went on again, self-assured that he had the upper hand. "As you are important to his plans, and he's paying me handsomely for it. I'll make her a gift, transfer her ownership to you. To solidify our partnership. All you have to do is say please." He held out his hand as if to make a deal.

John hesitated, for a second confused by this turn of events. Technically he could gain everything he was after by accepting this offer. It wouldn't fill his need for vengeance, but he could swallow his pride for Nikita's sake. Then he remembered. Remembered what he saw Aleski do to her. What he allowed to be done while he taunted and beat her. Remembered what he said to her… He looked up at the big man's eyes and understood. Aleski, John realised, was all about control. He got off on it, that's why he made Nikita beg. Why he wanted John to beg. If it was control he was after, John Wilson was the wrong mark.

He walked toward the big Russian, holding out his own hand. But at the last second he lunged forward with his right foot, firing a savage overhand left at the taller man with all his force. The blow caught Aleski on the chin, perfectly showing why that punch was favoured by shorter fighters against the tall. Aleski's head snapped back, his massive frame crumpling to the ground. John stood over him, chest heaving, fists clenched. The Russian's eyes were glassy, unfocused, but he was still conscious.

"You don't get to decide her fate anymore, you don't get to play games, you don't get to make deals," John growled. He reached down, grabbing Aleski by the collar of his expensive shirt, and hauled him to his feet. The larger man swayed, unsteady, but his eyes blazed with fury.

"You've made a grave mistake, Wilson," Aleski slurred, blood and spittle flying from his lips. "I'll destroy everything you care about. I'll-"

John cut him off, driving a vicious knee to the gut. Aleski doubled over, gasping for air.

"You'll do fucking nothing." John's right elbow crashed sickeningly into his target's face. "This ends here. YOU. End. Here."

"Wait," the battered man gurgled. "We can sort this out. Why should men like us fight and kill each other?"

"Men like us?" John laughed. "There are no men like us. You're a monster. A parasite feeding on the innocent."

Aleski managed a weak laugh, wincing as he wiped blood from his split lip. "Don't be naive, Wilson. We are cut from the same cloth, you and I. We both know what it takes to survive in this world. To take what we want." John's eyes narrowed as he took another step closer, his eyes burning with barely contained rage. "And what is it that I want?"

"What anyone wants. More," the Russian laughed. "Everyone wants the same thing. More."

"And you can give me that? More?"

"Well Nikita, obviously. A better apartment, and part ownership of a club I own. The Red Dragon. My previous partner passed not long ago."

John straightened slowly, considering the offer before tentatively offering his hand. Aleski extended his own hand, grasping John's. They shook. Up, down before John locked eyes with Nikita's tormentor, pulling Aleski toward him suddenly. The massive man instinctively pulled back. It was a mistake. John went with the momentum, folding Aleski's right arm in a figure four lock and wrenching it violently. John put his shoulder to the big man and pushed for all his worth.

By the door, De Smet had been waiting for this exact moment. He swung it open now just in time for John to give Aleski one final shove, sending him sprawling through the doorway before he slammed the door shut again. The bear of a man rose to his feet, furious. "What are you doing!?" he demanded. But John was past listening to demands. He locked eyes with his target now, his hand resting on a red lever, echoing the words he heard that fateful night at Nikita's apartment.

"All you have to do to end it, is say stop." John pulled the lever. Allowing Hondo, and four other chimpanzees into the back of house area. As De Smet and John left, careful to avoid any cameras showing they were there, Aleski's screams filled the air rising ever higher, before eerily falling silent.

"I'll drop you at the hotel to get ready," Jean-Paul said as they walked. "Although, and it's not my place to say, I do not understand why you don't intend to spend the night there."

"My payment is my own, leave it at that," John replied curtly.

De Smet spread his hands in a placating gesture, "I'll say no more. I've done my part tonight; it's your turn now."

John's night he knew, was not about to be any less complicated.

28

Chapter Twenty-Eight: Hermitage

Nikita-

The thought of John, surrounded and trying to make small talk with Russian politicians and autocracy brought a smile to Nikita's face during the ride, easing some of her tension. As the car pulled up to the museum, the grandeur of the building took her by surprise. A man opened the car door and offered his hand, assisting her from the vehicle. "Down the red carpet, the floor is straight ahead. One is free to take in the art in the west wing before dinner at eight pm. Unfortunately, the rest of the Hermitage is closed for this event." *There must be enough internationals that the greeters are speaking English.* She smiled her thanks and walked straight ahead, trying to look like she belonged there. *John would be at the floor* she thought, *they served drinks there and he'd surely be needing one.*

Nikita's heels clicked against the polished marble as she entered the grand foyer of the Hermitage. Artwork hundreds of years old sat on her left and right. The opulence of the surroundings threatened to overwhelm her, but she took a deep breath, remembering Kelsey's words. She belonged here.

She arrived at the top of an elegant staircase, a red carpet flowing down its centre, bracketed by carved and polished wooden bannisters that were artwork in their own right. Scanning the crowd, she searched for John's familiar figure. Her eyes swept past glittering gowns and crisp tuxedos, the chatter filling the air.

Then, she saw him.

He stood alone yet surrounded, his back to one of the ornate pillars, looking uncomfortable in a handsome black suit she didn't know he owned. His broad shoulders were tense, and he was clutching a spirit filled glass as though to lose it would be the death of him. Surrounding him in a semi-circle, several men and a woman attempted to converse with the obviously out of place Australian. He looked to her as a cornered bear, it's back to a wall, holding dogs at bay. She smiled to herself thinking that *he would probably prefer facing a hundred men then being here tonight.*

As if sensing her presence, John's gaze turned to the top of the stairs and Nikita saw the exact moment he recognised her. *Did his jaw actually drop?*

Kelsey had insured that Nikita was a vision in her elegant gown, her golden hair swept up in an intricate style; every woman in the building a crude imitation compared to her.

The woman who was a part of the group speaking to John followed his eyes, searching for what had stolen his attention. The man next to her did the same, one by one the whole room turned, eager to see what was going on. Until, slowly, the entire room was staring at Nikita as though she were the only woman in the whole world. If a pin dropped on the marble floor the entire room would hear it, she felt as though her heart would explode.

John silently gave his glass to the man beside him without even looking at him. His eyes never left Nikita as he strode purposefully across the room. The crowd parted before him, whispers and curious glances following in his wake. As he reached the bottom of the staircase, he paused, looking up at her with an intensity that made her breath catch.

As John approached, Nikita felt her heart racing. The room seemed to fade away, leaving only the two of them. His eyes were still on hers as he ascended the stairs, his movements purposeful and determined. When he reached a step below her, he paused, drinking in the sight of her.

"Nikita," he breathed, his voice low and filled with awe. "You look... I don't have words. I've never seen anyone, anything, so beautiful in my life."

"Breathe, John" she smiled softly, feeling a blush creep up her cheeks. Most men, Nikita had noticed, were wearing black tie in keeping with the invitation. John, however, was adorned in a black suit with white shirt, and a red tie and pocket square that matched Nikita's dress, invitation be damned. To her, her savage protector had never looked so handsome.

John offered his arm, and Nikita placed her hand in the crook of his elbow. As they descended the stairs together, the crowd's attention remained fixed on them. Whispers rippled through the room, but Nikita barely noticed. She was too focused on the warmth of John's arm beneath her fingers, the slight tremor she could feel running through his body. She glanced at him once more, knowing if he looked at her like that again, she would forever be his slave.

He glanced back and smiled. *John, smiling. Wonders never cease.*

As they reached the bottom of the stairs, he leaned in close, his breath warm against her ear. "I don't know how I'm going to make it through tonight," he murmured, "Every man in here wishes he were me, with you on their arm."

"None of them are knee high to you," she whispered in his ear, feeling a thrill run through her at their closeness. The crowd began to disperse, returning to their conversations, but their eyes kept darting back to the striking couple. John led Nikita toward the bar, his hand now resting protectively on the small of her back.

As they approached the bar, John's muscles tensed. She knew that the opulent ballroom, with its crystal chandeliers and polished marble floors, was a far cry from the rugged terrains he was accustomed to. He scanned the crowd, old habits refusing to die, looking for potential threats.

Nikita sensed his unease and squeezed his arm gently. "Relax, John," she murmured. "We're safe here."

He nodded, forcing himself to loosen his grip on her waist. "Sorry, force of habit," he replied, his voice gruff.

As Nikita ordered a glass of champagne for herself and bourbon for John.

"We've an hour until the dinner; there's over 300,000 pieces of art in this wing alone. Shall we get out of here for a bit?" she whispered to him. It was the best idea he had heard in days.

They wandered the halls alone. The west wing held mainly sculptures and Nikita was interested to see them. John was intrigued by each one. When she inquired, he explained. "I admire artists. My talents lie in destruction, not creation. My hands can't paint; I can't carve a sculpture. This is entirely foreign and out of reach for me and because of that I guess I find it even more beautiful."

Nikita's heart swelled with a mixture of sadness and affection at John's words. She reached out, gently taking his rough, calloused hand in hers. As they walked the halls, she wished this night, this walk, would never end.

***

John-

Forty-five minutes later they walked arm in arm into the dining hall, its grandeur befitting that of a state dinner with the president of Russia in attendance. The pair had never seen such extravagance in table settings or atmosphere. As they entered the room, John felt Nikita's grip on his arm tighten ever so slightly. He glanced down at her, concern etching his features.

"You alright?" he asked softly, his voice barely audible above the low hum of conversation filling the room.

Nikita nodded, a small smile playing on her lips. "Just… overwhelmed," she admitted. "I've never seen anything like this before."

John understood. The grandiose setting was a far cry from the life they both knew. Crystal chandeliers hung from ornate ceilings, casting a warm glow over tables adorned with fine China and gleaming silverware. Elaborate floral centrepieces perfumed the air, their delicate scent mingling with the aroma of gourmet dishes being prepared in the nearby kitchens.

As they made their way to their assigned table, John felt eyes following them. He resisted the urge to look over his shoulder, instead focusing on guiding Nikita through the crowd with a gentle hand at the small of her back.

They found their seats at a table near the centre, and John pulled out Nikita's chair for her, a gesture that didn't go unnoticed by the other guests already seated there.

As he took his own seat, he felt Nikita stiffen slightly beside him. He followed her gaze to a table near the centre of the room, where a group of well-dressed men were engaged in animated conversation. One of them, a silver-haired gentleman with a practiced smile, looked up and locked eyes with Nikita and then looked at John.

"Nikita," he murmured, his voice barely audible above the din of the crowd. "Do you know him?"

She nodded almost imperceptibly, her face a mask of carefully controlled emotion. "Know of him. That's Viktor Petrov, the President of Russia," she whispered back.

"Whatever happens when we have this conversation, go with it.

Show no emotion or surprise." He looked at her, willing her to understand the importance of their upcoming meeting. "Understand?"

"I understand. I'll translate, nothing more."

A waiter approached, pouring champagne into their flutes with practiced precision. Nikita made small talk with the couple seated across from them—a German diplomat and his wife.

The first course arrived, an artful arrangement of caviar and crème fraîche. John barely tasted it, his movements mechanical as he ate. His thoughts focused on what he would say to the President. How he would convince the man. He would have liked to have focused solely on that and not the people at his table. But he knew better, in this world John was a bit of a novelty. And he knew it was important that he was a novelty that was liked.

The meal progressed through four more courses, each more elaborate than the last. Conversation flowed around them—politics, art, the usual topics of the elite and Nikita gradually pulled John into the conversation at the table, translating when necessary as he regaled them with stories; showing off scars left by a leopard, explaining how poachers pick a spot to place a snare, showing photos on his phone of elephants wading through the river, or discussing which are the prettiest birds in the Okavango. The German diplomat's wife was something of an amateur ornithologist, so that was a big hit with her. Shortly after dessert arrived a man slightly taller than John, but not as solidly built approached the table. He wore an earpiece and John reasoned he must be part of the President's security detail. He leaned down and spoke quietly to Nikita who translated to John.

"President Petrov invites you to take a brandy and a cigar with him after the dinner."

"Tell the President I look forward to it," came John's reply.

Following dessert, they bade farewell to the company at their table. Nikita held the contact information for several of the members. She wondered if they would be invited to future dinners, as they seemed quite taken with her and John. John caught the eye of the security member who had come to their table, asking a question with his eyebrows. "Where?" To which the security member nodded through a curtained doorway.

John placed his hand on the small of Nikita's back, guiding her toward the indicated doorway. He could feel the slight tremble in her body beneath the silk of her gown—imperceptible to anyone else, but clear as day to him. He leaned close to her ear.

"You alright?" he whispered.

"Yes," she replied, her voice steady despite her nerves. "Let's get this done."

Funny, John thought, *she didn't even know what 'this' was.*

29

Chapter Twenty-Nine: The Conversation

Nikita-

The security detail led them through the curtained doorway into an intimate space. Dark wood panelling lined the walls, and leather armchairs were arranged around low tables. The scent of aged tobacco and expensive brandy hung in the air. Through wide French doors, a balcony overlooked the Neva River, its waters glittering under the night sky.

President Petrov sat in a corner booth, two security personnel standing at a discreet distance. When he spotted them, he rose with practiced grace, his silver hair catching the light.

"Mr. Wilson," he said in accented English, extending his hand. "I've heard much about you. Please, join me."

John's grip was firm as he shook the President's hand, his face a friendly mask. "Mr. President. Thank you for the invitation. May I introduce my assistant, Nikita."

Petrov's eyes lingered on Nikita a moment too long before he nodded cordially. "Of course. Please, both of you, sit."

The three of them settled into the leather chairs and a waiter appeared with a crystal decanter of deep purple liquid and a pair of balloon glasses. Another followed with a selection of cigars. Nikita noted how the President dismissed his security detail with a subtle gesture, sending them to stand by the doors. *He clearly wants some privacy for this conversation.*

"You've caused quite a stir tonight, Mr. Wilson," Petrov said as he selected a cigar, a Cohiba, examining it with practiced appreciation. "An Australian conservationist with the most beautiful woman in the room. People are curious." Nikita watched as John also selected a cigar, Montecristo No. 2, and utilised the cigar cutter to neatly cut the cap off. "It's just John. I get the impression most of our table led more corporate lifestyles. Some of my stories got so much of a reaction I was afraid to tell any of the good ones."

Petrov chuckled. "I understand entirely. I did a bit of work in Africa too, as a younger man. This is going back to the '80's." John didn't seem to need any explanation as to what kind of work Petrov did and kept his mouth shut, preferring to seem preoccupied with lighting his cigar.

"Yes," Petrov went on, "the people there are crazy of course. But the wildlife..." he spread is hands, palms upward, "it's something else."

"Nothing like it," John offered, ignoring the comment about the people. "It's hard to describe to others what it's like to be patrolling on foot only to accidentally come across a bull elephant in musth. You think, how could you not see something so big?"

Petrov laughed, a genuine sound that seemed to momentarily strip away the layers of power and politics. "Yes! Exactly this! I was once tracking a herd of buffalo with a guide when we came upon a pride of lions. Just like that—" he snapped his fingers, "—out of nowhere. I still remember the way my heart stopped." John nodded, drawing deeply on his cigar. Nikita sat beside him. She hadn't yet been required to translate but remained alert to every nuance of the conversation. *Who knew the President spoke such good English?*

"It's humbling," John said finally. "Reminds you that we're not always at the top of the food chain."

"A valuable lesson for any man," Petrov agreed, swirling his brandy. His eyes, calculating and sharp, studied John over the rim of his glass.

"Which brings me to why I wanted to speak with you." Petrov leaned forward slightly, his voice dropping. "Your work in Africa was impressive. Your... military background even more so. And now you're here in St. Petersburg. A man with your particular skills doesn't simply retire to Russia for the architecture." The President waved his arm around the room as he said the last sentence. "Tell me, what really brings you to St. Petersburg, John?"

John's face remained impassive as he took another draw from his cigar, as if buying himself a moment to consider his response. The smoke curled lazily upward in the dim light of the private room. "You know, I think because of the life I lead people assume there's more to it than what there is. I had a job go south, in Sudan. proper south" John added with an inflection. "I'm not retiring here, just taking a step away for a while. When the chance came up to be a part of the expansion and show off African wildlife for a bit, I though why not?"

Oddly the explanation seemed to satisfy the President. "Even the best soldiers can use a step away from time to time," he said. The two men traded a few more stories of their time in Africa. Nikita sat almost dead still, her posture perfect, her mask firmly in place even though inwardly her mind and heart raced; each of her organs competing with the other for speed.

"I'm glad a man like you is onsite to help the zoo. I've long thought the expansion overdue. Tell me, do you think this new Africa wing will help put Leningradskiy back on the map?" Petrov asked.

John's eyes flicked to Petrov. "Funnily enough, yes. I can make it the envy of every zoo in Europe. But I'd need some favours."

Oh.... fuck Nikita thought to herself. *He did not just ask for a favour from the President of Russia?*

Petrov's eyebrows rose slightly, the only indication of his surprise. "Favours? From the President of Russia? You are either very brave or very foolish." His tone was amused rather than offended.

John held the man's gaze steadily but let out a small chuckle. "From the stories we've been sharing you already know I'm both." he admitted with a bit humour, tapping his cigar gently against the crystal ashtray. John drew from it again, the ember glowing bright in the dimly lit room. "The zoo has a chance to be something special, not just for St. Petersburg but internationally. To do that, we need certain animals—rare specimens that are difficult to acquire through normal channels."

"Go on," Petrov said, his interest clearly piqued.

"I can give the zoo a species no other zoo in the world has. That would certainly put it on the map, internationally." John offered. "Acquiring the animals is straightforward enough. What I need is a pair of doors opened back here."

Are you crazy? He's so casual. He had a harder time learning how to order coffee in Russian.

"Hypothetically, if we were having this conversation, what is the species and what doors would need to be opened?" Petrov asked.

"Mountain gorillas from the heart of Africa. No zoo has them, anywhere. Not only would Leningradskiy have something no one else has; but it would be the right thing to do."

"Mountain gorillas?" Petrov repeated, his eyes narrowing slightly. "They're critically endangered. Protected by international law."

"Yes, and we need to be the ones doing the protecting."

"Neither Uganda nor Rwanda would ever give them up."

"Agreed. Which is why they aren't coming from Uganda or Rwanda." John glanced at the security detail. "I can speak plainly in front of them?"

"What they've heard would make even your skin crawl, John."

"Right," he took a long draw of his cigar. "So here it is. Uganda and Rwanda have good solid protections. Stable governments. Good national parks and what have you. No gorilla's from them. The neighbouring Democratic republic of Congo however, is very different ball game. The civil unrest gets worse day by day and rebel groups grow stronger. There will be war soon. The current population of gorilla has been hit very hard and best estimates sit around thirty members, total. With open war coming it is thought they will be wiped out. The people who devote their life to protecting them have two options. Let them go extinct on their watch or do something crazy. They've reached out to me to see if I'm able to assist in doing something crazy."

Petrov's expression remained unreadable as he swirled the brandy in his glass. "So, you propose to smuggle endangered mountain gorillas out of a war zone and into my country against international conservation laws?"

"I propose to save a species from extinction," John countered. "And yes, make the Leningradskiy Zoo famous in the process."

Nikita felt her heart hammering against her ribs as she watched the exchange. The sheer audacity of John's plan was breathtaking—and terrifying. *This must be what De Smet put him up to.* She maintained her composure, even as her mind raced through the implications.

"And what doors would Russia need to open for this... conservation effort? Hypothetically of course," Petrov asked, setting his glass down with deliberate care.

"Two doors. The first is appoint me as curator of Leningradskiy Zoo. The previous curator, Aleski Sokolov passed away unfortunately this evening. There was a workplace accident involving a chimpanzee. Leningradskiy is a government zoo and the department needs to ensure I am appointed as the successor. Both to increase safety procedures so something like that doesn't happen again, and to ensure everything at the zoo is ready to receive our new arrivals. The second, when the flight arrives with the cargo, it needs to pass inspection. The paperwork must be accepted and stamped."

Sokolov is dead? John wouldn't say that if it wasn't true. With a chill down her spine, she realised she knew somehow the accident was arranged by John. She wondered if that was the errand he had to run while she was getting her hair and makeup done.

Petrov leaned back in his chair, studying John with renewed interest. The silence stretched between them, filled only by the soft crackle of burning tobacco. Finally, the President's face broke into a smile, not a warm smile though.

"Mr. Wilson," he said, "you continue to surprise me. Most men who sit in that chair ask for money, for power, for influence. You ask to save gorillas and run a zoo." He tapped his cigar against the ashtray. "Curious priorities."

John held his gaze steadily. "My priorities have always been straightforward."

"Yes, I imagine they have." Petrov glanced at Nikita, who had maintained her perfect composure even as her mind screamed with questions, even as her heart raced in wild emotion realising that John might in fact have freed her, as he said he would. *The rules were different with John.*

"Your first request is simple enough." Petrov spoke. "A curator's position can be arranged. The second, I would need to know some more details."

"Fair enough. Hypothetically, the gorillas would be officially listed as deceased in Congo due to poaching. The paperwork would show they were killed—a tragedy but not uncommon. In a completely unrelated incident, a plane carrying Western lowland gorillas from the Republic of Congo will arrive here, with their paperwork."

"And these conservationists—they're willing to falsify records? To lie to their own governments?"

"They're willing to do whatever it takes, and they understand that sometimes to do the right thing you have to do some wrong things."

Petrov chuckled at John's words, a deep sound that resonated in the small room.

"A pragmatic philosophy," he said, raising his glass in a subtle toast. "I've always appreciated men who understand that particular truth." He set down his glass and leaned forward, his demeanour shifting to something more business-like. "Your plan is audacious, Mr. Wilson. Some might even call it foolish. But I find myself… intrigued."

John remained silent, waiting. Nikita knew he could feel her tension beside him, though she betrayed nothing outwardly. *I would call it foolish too. Are you insane?*

"I will need to know exactly when this flight would arrive, and what documentation to expect," Petrov continued. "These details would be necessary for any hypothetical arrangement."

"Of course," John nodded, carefully tapping ash from his cigar. Petrov motioned for one of his guards, who placed a small black card on the arm of Nikita's chair. Petrov stood, and John followed. "You'll have to excuse me. I'm a busy man. Have your assistant send the details as you know them. The doors will be open, walking through them will be up to you."

"Thank you, Mr. President."

"Mr. Wilson. If you pull this off, expect to hear from my office. A man of your talents will never be short of work."

John smiled and nodded before the guards ushered him and Nikita out.

30

Chapter Thirty: The non-gift

Nikita-

The hotel John had booked was walking distance from the Hermitage. Nikita's head was swimming with questions. *Aleski dead, John promoted to curator, smuggling gorillas.... what had De Smet put him up to?* The conversation with the president had been the wildest thing Nikita had ever heard. Yet John had barely blinked as they discussed every detail. He said he would tell her everything when they got to the hotel. "I'll answer every question you have, about anything you want to talk about. No secrets," were his words. Tonight was a whirlwind. Her elegant red dress and its lace overlay whipped around her as they walked briskly toward the hotel. Nikita felt as though John would burst with the energy she felt barely restrained within him. They entered the hotel lobby.

The radiant chandelier cast a warm glow over the marble floors as John and Nikita strode toward the elevators. John's jaw was clenched, his eyes darting around the lobby as if expecting danger to materialise at any moment. Nikita could feel the tension radiating off him, his hand firmly grasping hers as they walked.

Once inside the elevator, John let out a long breath, his shoulders sagging slightly. Nikita studied his face, noticing the deep creases around his eyes, the weariness etched into every line. As the elevator ascended, she squeezed his hand gently, a silent reassurance.

"John," she began, her voice barely above a whisper.

He turned to her, his eyes softening for a moment. "Not yet," he murmured, his voice gruff. "Soon."

The elevator dinged, and they stepped into the most gorgeous hotel room Nikita had ever seen, not that she had stayed in many. The room seemed to hold its breath as she entered, a luxurious haven of plush furnishings and glittering crystal. The walls were a warm cream, adorned with intricate gold trimmings that caught the light from the chandelier above. Nikita's eyes widened in awe as she took in the massive four-poster bed draped in silky red curtains, the marble fireplace, and the stunning view of the city skyline through floor-to-ceiling windows. This was a room of luxury, and she could feel her heart flutter at the thought of spending the night here with John.

She took off her heels, allowing her feet to sink into the plush carpet as she walked toward the bed. She ran her hand over the smooth, silky sheets, enjoying the softness against her fingertips. The curtains were a luxurious velvet material, and she couldn't resist reaching out to brush her hand against them.

There was a loud 'pop' behind her as John opened a bottle of champagne, pouring two glasses. The bubbles tickled Nikita's nose as he offered her a glass.

"My last gift of the night," John said with a smile. "I hope you like it."

Nikita took another sip, savouring the effervescence. "It's perfect," she murmured, her eyes meeting John's. "Everything has been perfect."

John placed his glass down and rushed to her as tears threatened to loose themselves from her eyes. His arms wrapped around her, making her feel as though she were being held for the first time. "It's all been for you, everything I've done," he whispered. "I will answer every single question you have, but I need you to answer one first. Do you trust me?"

Nikita's breath caught in her throat as she looked up into John's intense gaze. She searched his face, remembering all they had been through together, all the times he had protected her, bled for her, saved her from herself and lifted her up.

"Without question."

"Hand me your phone."

She did so, confused as to why, but she did just say she trusted him. Her heart dropped as he deftly navigated to the hidden folder on her phone where she kept pictures and recordings of her abuse. She didn't know he knew where it was. He looked her in the eye and deleted it before she could react.

Nikita gasped, her eyes widening in shock as she watched John delete the folder. For a moment, she felt a surge of panic and anger. Those images, those recordings - they were her proof, her evidence of the horrors she had endured. They reminded her of what she was. But as she looked into John's eyes, she saw something there that made her pause.

"Why?" she whispered, her voice trembling.

John took a deep breath, his hands gently cupping her face. "Because you don't need them anymore. You're not that person anymore, Nikita. You're stronger now, braver. Those memories... they were holding you back, keeping you tied to a past that does not define you."

Tears welled up in Nikita's eyes as she sat, letting his words sank in. She had clung to those painful reminders, believing they were necessary to validate her suffering. Reminders of her place in the world, with or without Sokolov.

It had been the perfect night, and he had ruined it, trying to tell her she wasn't what she was. Tears fell softly, silently. But John brushed them away and handed her a box, black with gold ribbon.

"I though you said you had given your final gift?" she asked through her crying.

"This is not a gift," he said softly as he crouched in front of her, looking into her eyes. "I cannot give you what is already rightfully yours. Open it."

She lifted the lid, and a frown came across her brow. Inside were some papers, and a smashed up hard drive. "I don't understand," she looked at John.

He looked at her with an intensity that made her heart stop. "I said I would free you. Did you not think I meant it? The papers? Coded invoices used to keep track of the sale of merchandise. In plain terms, this paper was your bill of sale. Burn it," he gestured at the fireplace. "The hard drive? Where the originals of your videos were kept. Kelsey and I stole it. The three men in the video I saw of you? Gone, forever. Not able to hurt you or anyone else again… De Smet is also leveraging you a passport. You are free Nikita, to go anywhere, be anyone, have a life, choices…" Tears fell from John now, and he stopped. Unable to force the words out anymore.

Nikita's hands trembled as she held the box, her mind reeling from John's words. She looked from the papers to the smashed hard drive, then back to John's tear-streaked face as he stared at the floor. The weight of her newfound freedom crashed over her like a tidal wave, overwhelming and terrifying in its vastness.

"I… I don't know what to say," she whispered, her voice barely audible. "What do I do?"

John reached out, taking her hands in his. "Whatever you want, go anywhere you want, make choices for yourself. You become whoever you want to be someplace far away, someplace no one knows who you are. Live."

Nikita stared at the contents of the box, her hands trembling as she picked up the papers, documents that had bound her to a life of exploitation and pain. With shaking fingers, she stood and walked to the fireplace, hesitating for just a moment before tossing the papers into the flames. She watched as they curled and blackened, years of torment reduced to ash.

She looked back at John. "I will answer any questions you have, ask whatever you want," he said.

"All that can wait," she said breathlessly. Her feelings threatened to overwhelm her entirely as she crossed the room toward him, crashing into his arms and kissing him deeply, passionately. Her first as a free woman, able to choose.

"Stop," he said as they broke apart. "You don't have to do that. I did not mean for you to be free from one man, only to feel bound to another. You owe me nothing." He moved further away from her. "The room is paid for two more nights. On the morning of checkout there will be a parcel at the front desk for you. Passport, credit cards, some cash. And you've got mine and Kelsey's numbers if you run into any trouble. You owe me nothing, go and live your life."

Nikita stepped forward, her eyes searching John's face. She saw the conflict there, the desire warring with some sense of duty and honour she did not quite understand. He wanted her, she knew he did, but would not allow himself to give in. Her heart swelled with a mixture of gratitude and frustration.

"John," she said softly, her hand resting on his chest. "You're not understanding. This isn't about owing you anything. This is about me making a choice. My choice."

She took a deep breath, steeling herself for what she was about to say. "For the first time in my life, I'm free to want something – someone – for myself. And I want you, John. Not because you saved me, not because I feel obligated, but because of who you are. I have a choice now, to be wherever and with whoever I want. And I chose to be wherever in the world you are. And I know you want me too."

She felt his his ragged breathing beneath her hand. "You've given me freedom, yes. But you've also shown me kindness, respect, and… love. I may be free to go anywhere, but there is nowhere for me to be where you are not there."

John's eyes softened, "Nikita, I… I'm not a good man."

"Stop," she commanded. "You said you'd answer any question. So, answer honestly. What do you feel for me?"

John's jaw clenched, his eyes darting away from Nikita's piercing gaze. The silence stretched between them, thick and charged. Finally, he let out a shaky breath, his shoulders sagging as if a great weight had settled upon them.

"I'm not a good man, and I would see you with a good man…or none at all."

"John," Nikita interrupted, her grip on his shirt tightening slightly. "You love me, don't you?"

***

John-

He paused, not knowing if he should say the words. If he did, she would almost certainly return them.

He glanced at her and, the words he said weeks ago echoed in his own head. *I am not a good man, but for you I would be the worst.* He knew, on that staircase tonight, what he had fought off acknowledging for so long. He loved her. Despite wanting her not to want him, not to choose him, he loved her. Everything he had done, everything he hated most about himself, every terrible dark deed. He would allow them to pale into the actions of a consecrated altar boy compared to what he would do should she be threatened again. She would, he knew, say she wanted to be wherever he was in the world. And that couldn't happen. Still, he had to go soon, and it seemed poorly to do all this only to lie now. She would know it was a lie too.

"John…" her voice prompted, as though she could almost see the

247

gears of his mind clicking and whirring with what to say. There was nothing for him to say but the truth.

"When I met you, those months ago at the office, I saw an exceptionally beautiful woman. As days turned to weeks and weeks turned to months, I was shown your kindness, your strength, your resilience, your intelligence and your goodness. These things won me over and I came to realise that your beauty truly was the least of your qualities. Everyone I know is brittle and broken, strong on the outside but underneath all of us are hate filled and resentful, bitter and self-destructive. And then I met you, someone with more reason than any other I know to be bitter, angry, weak; and you choose kindness. Not just with me, but with Kels, after one night, you choose goodness, when you have every reason not to. You have this uncommon strength that makes everyone around you feel better for the mere fact of being in your presence. I knew I was in trouble the night you hosted me for dinner, and I knew I would do anything for you when you saved me from my own nightmares, playing through the night for me."

John's eyes met hers, filled with a storm of emotions. His hands trembled as he reached up to cup her face. "So, yes," he whispered, the word barely audible. "God help me, I love you." Nikita's heart soared at his admission, but she could see the pain etched in the lines of his face. She knew there was more he needed to say.

John went on, "I know you think people can't love another before loving themselves first. I do not think I could ever love myself. But when I am with you…I love you so hard I forget what it is to hate myself."

"I love you, too"

"Don't." The rebuke heavy and sharp. "Love someone else, anyone else." Even now, with her free and wanting him, his voice was soft and sad. He begged her to go, pleading with her to start a new life far away. Still trying to protect her from what he knew he was.

"I am a free woman." She stared into his eyes. "You can't tell me what to do, or who to love. I see you and I choose you."

"Nikita," John continued, his voice cracking. "I've lost everything I've ever cared about. I'm broken. And I'm afraid that if I let myself love you, I'll lose you too. Or worse, I'll drag you down into the darkness with me." Nikita stepped closer, tears falling as she heard his confession, unabated now. Her breath escaped her, her heart pounded so loudly that she was sure he could hear it. She leaned in, her forehead resting against his. "Then let me love you back," she pleaded softly. "Tomorrow, tell me every terrible thing you've done and let me love you any way. And I will tell you every single horror I have suffered and watch you cherish me anyway. You will not lose me, and I will not lose you."

John never stood a chance. His nose gently brushed hers before their lips met as if for the first time, powerful and unrepentant, raw and honest. As though finally giving in to what they had both wanted for so long but had dared not hope for.

Nikita melted into the kiss, her body pressing against John's as if trying to fuse their very souls together. The room around them faded away, leaving only the sensation of their lips moving in perfect synchronisation, their hearts beating as one.

When they finally parted, both were breathless and trembling. The walls he had built around himself were crumbled, revealing the man beneath. Soldier, man, protector, murderer, savage, damned, battered, broken….and hers.

He drew breath in to speak, and she placed a finger upon his lips, "You talk too much," she said softly. John thought he would melt as her green eyes, soft and pleading, met his. "I will stop if I want to, or if you tell me too. But I choose this, I choose you."

With a sudden, thrilling impulsiveness she kissed him again, her hands finding where the buttons met in the middle of his shirt and tore them apart, buttons bouncing across the carpet as Nikita's hands searched across his now exposed chest. John's heart raced, his body on fire at her touch, he paused looking at her again. "I want you," he said almost inaudibly.

Nikita stiffened at his words. "I want you to have me," she said slyly.

The two stared at each other in silence that was deafening. And then, as though a starting gun had signalled a race to begin, John shed his now torn shirt, struggling to undo his tie as they came together. Their lips met again, and Nikita's fingers traced the scars on John's chest, each one a testament to the life he'd led, enemies overcome, pain he'd endured. They stood out as rents in a knight's armour, not shining and untested, but damaged and battle won. Inscriptions almost, of everything that had tried to harm him, stop him, kill him, and failed.

"I want you to see me" she said almost breathlessly. "All of me." She took a few steps back, undoing the lace overly that had hidden her scars, that had allowed her to feel so beautiful at the dinner. She let it fall to the floor as she stood before him, still wearing her dress, but never more naked and vulnerable in his sight.

John's eyes traced Nikita's form, taking in every scar, every mark that told the story of her past. His gaze was reverent, filled with a mix of sorrow for her pain and awe at her strength. He walked toward her and Nikita knew from the look in his eyes that she would never be the same again.

"I see you," he murmured, his voice rough with emotion. His fingers ghosted over her shoulders, down her arms, barely touching. "Every part of you, and you are beautiful."

Nikita's breath escaped her. A small part of her still expected pity, maybe even disgust, but the look in John's eyes… no one had ever looked at her like this before, with such raw admiration and acceptance. She reached for the zipper of her dress, her fingers trembling slightly. "Allow me," he said softly.

With near reverent care, he slowly unzipped her dress, letting it pool at her feet. His calloused fingertips traced the lines of her scars, each touch a silent promise of understanding and acceptance, a vow to cherish and protect. Nikita shivered, not from cold but from the intensity of his gaze, the gentleness of his touch.

John's eyes met hers, dark with desire but tinged with a hint of hesitation. "Are you sure?" he whispered one last time, his voice husky.

Nikita nodded, her heart pounding. "I have never been surer of anything," she breathed. Her eyes welled with tears, overwhelmed by the tenderness in his words and actions. She pressed herself against him, skin to skin, feeling the steady beat of his heart against her chest. Their lips met again, this time slower, deeper, a conversation without words.

For a moment, they allowed herself to forget everything else – the pain of the past, the uncertainty of their future. In this moment, there was only each other, his strong arms encircling her, her hands roaming his exposed chest and shoulders.

Nikita arched into him, a soft moan escaping her lips. She could feel John's restraint, his careful control even as desire radiated from him. Gently, she took his face in her hands, forcing him to meet her gaze.

"It's okay," she whispered. "You don't have to hold back. Not with me."

He groaned, a sound that reverberated through her core.

Their lips met again, and this time there was no holding back. John lifted her effortlessly, her legs wrapping around his waist as he carried her to the bed. He laid her down gently, his body covering hers, strong and protective.

As they came together, it was more than just physical attraction. It was two broken souls finding solace in each other. Two people who had been found, even as the world told them they deserved to be lost.

It was a joining of two souls, a moment of perfect unity where past pains and future fears melted away.

In the aftermath, they lay tangled together, breath slowly returning to normal. John's fingers traced lazy patterns on Nikita's skin, while she nestled her head on his chest, enjoying the feeling of his arms safely around her. She was still enjoying that feeling when she fell asleep.

31

Chapter Thirty-One: Explanations

John-

"And Sokolov?" she asked, that devious grin still on her face. *Something had utterly broke free in her last night*, John thought. It was as if being truly accepted and made safe had given her the chance to become this playful creature beside him. He loved it, but it was exhausting. She had been teasing him most of the past hour. He had promised last night to answer all her questions. And Nikita was taking him up on it, stroking and teasing his body as she pulled every answer from his lips.

"What I said last night was true. He was in an accident at the zoo yesterday. He's not coming back," John explained. "When we first had that conversation at my apartment, you were protecting me from someone. It was Aleski, wasn't it?" he kissed her forehead, "You needn't have bothered. He was a coward, they all were."

"They're really all gone?" she replied, as though she hadn't quite believed last night. "All three," John shuddered at her touch.

"You saw me grab one the night we first slept together. I made him pay for every slight touch upon your skin; it took hours. And while at the end I had some information. I didn't quite have enough to go on to plan it. I was stuck-" he groaned as Nikita kissed his chest.

"Go on," she flashed that wicked grin.

"I was stuck until Jean-Paul came and Kelsey took you to dinner."

Nikita's eyes widened, a mix of surprise and curiosity dancing in her gaze. "Jean-Paul? What did he have to do with it?"

John closed his eyes, savouring the warmth of Nikita's body against his. He took a deep breath, steeling himself for the conversation to come "Jean-Paul… he was the missing piece. Nikita's fingers traced lazy circles on his chest, encouraging him to continue. John's voice was low, almost a whisper. "He had connections I didn't. Information that filled in the gaps. You see, it was Jean-Paul that had organised with Aleski for me to take the job here so that I could be at the zoo when he needed me, so I could convince the president. Sending you to be my assistant was entirely Aleski's idea, although Jean-Paul did know about it."

He took a deep breath before continuing. Nikita's hands were still teasing. "Stop that for a second, I need to tell you this." She stopped, concern on her face. "When Jean-Paul came the other night to pitch this batshit job at me, I knew I could use his connections. I wasn't aware how involved he already was. But that just meant it was easier to get to the bottom of things. He needed me, and he was willing to pay whatever for me to sign on. You saw me grab the first man. Well, the night we sent you to the ballet, Kels, De Smet and I went to the Red Dragon.

While Jean-Paul kept Aleski occupied, Kels and I broke into their offices and the safe the first guy told me about. That's how we got the hard drive and papers. The third guy, they called him Ghost, interrupted us and came down with a case of falling off a balcony. That just left Aleski, who Jean-Paul and I ensured had an accident at the zoo while Kelsey took you to get your hair done."

Nikita's eyes widened as she absorbed John's words. She sat up, pulling the sheet around her as she studied his face intently. "So, Jean-Paul was part of it all along? And Kelsey too?" Her voice was a mix of disbelief and awe.

"Jean-Paul kinda. He needed Aleski for this upcoming job. Then Aleski ran out of usefulness and Jean-Paul needed me more. You can always trust him, if you trust him to use you. He needs me, which allowed me to negotiate whatever payment I wanted. Kelsey not so much. She came to Russia to make sure I didn't kill Jean-Paul on sight for the Congo. But she is loyal to a fault and as soon as she sniffed you out and knew I was trying to free you, she was all in. But yes, this is how I know those three are gone, how we got the hard drive, your papers, passport, and the French cyber security unit has flagged all your videos to be taken down whenever they appear on a website. When you told me not to take Jean-Paul's job, and I said I got the right price…It was this, you, the only thing worth asking for…"

Nikita's breath caught in her throat as she processed John's words.

"John," she whispered, her voice thick with emotion. "I… I don't know what to say."

He reached out, gently cupping her face in his calloused hands. "You don't have to say anything," he murmured, his eyes searching hers.

A moment of silence passed between them, heavy with unspoken emotions. Then, without warning, Nikita launched herself at John, wrapping her arms around his neck and burying her face in his chest. Her body shook with quiet sobs, a mixture of relief, gratitude, and overwhelming emotion.

John held her tightly, his strong arms encircling her trembling form. He pressed his lips to the top of her head, inhaling the scent of her hair. "It's over now," he whispered softly.

"John? About Amy…"

"Hmm?"

"Do you know where she is? If she got in touch with you, would…

well would you maybe-"

But John was already shaking his head. "Haven't spoken to her since, you know. She wanted to get far away, put it all behind her and pretend it never happened. I don't keep track of her or reach out. I'm dead to her, the least I can do is stay that way. I'm yours, entirely, if that's what you're concerned about. Even if she came back."

Yours until I have to go with De Smet anyway,

Nikita leaned into his touch, closing her eyes for a moment. When she opened them again, there was a fierce determination in her gaze. "Tell me about the job Jean-Paul wants you to do. The one you agreed to."

"His plan is to relocate the gorillas, not just within the park but across borders. He wants to catch as many as possible and move them to our new primate exhibit, vacant because Monarto zoo is talking our chimpanzee troop. With their numbers dwindling and conflict brewing in Congo, he fears they won't survive without intervention. He's faced with a difficult decision: let the species go extinct or take drastic measures. And so, he's chosen to do something crazy. This means he needs me to lead a team on an expedition to track, capture, and smuggle them out."

Nikita recoiled in shock, now understanding what John had agreed to do to free her. "That…is… absolutely insane." she said, "And mountain gorilla can't survive in Russia, regardless of how good the enclosure is. They simply wouldn't survive."

"Yeah," he replied. "But I've already received payment. So, I guess I'm going."

Determination settled across Nikita's face. "Then I'm coming with you," she declared, her voice steady despite the tremor in her hands.

John's brow furrowed, "Absolutely fucking not. It's too dangerous. I can't risk—"

"You can't risk what?" she interrupted, her voice rising. "My safety?

My freedom? You've just given me both of those things. And now you're about to go on some trip that could get you killed." Her voice softened, but the intensity remained. "I won't sit idly by while you put your life on the line. Not after everything you've done for me."

He sighed, knowing that arguing here and now would be futile.

"Besides," Nikita continued, a hint of her earlier playfulness returning, "someone needs to keep an eye on you and Kelsey. God knows what trouble you two would get up to without someone to keep you in line." She flashed that grin once more as her hands resumed their teasing. "Now…I believe I was starting something earlier." she said coyly. "Why don't you wait five minutes and follow me into the shower, and I'll finish it?" She kissed his chest again and left. He could argue with her about going to Africa or follow her into the shower. The shower won out. There was time enough to argue later.

32

Chapter Thirty-Two: Trouble in paradise

John-

Two days later John unlocked the door and the new couple walked into his apartment. Kelsey had stayed there the last few nights while they were at the hotel but had left for Australia that morning.

John surveyed the living room, noting the subtle signs of Kelsey's presence - a half-empty coffee mug on the counter, a throw blanket draped haphazardly over the couch. The air still held a faint trace of her deodorant; Kels wasn't a perfume girl. John stood there for a moment, feeling the weight of the impending mission settle on his shoulders. The enormity of what he'd agreed to do—what he had to do—threatened to overwhelm him. He closed his eyes, took a deep breath, *I'll figure it out.*

"She didn't leave much of a mess," Nikita observed, her eyes scanning the room. "I'll make us some coffee," she said softly, disappearing into the kitchen. Her fingers trailed along his arm as she moved past him.

John grunted in response, moving to collect the mug. "Must've been in a rush. It's unlike her to not finish a coffee." A folded piece of paper held in place by the mug, caught his eye. He unfolded it, recognising Kelsey's messy scrawl immediately.

"What's that?" Nikita asked, peering over his shoulder.

John's jaw clenched as he read the note aloud. "Johnny boy, I've made some calls. My contacts in Kinshasa are expecting us in four weeks. They'll have the gear and intel we need when we arrive. Don't do anything stupid before I get there. And for fuck's sake, bring Nikita. You'll need her. - K"

He crumpled the note in his fist, frustration getting the better of him. "Fucking hell." Kelsey had always been one step ahead, planning and plotting even when John thought he had everything under control.

Nikita's eyebrows shot up. "Well, I guess that settles it," she said, a hint of smugness in her voice. "Looks like I'm coming with you after all."

John turned to face her, his expression stern. "This doesn't change anything. It's still too dangerous. Kelsey does not get to make this decision."

Nikita crossed her arms, her eyes flashing with determination. "And you don't get to make it for me either, John. I'm coming, whether you like it or not."

He ran a hand through his hair, frustration evident in every movement. "You don't understand what you're asking for. Congo... it's not like anything you've ever experienced. It is absolutely brutal, just unforgiving."

"Then teach me," Nikita interrupted, stepping closer to him. "Train me. Prepare me. But don't shut me out."

John's resolve wavered as he looked into her eyes, seeing the same strength and determination that had drawn him to her in the first place. He rubbed his forehead. "Kelsey had no right to do that," he sighed.

Nikita placed a steaming mug of coffee in front of him, her hand lingering on his arm. "She cares about you, you know," she said softly. "In her own way."

John grunted, taking a long sip of the hot liquid. "She's a pain in my ass," he muttered, but there was no real heat in his words. "She's going to be pissed when she finds out she's not coming," he laughed bitterly. Truth be told, he'd love for Kelsey to come. But this was his agreement, and he couldn't drag her into it even if she begged him. He sold himself, not her.

Nikita's brow furrowed. "What do you mean she's not coming? The note said—"

"The note doesn't matter," John cut her off, his voice firm. "This is my job, my responsibility. I can't drag either of you into this mess."

Nikita opened her mouth to argue, but John held up a hand, silencing her. "I made a deal, Nikita. I sold myself to Jean-Paul, not you, not Kelsey. This isn't up for debate."

Nikita's eyes flashed with anger. "So, you'll push us away to protect us? Is that it?" She set her own mug down with more force than necessary, coffee sloshing over the rim. "Dammit, John. When are you going to realise you don't have to do everything alone?"

John's jaw clenched, his eyes hardening. "This isn't about being alone. It's about keeping you safe. Both of you."

"And who's going to keep you safe?" Nikita challenged, her voice rising. "You think you're expendable? That your life matters less than ours?"

The words hit John like a physical blow. "Oh, what? Like my life is some precious thing!? You know what I am, what I've done." He fought back. "I told you to go, this is how things end for me, maybe this job, maybe the next, but eventually. There is no happy ending here."

Nikita's expression softened, a mixture of pain and understanding crossing her face. She stepped closer, placing a hand on his arm. "John," she said softly, "look at me."

Reluctantly, he turned to face her. The intensity in her eyes made him want to look away again, but he forced himself to hold her gaze.

"Your life matters," she said firmly. "It matters to me; it matters to Kelsey. We need you as much as you need us. And you do need us," she smiled at him.

"I do need you both… I need you alive, not dead on some mud-covered mountain in a shit hole of a country half a world away," he said not unkindly.

Nikita took a long pause as she studied his face.

"You don't think you're coming back," she finally said barely audibly. John's silence was answer enough.

"You bastard," she whispered, her voice trembling. "You're planning on not coming back, aren't you?"

John's jaw clenched, his eyes fixed on a point somewhere over her shoulder. "I wouldn't say I plan on it, but it's a possibility I have to consider," he said gruffly.

Nikita stepped back, shaking her head in disbelief. "No, no, no, I won't let you do this. You can't just… just throw your life away like it means nothing!"

"It's not throwing my life away," John snapped, his patience wearing thin. "It's doing what needs to be done. Sometimes, that means making sacrifices."

"Sacrifices?" Nikita's voice cracked as she continued, "Is that what I am to you? Just another sacrifice in your little personal quest for redemption?"

John's eyes flashed with pain. "No," he said firmly. "You're not a sacrifice. You're…" he trailed off, struggling to find the words.

"I'm what!?"

"EVERYTHING!" He ran a hand through his hair, frustration evident in every movement. "You're important to me," he finally admitted. "More important than I ever expected anyone to be again. And Kelsey is like my own damn sister. That's why I can't let you come, either of you. I can't risk losing you too. I couldn't bear it."

Nikita moved closer, placing a gentle hand on his arm. "And what about us? Do you think we can bear losing you?" Her expression softened slightly, but the determination in her eyes remained. "You think I can risk losing you? After everything we've been through together. Everything you and Kelsey went through together. You think it's fine to ask us to do what you're not willing to do yourself?"

John grimaced, his eyes stormy as he wrestled with Nikita's words. She was right, and he knew it, but admitting it felt like surrendering a piece of himself he wasn't sure he could afford to lose.

"It's not the same," he said gruffly, turning away from her intense gaze. "I've lived my life. Made my choices. You and Kelsey... you've got your whole lives ahead of you."

Nikita moved around him, forcing him to meet her eyes again. "And what about the life we could have together? Are you so ready to throw it away?"

Her words smacked into him, and for a moment, John allowed himself to imagine that future - a life with Nikita by his side, maybe even a family someday. It was a dream he'd only allowed in his head for brief seconds over the past few months, but now it flickered to life again.

"Do you think this version of me will exist with you gone?" Nikita asked, "Because it won't."

John's resolve wavered as he looked into Nikita's eyes, seeing the pain and determination there. He felt a tightness in his chest, a mixture of longing and fear that threatened to overwhelm him.

"Nikita," he said softly, his voice rough with emotion. "I can't promise you a future. I don't know if I have one to give."

She stepped closer, her hand coming to rest on his chest, right over his heart. "Then let me help you find one," she whispered. "Let me come with you. Let me watch your back."

John closed his eyes, feeling the warmth of her touch seeping through his shirt. The idea of her in danger made his stomach churn, but the thought of leaving her behind, of never seeing her again, was almost unbearable. He breathed deeply leaning into her touch. The walls he'd built around his heart were crumbling, and for once, he didn't try to shore them up.

"It's not just about the danger," he said, opening his eyes to meet her. "If you come, you're going to see things. See ME do things that I don't want you to see." He looked into her eyes, his gaze intense. "It's one thing for me to say I'm a bad man; but if you say it, then it's true. I don't know what I'd do if that happened. There would be nowhere for me to go from that."

Nikita's eyes softened, her hand moving from his chest to cup his cheek. "John," she said gently, "Do you think I don't know the things you've done?" She paused, her thumb tracing his jawline. "I am not Amy; you will not lose me. This won't be pretty. But I see you; you are a good man. You would never harm me, nor allow harm to come to me. You'd do anything for me, allow me to do anything for you."

"And if that good isn't enough?" his voice barely above a whisper. "If you see me out there and realise I'm beyond redemption?"

"We both know men beyond redemption. You are not those men."

John glanced at his watch. "We need to start getting ready or we'll be late for work."

They both knew he took the coward's way out.

33

Chapter Thirty-Three: Servitude

John-

That morning John and Nikita settled into his new office, moving what little he had across to the curator's building. They still went on rounds with the African section team, making sure everyone was on schedule with the upcoming move. It was made even more complicated by the departure of the chimpanzee troop and expected but secret arrival of a gorilla family.

John's jaw clenched as he surveyed the chaos of his new office, boxes stacked haphazardly against bare walls. Nikita moved quietly beside him, her presence both a comfort and a source of unease.

"We should get going," he muttered, avoiding her gaze. "The team's waiting."

Nikita nodded, her fingers brushing his arm briefly before she stepped back. "Of course."

They made their way through the winding paths of the zoo, the morning air thick with the calls of exotic birds and the distant chatter of monkeys. John's eyes scanned each enclosure they passed, assessing, always on guard. More so now with the weight of what was to come.

At the African section, they found the team huddled around a makeshift planning board. John cleared his throat, and heads turned.

"Right, let's hear it," John said gruffly. "Where are we with the chimp transfer?"

Mikhail stepped forward, clipboard in hand. "We're on schedule, sir. The transport crates are nearly finished should be two or three days, and we're using the two we have to condition the chimps for entry. Should be all set for the move in a fortnight."

John nodded curtly. "Good. And the new enclosure?"

Nikita spoke up, her voice soft but firm, as she translated into Russian for the others. After a brief conversation, parts of it John could grasp, she turned back to him. "The gorilla habitat is nearly ready. We've increased security measures as discussed. And vegetation will start arriving on Tuesday so should be well established by the time they arrive."

Their eyes met briefly, and John felt that unhelpful tightness in his chest again. He looked away quickly, focusing on the task at hand.

"Right. Listen up." John addressed the group, "What we're doing here has never been done before. It's secret and illegal, and there's a chance it's impossible. But it's still the right thing to do. It might not work; in fact, there's a good chance it won't. But if it does go wrong, it's not going to be here, it's not going to be on our end that it's all messed up. Understood?" Nikita translated beside him.

A murmur of agreement rippled through the team, their faces a sea of determination and nervous anticipation. John nodded, satisfied with their resolve.

"Good," he grunted. "Now, let's go over the security protocols one more time."

As they walked through the African section, John's mind raced with the countless variables that could go wrong. The gorillas' journey would be perilous, fraught with dangers both human and environmental. And even if they made it safely to the zoo, there was no guarantee they would adapt to their new home.

Nikita kept pace beside him, her presence a constant reminder of the complexities that now coloured his life. He caught her watching him from the corner of his eye, her gaze filled with a warmth he didn't deserve.

She seemed to sense his unease, occasionally offering a reassuring glance or a gentle touch to his arm.

As they came back to John's office, they found De Smet sat in a chair, waiting for them. Waiting for John, more accurately. "Congratulations on your promotion," he issued like a spider to a fly. "Would you mind giving the new curator and I a moment in private," he said to Nikita.

She nodded her head and left, glancing briefly at John as she did so. She shuddered as she left, as though De Smet had a way of making her skin crawl without even touching her.

"She's pretty," De Smet started. "Hope she was worth it"

John's jaw tightened, and he forced his hands not to clench into fist, forced himself to remain still, to not give De Smet the satisfaction of seeing him react.

"What do you want?" John growled, his voice low and dangerous.

De Smet leaned back in the chair, a smirk playing at the corners of his mouth. "Oh, I think you know exactly what I want, John. Your full cooperation and loyalty."

John's eyes narrowed. "You already have that. I agreed to your terms."

"Ah, but agreements can be... flexible," De Smet said, his tone dripping with false sincerity. "I need to know that you understand the gravity of your position. The consequences of any missteps."

The threat hung in the air between them, unspoken but palpable. John felt that hot fury building in his chest.

De Smet went on, "You've been paid for your services. But you're yet to render them. I just want you to understand what is at stake now if you refuse. Until you do what's required, I own you."

John's fists clenched at his sides, his knuckles turning white as he struggled to contain his rage. He took a step forward, looming over De Smet's seated form.

"I understand perfectly, and I have already opened doors for you here," John growled, his voice low and dangerous. "But let me make something clear to you. I may be in your debt, but I am not your puppet. I'll do what needs to be done, but if you think you can manipulate me or threaten the people I care about, you're making a grave mistake."

De Smet's smirk faltered for a moment, a flicker of uncertainty passing across his face before he regained his composure. He stood slowly, smoothing out his suit.

"My old friend," he said, his voice silky smooth once more, "I wouldn't dream of it. I'm merely ensuring we're on the same page."

De Smet stepped closer, his eyes gleaming with a predatory intensity. "But make no mistake, John. Your debt is far from settled. The gorillas are just the beginning. And your payment could be refunded should I choose."

John's stomach churned at the implication. He had known there would be a price to pay for Nikita's freedom, but the full extent of De Smet's plans was only now becoming clear.

"What exactly do you mean by that?" John asked, his voice tight with barely contained anger.

De Smet chuckled softly, a sound devoid of any real mirth. "All in good time, my friend. For now, focus on your new role. Make sure our... special guests arrive safely and discreetly. We'll discuss the rest when the time comes."

With that, De Smet moved to the door. He paused with his hand on the handle, turning back to John with a slight smile.

"Oh, and John? Do remember that walls have ears in this place." He glanced meaningfully at the thin partition before exiting with a self-satisfied smile.

John stood rooted to the spot, his breath coming in short, angry bursts. The implications of De Smet's words hit him like a physical blow.

Nikita.

She must have been listening. His mind raced, trying to calculate how much she might have heard, how much danger she might now be in because of him.

With a muttered curse, he strode to the door and yanked it open. Nikita was there, her face a mask of concern and something else - fear? Anger? He couldn't quite read her expression.

"How much did you hear?" he demanded, his voice harsher than he intended. "And what did he mean, your freedom could be reversed?"

Nikita flinched at John's harsh tone, but she stood her ground.

"Enough," she said quietly, her voice barely above a whisper. "I heard enough to know that you've put yourself entirely into servitude. For me."

John's expression softened slightly, but the tension remained in his shoulders. He glanced down the hallway, ensuring they were alone, before gently guiding Nikita into his office and closing the door.

"You shouldn't have been listening," he growled, running a hand through his hair in frustration. "De Smet is dangerous. The less you know, the safer you'll be."

Nikita's eyes flashed with anger. "And you think keeping me in the dark will protect me? John, I'm already involved. I've been involved since the day you met me, before even."

"What did he mean by the implication your freedom could be reversed?" He asked again, staring into her, "Are there others that might come for you now that Aleski is gone?"

Nikita's face paled, and she took a step back, her arms wrapping around herself protectively. "There... there are always others, John.

Men like Aleski, they do not work alone. They have networks, connections."

John's heart sank as he watched her retreat into herself, the weight of her past clearly visible in the slump of her shoulders. He fought the urge to reach out and comfort her, knowing that his touch might not be welcome in this moment.

"Tell me," he said softly, his voice losing its edge. "I need to know what I'm up against."

Nikita took a shaky breath; her eyes focused on some distant point beyond the office walls. "Property like me that has use and earns money doesn't just wander off. And De Smet seems to move into whatever circles suit his purpose. I think that if he needed to ensure compliance, or revenge, he could simply stop keeping secrets and point someone in my direction."

John sank into his chair, his mind racing. *The fuck was he going to do now?*

A thought worked his way to the front of his mind. "Earlier this morning, you said this version of you wouldn't exist with me gone. Is this what you meant"?

Nikita sighed, "It is a possibility that crossed my mind." She said, mimicking John's earlier line. "People like us do not get happy endings right?"

John's face hardened at her words, heart clenching at Nikita's words. The resignation in her voice, the acceptance of a fate she didn't deserve. He stood up abruptly, closing the distance between them in two quick strides.

"Listen to me," he said, his voice low and intense. "I'm not letting anyone take you back to that life. You understand?"

Nikita looked up at him, her eyes smiling sadly at the intensity written across John's face. "You can't fight everyone, John."

"Fucking watch me," he growled.

His hand moved as if to touch her face, but he caught himself, letting it fall back to his side. "I made you a promise that I would free you and that's useless unless I make sure you remain free." He looked directly in her eyes now, "I swear to you, anyone so much as breathes on a hair upon your head, and I will let everything I've ever done look like a fucking children's lullaby."

Nikita's eyes averted at John's fierce declaration, a sea of conflicting emotions wrestling across her face.

He turned away, pacing the small office as he spoke. "I need to be smart about this," he said, more to himself than to Nikita.

Nikita watched him, her brow furrowed with concern. "What are you thinking?"

John stopped pacing, his jaw set with determination. "Well, you can't leave my side until this is sorted. We need to get you trained." He looked at her again. "You're coming with me to the DRC."

Nikita's eyes widened in surprise, a mix of hope and apprehension crossing her face. "You're serious? You'll let me come with you?"

John nodded grimly. "I don't see that we have much choice. I can't leave you here unprotected."

He stepped closer to her, his voice lowering. "But Nikita, you need to understand what you're getting into. Congo isn't just dangerous physically. It changes people. What we'll be doing, it's not clean. Not legal. Not moral, by most standards."

Nikita met his gaze steadily. "I told you before, John. You will not lose me. I know who you are and I'm not afraid."

John's jaw clenched. "You should be," he muttered. "They all should be."

"When do we start training?"

"Today. This afternoon. We don't have time to waste."

Epilogue

The third of February. I celebrate it every year like it's my birthday. That's the date I met John in Sokolov's office. For me, that's the day my life begun.

My husband insisted I receive some form of therapy or counselling when I moved here. It was a good idea, as much as I hate it sometimes. I wouldn't say I'm over the part of my life before I meet John, but it's manageable at least. My scars will never really go away, and I still have bad days. Days where I can't be looked at let alone touched. But these days the shame is less in a way. I'm comforted by the fact that I didn't do that, it wasn't my fault, they did that to me-the shame belongs to them, not me.

But I get no such comfort about what happened next. It occurred to me that maybe if I had trusted John a little earlier, simply pointed those men out for him to deal with; he wouldn't have had to make the deals he did. The others disagree, but I consider everything that happens next to be entirely my fault.

I thought I knew shame.

I thought I knew what it was like to hurt, to lose.

I had no idea.

End of book one.

www.ingramcontent.com/pod-product-compliance
Lightning Source LLC
Chambersburg PA
CBHW020356120726
47904CB00002B/580